BLOOD LINES

BLOOD LINES

LIN LE VERSHA

This edition produced in Great Britain in 2022

by Hobeck Books Limited, Unit 14, Sugnall Business Centre, Sugnall, Stafford, Staffordshire, ST21 6NF

www.hobeck.net

A CIP catalogue for this book is available from the British Library.

ISBN 978-1-913-793-63-0 (ebook)

ISBN 978-1-913-793-64-7 (pbk)

Cover design by Jayne Mapp Design

https://jaynemapp.wixsite.com

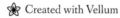 Created with Vellum

ARE YOU A THRILLER SEEKER?

Hobeck Books is an independent publisher of crime, thrillers and suspense fiction and we have one aim – to bring you the books you want to read.

For more details about our books, our authors and our plans, plus the chance to download free novellas, sign up for our newsletter at **www.hobeck.net**.

You can also find us on Twitter **@hobeckbooks** or on Facebook **www.facebook.com/hobeckbooks10**.

PRAISE FOR BLOOD LINES

'This is a cracking book ... It's a book that will keep you glued, and the twist at the end even surprised me!' Carole Gorlay

'An enjoyable read ... Believable characters in an interesting and entertaining story.' Sarah Leck

'Lin has captured the seemingly happy family who, when you dig deeper, are dysfunctional as well ... a very readable book.' ThrillerMan

For Gerry

SATURDAY 26TH AUGUST: 5.30 AM

'WHERE'S THE BODY?'

She nodded towards the half-open door. He reached for the black-and-white chequered scarf draped around his neck and dragged it up to cover his nose and mouth so he could breathe without throwing up. He gagged at the disgusting smell of urine, and worse, trapped at the bottom of the concrete steps leading down into the basement flat.

Standing in the doorway, he found it hard to believe she'd been in a dump like this. It was filthy. Crap everywhere. His phone torch beam revealed the floorboards littered with needles, overflowing ashtrays, old water bottles, burnt spoons and fragments of silver foil. He leaned in, flipping the light switch with his elbow, and the bare bulb stripped away all secrets.

The filthy mattress in the far corner was splattered with brown stains. Blood? How had she stayed here overnight? Where was the body? He turned to her, his eyes above the mask showing his puzzlement.

She answered before he could ask. 'I sat out here, on the steps, away from... Waiting for you... It's in the bathroom.'

She slumped on the bottom step, exhausted and shivering. Dawn picked out the grey shapes of cars and houses in the London street. The early morning light was getting stronger and hints of pale blue skies emerged in the rectangle above the stairwell, promising another hot day.

A car turned off the main road, and they ducked down as headlights shone above them and penetrated the stained lemon sheet pinned to the top of the window frame. For a moment, the room was filled with a noxious yellow gloom. The engine noise disappeared up the street. He climbed up a step to peer over the edge of the pavement and look up the road to check no-one was around.

'We need to get a move on.'

She nodded, but didn't move.

Aware that as soon as he stepped into the room he would leave his DNA, he pulled on his black leather gloves, walked over to the gun, wiped it with a rag he found on the floor and returned it to exactly the same spot. He shoved the rag in his pocket. Trying not to disturb the rubbish that carpeted the bare boards, he picked his way to the far end of the room and into the bathroom.

Bile erupted from his gut and he forced his hand over his scarfed mouth to keep it in. A dark red trail led along the floor and smeared down the inside of the stained enamel bath to a sticky puddle that framed what was left of the top of the man's head. His eyes were closed and the rest of his face looked asleep. Not even a splash of blood on his skin.

How had she managed to drag a body so big into the bath? He was over six feet and fit, with gym sculpted muscles on show where his tee shirt had ridden up under his armpits. His

2

skin was dull, his body empty. The metallic, stink of rancid dog-meat soaked into his scarf. He swallowed sick as he stepped back and gulped for breath in the less rank air of the stairwell. He leaned in, switched off the light and pulled the door to.

'Fuck! We should phone the police.'

Terror crossed her face. 'No. We can't. I wiped everywhere I'd been. They can't find out I've been here. If they find us, we'll say we left last night before it happened. I turned my phone off after I called you.'

'We should go.'

He climbed up to the second step and, looking both ways above the concrete wall, scanned the road. No cars yet. A few yellow lights glowed in downstairs bay windows. Lucky it was Saturday. Few early risers and no joggers. He gave in. No police.

'Right, let's go.' Had she heard him? He nudged her. 'You got everything?'

She nodded and indicated a bulging knapsack by her feet. He was impressed. She'd kept her cool despite everything. He pulled her to her feet, then helped her climb up the steps and into the car. Her hands wouldn't stop trembling. He leaned across and clicked her seat belt for her.

TUESDAY 3RD OCTOBER: 7.30 PM
STEPH

THE RAZOR BLADE sliced through the eyeball with clinical precision. A horrified intake of breath rippled through the cinema. Steph had bought the ticket by mistake for the arty Spanish film at the Electric Picture Palace, a jewel of a cinema in Southwold. The ex-cart shed transformed into an elegant 1930s plush red velvet and gilt cocoon, magnified the shock of the violent image. She felt the woman beside her grasp the arm of the seat and was aware of her lowering her head. Maybe her purchase was also in error?

Steph was a regular at the EPP, as it was known. Oakwood was cinema-free and the selection of films here, from the great Katharine Hepburn to the latest releases a little later than the large chains, suited her perfectly. As usual, she'd booked her ticket at the last minute and in her rush had written the wrong date on the form but after the shock of the opening few shots, it settled into a rather good film, and she noticed the woman beside her relaxing too.

Without warning, the room was plunged into darkness as

the film was stopped for the interval at what the manager had promised would be 'an inopportune moment'.

Steph turned to the woman on her right. 'That was quite an opening!'

'Terrifying, wasn't it? I'm not sure what made it so horrific. Maybe it's eyes – their vulnerability?'

They were interrupted by appreciative applause as a trap-door in front of the screen opened and a Whurlitzer organ rose from beneath the stage, with the organist playing a jaunty version of *I do like to be beside the seaside*.

'Perhaps not the most appropriate music?' Steph pulled herself up and out of the low seat. 'Would you like to join me for a drink?' She had noticed that the woman, like her, was alone.

'That would be lovely, thank you. I've lived here for three years but this is my first time here.'

Steph followed the petite figure into the bar. It was difficult to guess her age as her long dark hair, held back by a tortoiseshell barrette, framed a pale face with a perfect complexion and few wrinkles. Fixing on mid-forties, Steph admired her elegant, individual dress sense; long claret velvet dress and paisley shawl. This woman appeared to have the confidence to be her own person and presumably she didn't need to visit Miranda Modes for professional advice, as Steph had done when she started her new job.

During the interval, Steph discovered that Esther was originally a local who had moved around the world with her husband's job but returned when she inherited her grandmother's Edwardian house on North Road by Southwold pier. Steph found Esther easy company, decided she was her blood group and was pleased that she'd met her by chance.

They watched the rest of the film and stood obediently for

5

the National Anthem, with accompanying film extract of a tiny-waisted Queen leaving Westminster Abbey after the Coronation. Esther looked puzzled.

Steph smiled. 'Traditions of the silver screen are honoured here.' Shuffling out of the tiny cinema, they bid 'Good night' to the dinner jacketed manager and stepped through the tiny double doors into torrential rain.

Steph looked up at the sky, now iron grey with no promise of the downpour relenting. Esther pulled her shawl around her shoulders and shuddered. 'Oh no! I'd no idea we'd have a storm. I decided to up my step-count so I walked here.'

'Don't worry, I'll give you a lift. My car's parked opposite.'

They drove down a deserted High Street, past several shops with *To Let* signs stuck to their windows. Where had all the little independent shops gone? A man who appeared to have given up the struggle to ride his bike against the fierce October wind waved his hand as they stopped to let him cross the road.

'He didn't plan on this storm either,' said Esther, nodding towards the transparent tee shirt glued to his chest. 'How stupid thinking I could walk! I'm so grateful, thank you.'

'We've gone from salad to soup in a day!' Steph passed a pub, lights blaring into the dark but no one inside. They drove beside the boiling sea, the waves whipped up by the wind and past the dark pier, then Esther directed Steph into a tunnel of dripping trees beside a row of elegant Edwardian houses.

'Over there.' She waved her hand. 'The light in the porch.'

Steph parked opposite some ornate metal gates, through which bleached blobs of dripping hydrangea blooms glowed in her headlights. The crashing of the waves against the piles of the pier sounded loud enough to uproot them. She envied Esther, living within the sound of the sea.

'You've been so kind. Thank you, Steph. Fancy a drink? It's not late.' Esther's warm voice was persuasive.

Steph paused. She had to be up early the next day as they were expecting visitors from the Department for Education at the college, but just one wouldn't hurt, would it? 'Thank you. That would be lovely.'

Steph followed Esther to a brick porch, large enough to be a room, and they were just about to go through the front door when a Fiat Uno sploshed into a huge pothole, scrunched out and parked behind her car. A girl with a jacket draped over her head dashed into the house through the driving rain, followed by the driver, also trying to keep dry. The wind caught the door, and it slammed behind them.

Esther tutted. She had stepped aside as they dashed past. 'Sorry. Children! Hopeless, aren't they?' She opened the door once again. 'Just dump your mack on the newel post at the bottom of the stairs and let it drip there.'

Steph shook it, splattering tiny drops over the tiles, and did as she was told, slightly concerned about leaving her soggy coat on the delicately carved acanthus leaves at the end of the oak staircase. She raked her hands through her damp hair, glanced in the gilt mirror to check she was half decent and followed Esther down the black-and-white diamond-tiled hall into a massive sitting room full of antique furniture. The old oak floors glowed and were softened with enough rugs to fill a Persian market stall. Steph gasped as she walked towards one of the enormous sofas. 'What a beautiful room!'

'Not so fashionable now though – all this brown furniture. Gin? Scotch? Wine?'

'G&T, please.'

Esther appeared to have become more confident and relaxed in her hostess role. She'd seemed a little tense at the cinema. The clink of glasses and the bashing of an ice cube tray against something sounded promising.

She looked around the room with her practised eye, sussing out who lived there and how. Oil paintings in gilt frames and gentle watercolours filled every space on the long walls and ranged from Constable-type Suffolk landscapes to modern, brightly coloured abstracts. An eclectic mix, but somehow it worked. No photos of weddings, babies or holidays were displayed anywhere in the room.

The bookshelves on either side of the marble fireplace were crammed with books on Jane Austen. She couldn't resist it – she had to have a closer look. First editions, or anyway, very old copies of all Austen's books, filled the top shelves with folio editions and newer hardbacks of her novels below. The bottom three shelves housed a collection of biographies alongside about thirty DVDs of film and TV adaptations.

'I see you've found my collection.' Esther returned carrying two large cut glass tumblers, ice cubes clinking tantalisingly.

'Sorry. I hope you don't mind? It looks fascinating.'

'Not at all. My grandmother started collecting and I've carried on. I'm a passionate Jane-ite. Constantly have one of her books on the go and lose myself in a film or series at least once a week. So calming. Do you read her?' Esther's delicate hands were constantly moving to emphasise her speech.

'Well, I did *Pride & Prejudice* for GCSE but that's it.'

Steph resumed her seat and sipped the rocket fuel G&T Esther handed to her. She had only drunk fizzy water at the interval, so she shouldn't be over the limit.

Esther fiddled with a discreet brass tap beside the fireplace and a gas log fire popped into life, the blue flames rapidly turning yellow. In the firelight, with her long dark hair, her elegant velvet dress and dangling pearl earrings, Esther could easily be one of the Jane Austen women on her bookshelves.

'Have you lived in Oakwood long?' Esther cut through Steph's thoughts.

'Just over a year. Moved from Ipswich. Lived there for almost fourteen years and before that London.'

'Oh, where? We lived in Kensington before moving back here.'

'Wandsworth. Just south of the river. Our first house, a small Victorian terrace – quite close to the river. Be worth a fortune now.'

'What did you do in London?'

'Mike, my husband and I worked in the Met, you know, the Metropolitan police? That's where I met him. Then he got promoted to Suffolk, so we moved.'

Esther stood up, the firelight enriching the deep wine colours of her dress. 'First time this year. Helps take the chill off the room. Your gin OK? I do like it to taste of something.'

'Fine, thanks,' The vertebrae at the back of Steph's neck, where dark chocolate and gin always hit, relaxed, and she felt warm and comfortable by the fire.

Esther sighed. 'We moved back when Dickie's consultant suggested we contact a hospice for support. We'd both lived in Suffolk as children and he wanted to be here when he... Well, our tenants moved out and he spent six months here before moving into the hospice.'

'I'm sorry.'

'Yes. Hasn't been wonderful. Diagnosed with Motor Neurone Disease almost three years ago. He's done well – we've been lucky he's lived so long, although it doesn't always feel like it sometimes. Gets fed through a tube in his stomach, has help with his breathing and speaking is getting difficult. I sit with him most days and do most of the talking, watching him slowly disappear.'

They'd known each other about three hours and this woman was pouring out her life story, but Steph recognised the desperate need to re-live her husband's history and keep him part of her. 'You don't plan for it, do you? Just have to get on with living the days. Mike collapsed at work. Left one morning as usual, never came home again.'

Steph found it easy to share confidences with the woman who sitting curled cat-like on the armchair. She didn't normally go around telling anyone anything about herself, having learned over many years to ask questions and get others to talk. Esther had a talent few possess. She listened.

'You're right. You don't know how it feels until you live it.'

Steph admired Esther's ability to manage the emotional tone of the conversation so well. She was right. Living through terminal illness and bereavement was a sort of club you thought you'd never join and when you did, you wanted out. Poor Esther had been a member a long time from the sound of it. One of Steph's colleagues in the Met had MND, and it had been grim to watch him waste away.

She was jerked out of her recollections by the sudden opening of the door; a girl with long blonde hair, wearing a black mini dress over leggings and red converse boots, bounced towards Esther and sat on the arm of her chair. For a moment, Steph couldn't place where she'd seen this girl before. Of course, out of context it was difficult, but she recognised her as one of the college reps. Marianne – yes that was her name. Peter Bryant, the Principal, thought she was one of the most reliable and impressive of the year group. As Marianne leaned over to adjust Esther's shawl, Steph smiled at the two identical profiles, indisputably mother and daughter. They seemed so close.

Marianne turned to face Steph. 'Steph! I didn't know you knew Mum.'

'I didn't – not until this evening.'

'And how do you two know each other?' asked Esther.

'I work at Oakwood College, receptionist and PA to the Principal.'

Marianne draped her arms around her mother's shoulder. A puzzled look passed across Esther's face as she gazed up at Marianne, and Steph wondered if this demonstrative behaviour by her daughter was unusual. A movement to her right caught Steph's eyes, and she spotted the Fiat Uno driver lurking in the doorway. He appeared to be sussing out the scene before he stepped in and sat down in the armchair on the other side of the fireplace.

'And this is Darcy, Marianne's brother.' Esther turned to face him. 'You must know Steph too?'

'Hi, Steph.' He lifted his right hand in a half wave.

She knew this tall boy with the most beautiful smile and perfect manners very well as he often visited reception for a chat

'Yes,' she said, 'Of course I know Darcy. We're both fans of the Canaries and think they were robbed last season.'

Darcy grinned across at her. 'Absolutely right. Their manager has done—'

'Good night, Mummy.' Marianne kissed the top of her mother's head. 'Steph, good to see you. Need to be in early. Mr Bryant asked me to take some visitors on a tour of the college.' Marianne waved as she floated out of the room, while Darcy, trailing behind her, smiled good night to his mother and Steph.

Feeling told off for being up late, Steph replaced her glass on the side table and looked at her watch. 'Look at the time! I'd better get going, too. It's been lovely to meet you and to chat.'

'Yes. It has. I've been so involved looking after Dickie that I haven't made many friends since we came back. Perhaps you'll come over for a kitchen supper one evening? I know Darcy would love to have someone to talk to about Norwich City – neither I nor Marianne know the first thing about football.'

'Thank you, I'd love to.'

Reluctantly leaving the cosy depths of the soft cushions, Steph followed Esther, who lifted her coat from the newel post and held it out. 'It's a little drier than when we arrived.'

'Yes, a lot better. And thank you once again – a lovely end to the evening.'

The rain had stopped and the wind no longer whirled the brown leaves around the lane. Steph climbed into her car and looked across at Esther, her face and hair back-lit by the glow of the porch light. As she wrapped the shawl around her against the chilly night, she once again became a silhouette of one of her nineteenth-century heroines.

3

WEDNESDAY 4TH OCTOBER: 7.40 AM

STEPH

WHEN STEPH WALKED INTO RECEPTION, she found Marianne sitting beside Darcy on one of the black leather sofas. He leaned across her, picked up his sports bag and left, bowing his head to Steph as he passed. Was he taking the piss or being chivalrous? Steph wasn't sure.

'You're up early!'

'Not sure what time Mr Bryant needed me. Do you know, please?' Marianne rose and stood opposite Steph in front of the long desk, bright eyed and ready for action.

Feeling told off again, Steph checked the college diary on her desk. 'Let me see, they're due to arrive at eight forty-five, then tour the college with you at nine thirty. Why don't you grab a coffee in the canteen and come back later?'

Marianne walked towards the corridor, hesitated and returned to the desk. 'It was lovely to see you with Mummy last night. She hasn't got many friends since... you know... She spends all her time with Daddy. She doesn't go out much.'

'I'm pleased to have met her too.'

Desperate to get on with her morning routine and even

more desperate for a coffee, Steph made a tour of reception checking all was in order. After working in the college for the last year, she now felt she owned this glass box fixed on to the old 1930s building. She'd thought it bizarre at first, but it made a good impression on visitors. Modern sliding doors led to Steph's long oak desk on the left, while on the right, the two black leather sofas, tucked away in the top corner of the box, created a more private waiting area.

Steph checked her reflection in the glass and pulled in her stomach. Her blonde spiky hair, re-styled for her new job at the college, still suited her and she'd kept off the weight she'd lost during her illness, following Mike's death. She returned to her desk past the modern light oak door that led to the Principal's office. Opening that door was like stepping back in time. Peter's office resembled an early twentieth-century gentleman's study; old oak, red leather chairs and slightly threadbare Persian rugs.

She was opening the visitors' book for the day when it was grasped and turned upside down so that Paul Field, the Vice Principal, could read it. Forced to breathe in his musky cologne, she stepped back. He leaned over, and Steph thought one again that his carefully arranged and gelled black hair must be dyed. The colour was too solid to be natural. He scanned the previous day's entries, snapped the book shut and pushed it back towards her. 'Is the Principal in?'

'Not yet, Mr Field. Shall I tell him you want to see him when he arrives? He's expecting visitors first thing.' Trying to squash her irritation, she re-opened the book, found the right page, and once again placed it on the desk in front of her. He gave no reaction but spoke as he walked away.

'Oh, yes, I knew that.'

After reorganising the magazines on the coffee table, which Steph had tidied moments earlier, he stood by the entrance, hands behind his back, waiting for what? She wasn't sure what it was about him, but he always rubbed her up the wrong way. He often appeared when she was in Peter's office, demanding his urgent attention for something of academic importance, while letting her know it was nothing to do with her, a member of the lowly admin staff. She wasn't sure how Peter had the patience to put up with this fussy little man, but he'd inherited him when he arrived at the college as Principal. Gossip had it that Paul Field had also applied for the top job, assuming it was his, and when he didn't get it had been difficult ever since.

A group of five students piled through the doors, laughing and chatting on their way to the canteen before lessons, but his frown soon silenced them. Their dark coats and additional layers reflected the sudden change in the weather and Steph mourned the disappearance of the bright colours of their summer clothes.

Steph turned to her computer and searched for the student records on Marianne and Darcy Woodard only to be distracted when a whirlwind of bright red pranced in, stopping in front of her. Caroline, the Head of Art, beamed at Steph and gave a twirl in her floor-length crimson cloak which rippled out at least ten metres of woollen cloth. Paul Field appeared to be hypnotised by Caroline's entrance for a moment, then shook his head, clearly disapproving of her ostentatious display, tut-tutted and tottered off down the corridor.

Caroline had either not noticed or ignored him. 'What do you think? Got it in London last weekend. Desperate for the colder weather to come so I could wear it. It's stunning, don't you agree?'

'It's bright.'

'Not too much, darling?'

'No, Caroline, you look wonderful. I'm pleased you've

dropped by. So tell me, what do you know about the Woodard brother and sister?'

Sweeping the edge of her cloak dramatically over her left shoulder, Caroline paused, or rather posed, thought and said, 'Darcy's a talented artist, destined for Ruskin, Oxford. Produces the most sensational abstracts, exquisite pieces. Such a creative boy – most impressive from the star of the rugby team.'

'Marianne?'

'Outstanding organiser, superb at English. Her poems always get in the magazine. I was great friends with their mother, Esther, you know, before she married Dickie and moved to London.'

'But the children are so... so different.'

'Of course, they are, my dear. Darcy's mother was Nigerian. Dickie was finance director of some oil company in Nigeria and they rescued Darcy after his mother died in childbirth. His father, a French diplomat, I think, disowned him. They returned to the UK for Marianne's birth and adopted Darcy, who I think is a few months older than Marianne. Lovely family. And Esther's coped well with some real challenges.'

'Really?'

'When Darcy was in primary school, they discovered he was diabetic and now there's Dickie's illness. She manages so well. Never complains. Must dash, darling; students waiting.' Caroline spun round again, making the yards of fabric swirl around her feet, swept across reception and up the stairs to her studio.

Steph's assessment of Esther moved up a further notch. Not only was she a woman happy in her own skin, but she'd spent her life looking after an adopted son as well as her own child. What a strong woman she must be.

She checked on the student files and saw that Caroline was right. Darcy had turned eighteen in August, one month before Marianne's birthday in September. Both were among the older students in their year – no wonder they came across as so mature.

The VIPs, three men and one woman in dark uniform suits, just missed Caroline's dramatic performance and disappeared into Peter Bryant's office. A shadow fell across Steph's desk and she looked up to greet Jake, an eighteen-year-old who often came to chat with her. They'd formed a strong bond after she'd ferried him home, very drunk, from a beach barbecue.

After the usual pleasantries and debate about Norwich City, an essential skill required to survive student conversation, he leaned over the desk and asked, 'Are you taking Derek for a walk after college?' Derek, her rescued black-and-white collie-lurcher, had become a firm fixture in her life since she moved to Oakwood a year ago.

'Not tonight, I have a dental appointment, but I will tomorrow when I get back from London. I'm going on the Art trip.'

He lowered his voice. 'Could Mum and me join you then, please? She wants to ask your advice about something... something really nasty she thinks is going on.'

Intrigued, Steph agreed to meet them by the pond on the common at half-past five. She should be back by then. As she worked through her 'to do' list, Peter opened his door and beckoned to Marianne, who had magically reappeared, to take the visitors on a tour of the college.

As Marianne led the group up the corridor, Peter raised his

eyebrows, sighed and shook his head. 'Thank God, they've gone. What a load of stuffed shirts! They think they know all about sixth form colleges, despite all of them going to public school.' He started to walk back to his office, but paused. 'Will you come in for a chat, please? Oh, and bring some coffee – I need one.'

Steph carried two strong coffees into Peter's room. He nodded towards a chair. She sipped hers, waiting for him to finish emailing on his desk computer. The room was typical of the 1930s grammar school from which the college emerged in the 1970s. A copper hooded grate, now filled with pinecones, red leather button-back chairs and oak-panelled walls gave the room a solid, business-like feel.

She loved her job at Oakwood Sixth Form College and knew, after her illness and departure from the police, she was lucky to have landed such a great opportunity in her mid-fifties. The constant stream of staff asking for help with admin tasks or students coming for a chat meant she knew just about everything going on in the college and Peter usually came to her if he wanted to know anything. She didn't like to think of herself as a gossip, but she found she knew about most things first.

Peter plonked himself down in the chair opposite and gulped his coffee. 'Ah! So good! Now tell me everything you know about drugs in the college.'

'Sorry?'

'I went to a conference yesterday on county lines and couldn't sleep last night. It's bound to be here, in the college. If you look at the national stats, with so many sixteen to nineteen-year-olds, we can't avoid it.'

'I'm afraid you're right.'

'It's horrific. Your Chief Inspector Hale made a powerful speech.'

'Yes, he mentioned he'd met you.'

'Gosh, that's quick. We didn't leave Ipswich until nine o'clock last night... Ah! I see.' Peter blushed.

Surely news of their relationship had reached Peter's ears? Everyone else seemed to know. Steph didn't exactly live with Philip Hale, but they spent most nights together at her flat. A divorcé and a widow seen regularly together walking her dog, in local pubs and at concerts. How had Peter missed the gossip?

She had been reacquainted with her old boss Hale, as he was affectionately known by all his colleagues, when there had been a murder in the college a few weeks after she started working there. With Peter's agreement she had been appointed as a Civilian Detective, a role created to help with the manpower crisis in which ex-detectives were given contracts to work on individual cases. Her position in the college gave her ideal opportunities to investigate the murder, and Peter now assumed she was the first person to turn to for advice on police matters.

Peter recovered himself and continued. 'Hale said county lines are well established in Ipswich and now moving further out to towns like Oakwood. So far, we've avoided much of the action, but he thinks we need to be ready for it.'

'Right.' Steph had no idea why he was telling her.

She soon found out as he went on, 'I thought you could do additional tours of the college, especially the canteen, and keep an eye out. I mean you'll know what to look for with your experience.'

Steph nodded. She had thirty years' experience as a police officer, twelve of them with Hale as her boss, but she'd hoped to leave that life behind when she'd moved to the college. Peter was right, though. She was best placed to find someone dealing on campus.

LIN LE VERSHA

'Of course. Should I explain this to Jane, as she'll need to cover reception?'

He paused and looked thoughtful. 'No, don't say anything to her about drugs. We don't want it getting around. Just say something about making sure the new students are settling in as we want to improve our retention rates.'

Not convinced, as the new sixteen-year-old students had been in college well over a month, Steph added, 'Or perhaps to check they're only smoking in the smoking area? The cleaners complained to us both the other day.'

'Great idea. Break over in the canteen would be a good start. I know we can't do much to stop it in the evenings and weekends, but we should be able to offer protection to our students here. Make sure you take a walkie-talkie with you to get help if you need it.'

As she turned the door handle, she found it was already moving and was forced to step back as the door flew open to reveal Paul Field, who made a pathetic attempt to knock as he trotted into the room. His hands raised in melodramatic shock, he jumped back and lowered his head in a mock bow. 'Sorry. Didn't mean to scare you, Mrs Grant. Have you finished?' His beady eyes darted from Steph to Peter. 'Don't want to interrupt anything.'

Why did he always make it sound as if they were up to something?

Peter smiled. 'Do come in, Paul. See you later, Steph.'

4

WEDNESDAY 4TH OCTOBER: 11.00 AM
STEPH

AT BREAK, Steph walked down the corridor, through the old entrance hall and out into Main Quad, the grass square at the centre of the campus. The storm had passed, but the autumn winds were tugging at the mustard-coloured leaves on the silver birches and shunting the solid clouds across the grey sky at a ferocious pace. She looked across at the groups of chatty, laughing students, most with their phones glued to their hands. Phones made great props when you were nervous, as Steph knew only too well.

She recognised most of the students milling around and several stopped her for a chat. By the door to the drama studio she noticed a tall boy, well over six feet, leaning against the wall, wearing a designer hoodie and expensive trainers. He had that look she recognised so well. Sensing he wasn't a student and shouldn't be there, Steph stopped to have a quick word with three girls who had recently put on a fashion show for charity. Well-practised at talking to someone while using her peripheral vision to observe someone else, she watched the tall boy.

The girls chatted away, apparently flattered by her fascination in their next project, a gigantic sculpture made from single-use plastics. She saw the boy turn to greet Fred Castle, his face an angry mass of spots, with the now familiar man-hug. As they moved apart and laughed, they slapped right hands before Fred mooched off towards the canteen. The tall boy turned towards the wall, his back to her, and fiddled with something in his jeans pocket, before pulling up his hood against the wind.

He slid around the corner of the building, head down as he passed the CCTV camera, and leaving college on the footpath, he greeted another boy. Was that Darcy? Steph could see the top of their heads bouncing along the hedge and she waited until they'd disappeared. It hadn't taken long to spot a deal, had it?

Wishing the girls luck with their ambitious project, Steph hurried to the canteen after Fred Castle. Chatting in the middle of a group of four boys from his year, he looked around and his head went down as he noticed her coming through the door. She grabbed some shortbread biscuits from the counter so she could get closer to him and hear what he was saying. They'd stopped talking when she'd arrived, but now Fred had become animated about some new video game he'd played and his friends were joining in with cheats and ways to get armour. Relaxed, hands in their pockets, they appeared open and carefree. No dealing going on there – at least not since she'd arrived.

Aware of a figure moving beside her, she looked down to see Paul Field reaching across her for a packet of biscuits. That man was so rude. 'Unusual to see you slumming here, Mrs Grant. Need to raise your blood sugar? I find I need a lift mid-morning, don't you?'

'You're right, Mr Field. Afraid I got tempted today.'

'Oh, my goodness, you're the last person who needs to worry about their waistline.' What a creep! At least he could have thought of something more original, especially when it wasn't true.

'Walking back to reception?'

Where you belong were the missing words that hung in the air. After twenty-one years as VP, he was going nowhere fast. Very different to Peter, he spent his life upholding the old, outmoded values of Oakwood College, regularly coming out with stuff like, 'Oh no, that's not the way we do things here', or 'Not quite the Oakwood Way, is it?' The college he thought he was running no longer existed, but he kept insisting it should be preserved.

'Peter was telling me you had a jolly useful chat this morning.'

'Really?'

The walkie-talkie in her hand buzzed, and she pressed the receive button. 'Steph, you're needed in reception.'

'Thanks. On my way.' She turned to Paul Field. 'Excuse me, must dash.'

'Of course. Don't let me keep you from your job.'

Saved by the tinny voice, Steph returned to reception, dealt with the phone call that had enabled her to escape from Paul Field's probing, then watched the CCTV recording, hoping to identify the tall boy and the student who'd left campus with him. She downloaded the relevant section and sent it to Peter. Despite playing it several times, they couldn't identify either of them. Steph couldn't shake off the thought that it could have been Darcy who'd joined the tall boy, but she had no actual evidence.

Once again she pulled up Darcy's record and discovered

he had excellent attendance and top grades. She recalled that Caroline had said she expected him to go to Oxford. Steph didn't know they did art at Oxford, but when she looked up Ruskin School of Art, she realised Darcy must be a very bright boy as he would need three A grades at A Level to get in. No hint of involvement in drugs – no lates or absences on Mondays or Tuesdays, the giveaway, and no disciplinaries. Like Marianne, he appeared to be a top student. Steph decided she was becoming obsessed with the Woodard clan and was pleased when red-cloaked Caroline swooshed in, taking her off to the canteen for lunch.

5

THURSDAY 5TH OCTOBER: 7.30 AM
STEPH

STEPH WAS the last one on the minibus and spotted that the only empty seat was beside Darcy. Caroline had moved Fred Castle from there to the front to sit with her as he'd started mucking about even before they'd set off. She'd told Steph she knew he would be trouble, he always was, and despite the attempt to terrorise him at the end of the last art lesson, he'd started playing the clown the moment he got on the bus, throwing crisps around like a child. Caroline was tempted to leave him behind, but if he was going to get his A Level, he needed to go to Tate Britain with the others.

Steph was disappointed as she'd looked forward to chatting with Caroline on the three-hour drive to London. Perhaps they'd be able to travel back together if Fred had calmed down by then. Peter had suggested that Steph should be the second adult on the visit, rather than taking a teacher out of the classroom. No doubt he also hoped she might overhear some student gossip about drugs, but with Fred being guarded by Caroline, there was little hope of that.

As she sat beside him, Darcy looked up from his phone.

'Oh! Hi, Steph. How are you?'

'Fine, thanks, Darcy.'

'I didn't know you taught art?' He slipped his phone onto his pocket and gave her his full attention.

'I don't. Can't draw a thing. Caroline needed an adult to make you lot legal, so she asked me. It's quite a treat to spend a day in an art gallery!'

'Yes, I'm really looking forward to it. We're going to have a special tour of the Prints and Drawings Room. Caroline said the sketches by Durer and Turner are inspirational.'

'Really?'

He handed her the worksheet Caroline had prepared for them with a map of the rooms they were to visit before he continued.

'We're concentrating on drawing this term, you know. It'll be amazing to see the creative process of some of the greats – you know, the way they use their sketch books – not just the final picture. Caroline always marks our sketch books, as she says that's where our real creativity lies.'

Steph handed the sheet back to him. 'You're so right. When I went to a Constable exhibition some years ago, I saw pages and pages of cloud studies he did to prepare for his landscapes.'

'Yet his pictures look as if he's caught a moment, don't they? That's genius, I suppose. Caroline says genius is ninety percent perspiration and ten percent inspiration.'

He folded up the sheet and inserted it inside the cover of the sketch book on his lap.

'You think a lot of Caroline, don't you?'

'She's a brilliant teacher, great fun and she knows what she's talking about. The other day she was telling us about

Moore, you know — the sculptor, and how he used his sketchbooks...'

His enthusiasm was contagious and, as he described Turner and Moore's creative process, she felt privileged to be let into the secret life of the artists through his eyes. She always enjoyed listening to Darcy away from his sister. When Marianne was there, he deferred to her and remained quiet. He often wandered into reception to wait for Marianne to drive her home and they had the ritual Canaries chat, or he'd reveal the latest exploits of the rugby team. Sitting beside him, she valued this opportunity of getting to know the artistic side of Darcy better but knew with this age group not to push or they'd clam up. So, for about forty minutes, she enjoyed driving through the Suffolk countryside and dreaming – mostly about Hale.

Just beyond Colchester, she noticed a sudden intake of breath beside her and looked across to see Darcy transfixed by his phone. She caught the image and words on the screen, and even with her extensive experience in the police, she was shocked. He sighed, closed it and realised she'd seen it too. He put his phone away and faced forward.

'That looked nasty.'

'It was nothing.'

'Really? Looked like racial abuse to me.'

'No, not that bad.'

'Sorry, Darcy, I know it's nothing to do with me, but I can't bear to think of you getting stuff like that. It's illegal, you know. Is that the first one or do you get lots of it?'

'It's nothing. I ignore them.'

'You've had more than one then?'

He didn't reply but stared out of the window, not wanting

to engage further. She waited for a few miles of crispy brown hedgerows to pass before deciding she wouldn't let it go.

'Do you know who sent it?'

Darcy didn't answer.

'You shouldn't have to put up with it, you know. It's wrong. We should call it out and stop it.'

His jaw tightened. She suspected she'd gone too far, but was so angry to see what this lovely boy was receiving.

'How often do you get filth like that?'

At last he turned, and she could see the pain in his eyes. He slumped slightly, sighed, and gave in.

'Most weeks. It started after I won a national art competition. Someone must've been jealous their picture wasn't chosen. It was the obvious way of getting back at me.'

'That's not on.'

'It happens. It's a fact of life. Well, my life anyway. I try to ignore it.'

'But it's revolting and vile and illegal. Every week, you say?'

'Normally after every rugby match.'

'Rugby? Why?'

'Well, last week I scored two tries, but my second one was disallowed as there was a forward pass before I got the ball, so the ref wouldn't give it. That was the worst one I've had so far, as the other team won on points following a drop goal in the last minutes. They went through to the county finals. We didn't.'

'But that wasn't your fault.'

Darcy looked at her as if she was being stupid.

'No, it wasn't, but that doesn't matter, does it? I'm not one of them, so everything I do is wrong and they get at me like this.' He fiddled with his phone, now turned off. 'It's easy for them, isn't it? They get to say what they want, send me disgusting images and I can do nothing.'

'We could look into it. Tell Mr Bryant.'

'Nothing will happen. It's almost impossible to trace this stuff unless it's linked to a particular account and they're not that stupid. So, I get it, delete it, try to forget about it. The only way I can survive is by pretending it hasn't happened. I assume at some point they'll get bored and move onto someone else or I'll leave college and it'll stop.'

'But that's dreadful. We must be able to do something.'

'Leave it, Steph. It's a fact of my life. I appreciate your concern, but I won't take it to Mr Bryant or anyone else. He can't stop it, and if they find out, it'll get worse.'

'If you're sure...'

'I am.'

She wouldn't give up. 'But that's how bullies work.'

'I know, but I can't do anything. It's nice of you to be concerned but I'm not going to do anything about it.'

'Right.'

Dismayed and defeated, Steph replayed his argument. Darcy was right to a certain extent. It was difficult to do anything about it, but not doing anything didn't feel right either. That's how bullies got away with it. Maybe Hale could help. She was angry that the people who controlled the social media sites allowed this disgusting abuse to be sent, with no one held accountable.

Calming down, she chatted to him on and off the rest of the way to the Embankment about his favourite artist, music – anything other than the disgusting filth on his phone.

Outside Parliament, Steph took her chance, if it backfired it would only be for a few minutes.

'I know I'm still new to the college, but I expected there'd be more drugs there somehow.'

'Really?'

'Yes, according to the papers and TV, your age group can't avoid them?'

'They're around. I mean, I know where I could get some, but the most sensible students don't get involved. Not everyone takes them, you know.' He paused, clearly trying to work out what she was after. 'So do you think there are drugs in our college then?'

'Are there?'

'Outside mainly, I'd say. Most students are too worried to risk losing their place at college if they get caught dealing or even using. The kids who get involved are the ones who don't care about their future or for the weaker ones it's FOMO.'

'FOMO?'

'Fear of missing out. Oh, look, we're here.'

How clumsy was that? She'd have been better off not mentioning drugs at all. Had she really thought that he would reveal a few names? She wasn't sure what she'd expected and realised she shouldn't have embarked on a fishing expedition without planning it first. It would be interesting to see if he came to chat again or if he now avoided her.

As she got off outside Tate Britain, Caroline came up to her. 'Enjoyed your chat with the wondrous Darcy?'

'Yes, I did. Lovely boy.'

'Well, you had a better deal than I did, my dear. Fred only converses in grunts and he could do with a shower! Let's hope he's better behaved on the way home and I can get rid of him.'

She turned to the art group milling around beside the minibus. 'Right! Everyone ready? Great. Now let's go in and don't wander off anywhere. You'll have time to go off by your-

self after our session. You all have your sketch books? Great.'
She scanned the group. 'Oh, it would be you, wouldn't it, Fred?
Get back on that bus and get your sketch book, will you?'

Several students tittered as Fred made a drama of climbing
up the bus steps and bowing to them at the top. He really was a
total idiot. Steph suspected it was a deliberate ploy to get even
more of Caroline's attention. Could this boy, who behaved like
a twelve-year-old, really be a major dealer in the college? Or
maybe his childish behaviour was a way of putting people like
her off his scent. Was he the one Darcy described as not caring
about his future, or suffering from FOMO? Useful phrase that!
Well, she'd tried and failed. She hoped she hadn't alienated
Darcy or that he'd say anything to Esther. Too late now. In the
meantime, she'd make the most of the opportunity to go behind
the scenes of this sensational gallery.

6

THURSDAY 5TH OCTOBER: 5.30 PM
STEPH

DEREK BOUNCED into the muddy pond, looking pleased with himself as two ducks scuttled out of his way. The storm had diluted the grey mud and dumped a reasonable amount of water in the pond so he could swim, but Steph would still have to hose him down when she got home and he'd stink of rotting vegetation until he dried.

'Hi! Derek looks as if he's enjoying himself!' Jake and his mother arrived beside her, smiling at the soggy dog eyeing another pair of ducks. 'This is my mum, Debby.' Looking embarrassed, he grinned. 'I think you've met?'

Debby gave Steph a wide smile, rolled her eyes and nudged her son. 'At least this time he's sober.'

'OK, Mum, enough.'

Steph recognised the neat, friendly woman she'd met almost a year ago when she'd delivered a very drunk Jake home. Her short dark bob blew around in the wind, which caught the edge of her navy raincoat, revealing her stylish olive-green casual trousers and beige top. Jake's mum was good news, and clearly she and Jake were relaxed in each other's company.

'Let me get this animal out of the pond and we can walk together.' Steph turned towards her dog, who was prancing around and chasing a stressed duck. 'Bone, Derek! Bone!' At the magic 'bone' word Derek stopped, alert, and paddled through the grey sludge to the edge, tail wagging, anticipating his reward. Steph hooked him onto his lead and gave him a small bone-shaped treat. 'Want to take him?'

'Please.' Jake, transformed from eighteen to eight, trotted off with Derek through the undergrowth while Steph and Debby followed at a more sedate pace.

'How's Jake? He looks fine when I see him round college.'

Debby frowned. 'It was the right thing to get him to repeat Year 13 after Justine's death last year. He resisted it like mad but eventually realised that for several months he'd been out of it, and he wouldn't get the grades he needed for Uni.'

'Bereavement's hard at any age but at their age it's appalling.'

'It's been tough but he's doing OK now, thank you.' Debby smiled.

'Jake said you're worried about something nasty?'

'I hope you don't think I'm being a gossip, but I'm worried about my neighbour, Julie, in the house opposite.'

'Go on.'

Debby looked down at the ground, apparently considering how to continue. She took a deep breath. 'You need to know Julie has always been a – how should I put it – a party animal. Always on the lookout for a good time, friendly, sociable and puts herself out there. Know what I mean?'

Jake jogged some way ahead with Derek, so Steph felt she could probe a little. 'She has lots of... boyfriends?'

Debby looked relieved. 'Exactly. Most of them don't last long. I often have her kids at mine when she's out on the town.

They're great kids – one of them is at your college – David Richardson?'

'Oh yes, I know him, a friend of Fred Castle. Enjoys playing computer games.'

'I'm impressed.'

Steph didn't tell Debby that life sometimes throws up these coincidences, and she'd overheard their conversation in the canteen.

'Anyway, David and his sister, Josie, are now coming over most evenings as their mother's taken up with this new man. Except this time, it's different. He's posh and not nice.'

Steph nodded, to encourage her to continue. 'She looks ill, so thin there's nothing of her, and gets irritable with the kids, loses her temper with them all the time.' She paused and glanced at Steph. 'And recently, I've noticed bruises on her face. She told me she'd hit her head on the corner of a cupboard, but she would say that, wouldn't she?'

Steph knew only too well the situation Debby described. It sounded grim. 'How long's she been like this?'

'Ever since that man arrived on the scene. He's a lot younger, and Julie thinks she's so lucky to have him, she won't stand up to him. She's always loved chatting, but now she's shut up in the house and inside herself. And then there are the others...'

Steph turned to face her, 'Others?'

'Visitors all hours of the day and night. And now I think he's making her do things – you know – with other men.'

Steph was convinced from Debby's description that Julie had got herself in deep. As they reached a clearing, she pointed to a bench, and they sat side by side, watching Jake throw sticks for Derek. Debby laughed. 'Look at that boy playing with your dog. He's like a kid again.'

Steph pulled the edges of her coat together as the wind forced its way through the gap. A few oak leaves, a shade of dark marmalade, fluttered around their feet. She waited for Debby to continue. She appeared to be doing a great job supporting Julie through this crisis. Jake was right. It was nasty.

'When you brought Jake back that night, you came with a police officer friend of yours. I don't want to get Julie into trouble, but I think someone needs to help her get out of this mess. If she's not careful, the Social will take the kids away and that'll kill her. Until now, she's always put them first. Now it's as though she's forgotten they exist.'

Debby stopped talking as Jake raced over with Derek at his heels. Steph picked up a small oak branch and lobbed it to the far side of the clearing. Derek chased off after it, along with Jake. Debby waited until she knew he couldn't hear her. 'Could you have a word with your friend and see if he can do anything to get rid of this man without... you know... making it formal? I don't want her to get into trouble. It could make it worse for those kids.'

Steph knew that as soon as Social Services got involved, they would have to put the safety of the children first and, from the sound of it, that would mean taking them away from their mother.

Jake panted up, with Derek behind him. 'Does he ever slow down?'

'Not very often. Sometimes after a long fight with the waves in Southwold he'll collapse for a bit, but otherwise, no.'

Debby stood up and shivered. 'Oh, it's getting chilly now, isn't it? We should go, Jake. We've taken up enough of Steph's time.'

'Not at all. It's been lovely to see you again.'

Once again, Steph hooked Derek back on his lead, and the

three walked through the gloomy tunnel of oak trees and silver birches, still clinging to most of their leaves. It wouldn't be long until their branches were stripped and let in the light and the wind.

When the path became too narrow for them to walk three abreast, Steph dropped behind and watched as Jake and his mother chatted and laughed together. She'd been touched by Debby's concern for her neighbour and the way she took care of those children. Steph feared Debby had reached the right conclusion about the man, who must be a cuckoo running his drugs empire from Julie's home. That poor woman would be dropped as soon as she was no longer useful.

She felt comfortable chatting with Jake and Debby as they walked through the common towards Oakwood. As soon as they reached the first street of Victorian terraces, Debby smiled and said, 'There's my car. It's so kind of you to listen, thank you.' She put her hand in her pocket and handed Steph a folded piece of paper. 'My mobile number. Contact me any time.'

'Will do, Debby. I'll be in touch.'

7

THURSDAY 5TH OCTOBER: 9.00 PM

STEPH

Collapsed in an armchair, reading a novel, Steph relaxed at last. She'd fed Derek, cleared up the breakfast things, taken a lasagne from the freezer and put it in the oven for when Hale arrived, and was deep in a snowstorm in Shetland when a bottle of champagne appeared around the edge of her front door and waggled at her. Derek dutifully barked at the invader before recognising him and returning to curl up on the rug in front of the fire. Hale stepped in, holding the bottle out to her.

'Happy Thursday! It's good to be back.' Leaning over, he kissed her hard on her lips, the cool bottle between them. He was so sexy. She was surprised how much she'd missed him, and it had been only one night. Hale had been at a conference in Norfolk, where the two forces were cooperating to close down the drugs lines invading their counties.

'What are we celebrating? Have I missed something?'

Moving to the island in the open-plan kitchen-sitting room, Hale put the bottle down, took off his coat and, as usual, threw it over the back of a dining chair.

'It's been a year since we got together and I think it's

worth celebrating, don't you?' He opened the cupboard, took out two champagne flutes and wrestled the cork out of the bottle.

'Is it really a whole year?'

Steph thought back to re-meeting Hale when he'd arrived to investigate a murder in the college; they'd been together ever since. After her initial panic at dating again and 'getting her kit off' in front of a new man, she'd settled into a comfortable, easy relationship with him. They enjoyed spending time together and just being. He'd kept his flat and hadn't moved too many things into hers, just enough to re-assure her and help her re-gain her confidence following what he called her 'illness', and she now called her 'breakdown'.

Handing her a glass, he leaned over and clinked his against hers. 'Cheers. Thanks for a lovely year.'

She was touched by his romantic gesture and realised how much she valued having him there. She'd always found him sexy. He'd aged well too. Grey bits in his hair and a few more wrinkles had improved him, if anything.

She raised her glass to him. 'Been good, hasn't it? Thanks, Hale.' She sipped the pale golden fizz. 'Umm! So good. We should celebrate more often. There's a lasagne in the oven. Should be ready in a few minutes. While we wait, I've a couple of things to tell you.'

They sat on either side of the fireplace as she unloaded her last two days to Hale. It was good to have him there, listening.

'I'm convinced I saw a drop yesterday outside the drama studio by a tall boy. I've never seen him before and he looked too old to be a student. Met a boy called Fred Castle – come across him?'

He shook his head. 'Not a name I know, but I'll check with the team tomorrow.'

'In the canteen he shut up and acted all innocent the moment he saw me.'

'Not easy picking up information there, is it? We need someone of student age.'

'Not an old woman like me, you mean.'

'Come off it! I mean, anyone who looks over twenty-five is old to your students. Maybe I should explore putting an under-cover cop in your college? You know, someone who looks like your students and could find out who's dealing?'

'Peter would take a lot of talking round – and isn't it a bureaucratic nightmare – especially with a college?'

'Yeah, it's a mass of paperwork but could pay off if Peter agrees. I mean, we know it's going on there, you saw it and he wants to stop it.'

'Could work.' She got up to check the lasagne. 'Actually, there is a student who's on our team. Remember Jake?'

'Not that lad who threw up in my car!'

'That's not fair – it was out of the window.'

'Anyway, what's he done?'

Hale walked past Steph, grabbed some cutlery, two place mats and napkins from the draw, arranged them on the table then sat in his place looking ready for supper. 'I'm starving!'

Steph slid the hot dish onto a trivet, prodded the lasagne with a skewer and nodded. 'Good, that's done.' She started dishing up, trying to preserve the delicate layers of meat, pasta and cheese sauce that Italian restaurants always achieve. She failed. 'Oh well, it'll taste fine.'

Hale smiled at her. 'Go on, you were saying.'

'I met him and his mother this evening at the common and she told me she's worried about her neighbour, Julie. Appar-ently, a few weeks ago a much younger man moved in, she lives over the road from Debby, that's Jake's mum, and there are people coming and going all times of the day and night and she suspects he's pimping her out too.'

Hale carried their plates, loaded with steaming lasagne to the table. 'Umm! Smells great! Sounds like she's got a cuckoo. They move quickly. It's difficult to keep up with them. As soon as we shut down one house, another pops up. Give me the address and I'll get someone to check it out discretely.'

Bringing the bowls of salad and parmesan cheese with her, Steph joined him at the table and continued. 'Thanks. Debby was worried about the two kids, David, at college and his sister, Josie, I think she said, at primary school. She's concerned Social Services will get involved and wondered if you could get rid of this boyfriend without bringing the kids into it?'

Hale looked around as if something was missing. 'You know as soon as we have any concerns for the kids' safety, we have to inform them, and it sounds as if their mother isn't coping too well, anyway. Ah, there it is.' He fetched the bottle from the hearth and topped up their glasses. 'I'm not surprised by any of it. Oakwood's now a target – we suspect two houses are already being used and there's some contaminated stuff going around. It could kill.'

'Really?'

'Your Peter—'

'He's not my Peter.' She thrust the dish of parmesan at him.

'Peter looked shocked when he saw my slides with the local stats of drugs use now, never mind the expansion we expect.'

'Yes, he said he hadn't realised how big a problem it is. I've now got the job of cruising round college to spot the dealer.'

'I'm glad they're making good use of your extensive skill set!'

She grabbed the oven glove beside her and threw it at him. He caught it and lobbed it back. 'Piss off, Hale. I moved there to have a change and what happens? I do the same stuff as I did in the police.'

'Seriously, this county lines threat to your college shouldn't be underestimated. Your students are bound to be involved. I think we should resurrect your status as a Civilian Detective again before something dreadful happens. It sounds as if Peter has beaten me to it.'

'OK. I'll tell him tomorrow. I suppose it clarifies the situation and may re-assure him that you're taking positive action to protect the college.'

After supper, they'd planned a gentle evening of wine and chat and two further instalments of their box set, but that was blown apart by the trilling of a mobile.

'It's not mine.' Hale held up his silent phone as evidence.

Steph grabbed hers from her bag. 'Whoever phones at this time?'

'Maybe Peter, to kiss you good night?'

Steph ignored him. 'Hello... Oh, it's you Esther... What? Are you sure? ... No, I'll be right over.'

8

THURSDAY 5TH OCTOBER: 10.00 PM
STEPH

THE FRONT DOOR was wide open and Steph could hear screaming from the sitting room as soon as she stepped into the hall.

'It's better like this!'

Could that ugly screeching be Marianne? Steph found it difficult to believe such aggressive sounds could be made by this perfect student. Her face reflected her voice. It was a contorted mask of anger and hate directed at her mother, who cowered behind an armchair. A dishevelled Marianne, her pale blonde hair in rats' tails, her mascara now clown eyes and the side seam of her short red dress torn up to her waist, stood in the centre of the sitting room, which appeared to have been hit by a tornado.

Pictures, if they were still on the walls, dangled at crooked angles, with about ten of them scattered across the floor. A crazed glass spider hid one of the largest Suffolk landscapes, while an oil portrait had lost two sides of its frame. The bookcase was almost empty, the books strewn around the room. Steph gasped as she took in the valuable first editions close to destruction, some with covers coming apart from their pages, others completely detached and lying at odd angles far away from the stories they'd encased. Chairs, sofas and tables had been rearranged in a higgledy-piggledy fashion, closer to a surreal art installation than the elegant sitting room she'd admired.

'Marianne, stop! Please stop it! You're right, it's better like this. Please stop now!' Esther pleaded from behind her chair. She was strangely calm in the midst of this chaos and didn't appear to be panicking. Was this the first time Marianne had behaved like this? A book thrown at Esther's head bounced off the window behind her and she ducked down behind the chair again.

Marianne was placing two antique chairs on top of each other to form a rickety sculpture. 'It works. It looks better this way. But I can't find it. Where have you hidden it?'

'Stop, Marianne, please. I haven't hidden anything, honestly I haven't.'

'You wouldn't listen to me – I'm right. I've looked but I can't find it. You've hidden it like you do everything! You didn't come! You didn't care!' Marianne fell to her knees sobbing, raking the rug with her fingers and tugging at a loose thread.

'Now why don't you go to bed, darling? You need some rest.' Esther's soft voice cut across the mayhem. How was she staying so calm while her beautiful room was being destroyed around her?

Steph crept into the room, trying to move without moving. Her feet slid on the floor and her body slithered along the wall as she tried not to startle Marianne. If only she could reach her.

Leaping to her feet, Marianne swivelled on her toes and threw herself on a pile of books in the centre of the room, chucking them up into the air as she searched for something on the floor beneath them.

Steph took advantage of her burrowing and made it as far as Esther before Marianne noticed her. Twisting round towards Steph, Marianne held out her arms in an exaggerated embrace and appeared pleased to see her. 'Hi, Steph! Why are you here?'

'I thought I'd—'

'Oh no! Am I late for Mr Bryant?'

Again panic invaded her voice. Marianne darted around the room, looking under tables, re-arranging the shambolic piles of chairs to check beneath them. Jerking upright, she stopped rigid and peered across at Steph, puzzled. Her face changed, and she fixed Steph with an accusing stare, as if seeing her for the first time.

'We all know, you know. That you sleep with him. Have sex on his desk after we've gone home. I can smell the sex.' Marianne held up her hands to shield her face, as if Steph was about to attack her, and turned towards Esther. 'Mummy, listen! You mustn't believe anything she says. She's a whore! She has sex in college with him all the time.'

Esther crept from behind the chair, holding out her arms in surrender to Marianne. 'Marianne, you need a rest.' Her soothing voice contrasted with the animal screams that followed.

'I do *not* need a rest. I must find it first—'

Esther continued her gradual advance towards Marianne, and as she reached out to touch her, Marianne rushed towards her screaming, 'No! Don't touch me!' and wrestled Esther to the ground in an ugly tackle.

Esther hit her head on the delicate legs of a mahogany dining chair, and the piercing crack of the wood stopped Marianne for a moment, as she stared, fascinated by its jagged end. She bent down to pick it up, but Steph beat her and grabbed it first. Marianne growled, screamed and jumped at Steph, pushing her down on the floor beside Esther. Steph stumbled to her feet. Keeping Marianne in her sights, she helped Esther to stand.

Marianne ran around the room howling, not caring how many books and ornaments she crushed as she scrambled through the mayhem. Looking terrified, she threw herself on a pile of books, burst into tears and scraped the pages and covers towards her, building a barricade. With incredible strength, she pushed an armchair on top of the pile of books, added a small wine table and hid behind it sobbing, 'Don't let him... He's coming. He's there... Stop him. Please! He has a gun!'

'Marianne, let me—' Once again Esther attempted to soothe her.

'You don't care!' She threw the wine table across the room. As it landed at Esther's feet, the top came off its stem and wheeled across the floor until it hit the upturned sofa.

Marianne screamed and shouted at her mother. Steph hunched down low and crept behind the barricade. Within reach, Steph lunged towards Marianne but, as she grabbed her by the waist, Marianne swung round and smashed her arm across Steph's face. Falling back beside the fireplace, Steph's head narrowly missed the sharp edge of the marble hearth. Marianne threw herself on Steph, pulled at her hair and scratched her face, screaming, 'You're one of them. You've hidden it. Where?'

Somehow, Esther pulled Marianne off Steph and slapped her face to break through her hysteria. Marianne froze, stared at her mother and screamed so loudly Steph's ears tingled. Marianne dived on a scrunched-up rug beside the sofa and, sobbing, drummed her feet on the wooden floor in a child's tantrum. All at once, she stopped and lay still. The silence was painful, wrapped around them, a sudden shock after the noise.

Esther and Steph moved as one towards Marianne's body. Steph felt her pulse, lifted her eyelids and placed her in the recovery position. 'Get an ambulance, quick. Tell them she's breathing but unconscious.'

Panicked, Esther delved into a pile of books near her upturned chair. 'My phone! It was here! My phone!'

'Get mine. Bag on the hall chair.' Steph grabbed a tartan throw from the back of a sofa, laid it over Marianne, then took a small cushion, and placed it under her head. Steph was convinced that no bones had been broken, but she was concerned that Marianne might throw up what smelt like spirits. From the size of the girl's pupils, she also assumed Marianne had taken something – ecstasy, possibly?

Esther dashed in. Now that Marianne was still and quiet, Esther's voice had become shrill and she took rapid steps in circles in the space by the door. 'They're on their way. They said they'd come. They will come soon, won't they? I've turned the porch light on. Left the front door open. How is she?'

'Unconscious, but her breathing's steady and not too shallow – a good sign.'

Esther stopped pacing and focussed on the room, as if for the first time. 'Oh my God! Look at this mess. Whatever will they think? They can't see it like this!'

'They'll have seen much worse.'

'I must get it tidied.'

Esther scurried around the room, gathering books and pictures into neat piles.

'Leave it. Do it later. It doesn't matter.'

Esther ignored her. She grabbed armchairs and pushed

them back where they came from. A sofa was harder to move, but with a great effort, Esther shoved it with her hip until it was back in front of the hearth. Handfuls of books she piled onto the shelves, pictures hanging at odd angles she straightened and those thrown to the floor she re-hung. The broken pictures she hid behind an armchair. It was all in the wrong order, but good enough. Anyone coming into the room for the first time wouldn't be aware of the extreme chaos Marianne had created.

Steph felt uncomfortable sitting on the floor beside Marianne while her mother flitted around in her tidying frenzy, but she didn't want to leave the unconscious girl. She sat beside her, stoking her head, and every few minutes felt her pulse, which appeared to be getting faster. She noticed a wet patch on the crotch of her leggings, which had spread down her dress, and made sure the throw hid it before Esther noticed. Where was Darcy? He must have heard this row even if he'd been asleep.

'Where's Darcy?'

Esther looked up in surprise, as if she wasn't sure who Steph was talking about. 'Darcy? He left. Yes, he left.' Esther hung another picture in the wrong place and bent to pick up two books that had fallen behind the sofa.

'Left? Where?'

Replacing the books on the shelf, Esther paused, then turned to Steph. 'Sorry? Darcy? Oh, he'll have gone to visit Dickie.'

'At this time?'

'Strange I know, but the hospice lets him in at all hours.'

How could Darcy have left with Marianne and his mother in this state? Had he left before Marianne started throwing furniture around? He couldn't have been here when Esther phoned her or she wouldn't have needed to, would she?

47

By the time they heard the ambulance draw up at the front door, Esther had almost returned the room to normal. Steph was amazed at Esther's behaviour, but she knew that grief and dramatic incidents made people act bizarrely. Some went into shock, were numb and couldn't move, while others went into overdrive trying to regain control and pretend life was normal. Esther must be one of these.

The paramedics wheeled Marianne out into the black, and up the ramp through the open doors of the ambulance. Wrapped in her shawl against the strong wind, Esther followed the trolley, not able to walk straight. Steph grabbed her arm and held her up as her knees gave way. She looked desperate. The crashing waves sounded as if they might flood the lane.

'Oh Steph! Will you come with me, please? I'm so scared.'

'You go with her. I'll follow.'

Esther stumbled up the steps, the doors closed and the ambulance, blue light flashing against the wind-churned black trees dripping over the lane, zoomed off into the night. Steph drove behind it, not sure what had happened in the last surreal hour or how she'd become the only person Esther felt she could call on for support in a family emergency.

By the time Steph arrived at the hospital, Marianne had already been triaged and was being moved up to a ward. On the trolley, still unconscious, Marianne resembled an etching of a Victorian heroine ravaged by consumption. Her hair, now brushed, lay over her pillow and highlighted her porcelain-pale skin. She looked peaceful, but so fragile. Esther turned to Steph as the lift doors were closing. 'I'll be back when they've settled her. Please wait.'

Steph watched the doors close, scanned the rows of blue plastic chairs and chose one where she could see the lift. The hospital was now eerie and quiet, with no drunks or bustle, and the only movement came from a blue overalled, tired-looking cleaner splashing his mop over the grey-tiled floor of the empty waiting room. The harsh strip lights were reflected in the puddles he left. She watched them shrinking as they dried.

Marianne collapsed, unconscious. At hospital. Will let you know when I'll be home. Steph XX

Steph texted Hale hoping she wouldn't be too long as she had to be in college early the next morning.

She picked up a tattered gardening magazine, published in March, which gave all sorts of useful pointers on how to turn her garden into an autumn paradise. A shame it was at least six months out of date. Now Steph had a garden, she thought she ought to be interested in reading about what to do with it, but perhaps the middle of the night wasn't the best time, and anyway Derek dug little holes all over it looking for bones. She threw the magazine back on the pile of scruffy Sunday supplements and celebrity photo weeklies and waited. The puddles on the grey tiles had dried and the cleaner had moved up the corridor.

Whatever was wrong with Marianne looked serious, and Steph worried she might not wake up. What if she died? That beautiful girl, so talented and with a glittering future floored by – floored by what, exactly? Steph was convinced it was drugs. Hale's words about contaminated drugs kept going around in her head. Not Marianne, surely? But why not Marianne? Loads of kids got involved in it now. Did Esther know? She'd said nothing, but then, there hadn't been time in that madness, had there?

Yawning, Steph looked around the deserted waiting room, trying to keep awake. She re-wound how she'd got there. A chance meeting and it appeared she had become Esther's best friend, the first person to call on in an emergency, and such an extreme and personal one at that. How did Esther know she wouldn't gossip at college? Surely, she had other friends who were closer? Perhaps she hadn't wanted to re-kindle her old relationships. Esther had said that she spent so much time with Dickie that she didn't have time for anything else. Perhaps it was true.

9

FRIDAY 6TH OCTOBER: 12.45 AM

STEPH

DESPITE TRYING HARD, Steph's eyes had closed and, with her head on her chest, she was drifting off to sleep when the clunk of the lift door made her wake up with a jump. Esther emerged, her head bowed. She looked empty and exhausted, and Steph feared the worst.

'Thanks so much for waiting. They told me to go home and come back in the morning when they've got the results of the blood tests. They'll do a brain scan first thing if she hasn't woken. She's still unconscious.'

Relieved that at least Marianne was still alive, Steph put her arm around Esther's shoulders. 'If there's nothing we can do here, let's get you home. They'll look after her.'

Silent on the drive home, Esther didn't seem inclined to talk about what had happened before Steph had arrived, which struck her as strange. Used to people re-living and repeating the events leading up to an accident, sudden illness or a death, Steph was surprised that Esther said nothing but quietly rocked herself back and forth as they drove to Southwold.

Once inside the house, Steph took charge and Esther let

her. She made them tea and lit the fire and they sat in its glow in that weird time of night inhabited by young mothers and the sick. Still Esther said nothing.

Steph looked around the room, which almost resembled the elegant sitting room she'd admired the first time she'd visited, not the carnage Marianne had created.

'It must've been such a shock when Marianne collapsed after all that mayhem.' Steph moved across to pour more tea into Esther's cup, hoping she'd open up.

'Yes I—' Esther cleared her throat as she struggled to speak. 'I need a proper drink after... after all this.' Trying to pull herself out of her chair, she fell back, exhausted.

Although tired, Steph got to her feet and stood in front of Esther. 'Good idea. Tell me where to find it.'

'The kitchen cupboard below the one with the mugs – scotch would be good – splash of water, please.' Esther's voice was a whisper, and the hand that waved vaguely towards the kitchen flopped to her side.

Steph returned to the kitchen, which typical of everything else in this house, was the height of perfect taste. Hand painted wooden cabinets in a misty green topped by solid oak gave the kitchen a timeless appeal. Drying herbs hanging from a rack above the Aga, infused the room with breaths of rosemary and thyme. Steph found the well-stocked drinks cupboard, poured a large malt whisky, added a little water and went into the hall. She paused, retraced her steps and grabbed the whisky bottle and a small jug of water, as she suspected Esther might need to talk.

As before, Esther was curled up in the armchair, hugging a purple velvet cushion and staring at the flames. She took the glass and gulped it down. 'Ah! Much better!'

Steph immediately poured her another, pleased she'd the

foresight to bring the tray. This time Esther sipped it, her breathing slower as she calmed down. Steph said nothing and waited for what she felt was going to come.

'Thanks, Steph.'

'Can I get you anything else?'

'No thanks.' She paused and scanned the room. 'What a shock. I can scarcely believe it happened. I sat here after supper, watching *Emma*. You know the film with Bill Nighy – does a splendid job acting with his eyebrows. Marianne came back from some gathering they call it, somewhere in Oakwood. She's normally so sensible, so reliable, you know. I've never had a moment's worry with Marianne, unlike... Well, anyway, she arrived home early.'

Esther looked up at Steph, who nodded and encouraged her with a smile. The whisky was working.

'She acted strangely. I thought maybe she was drunk – they all drink far too much now, don't they? She said she wasn't, but she had such a loud voice, almost shouting, and she couldn't keep still – sat down, stood up, was so excited, pacing around the room. She held a large bottle of water and kept gulping it.'

Steph nodded and wondered if Esther had told the doctors all this.

'I thought it was best to leave her and went upstairs to bed. I was in my bathroom when I heard the most fearful crash and something being dragged across the floor, so I came downstairs to find Marianne re-arranging all my pictures, books on the floor and the sofa over there.' She pointed to the bay window. 'It's so heavy. I've no idea where she got the strength to shift it. I tried to stop her, but she was determined to move everything around, saying something about finding a body or a gun. You heard her. It was like a horror film, here, in my house.'

Steph nodded again in sympathy, which encouraged Esther to continue.

'Marianne talked nonsense and was panicked by something she'd seen beside the fireplace. It terrified her, but I couldn't understand what she was saying. I tried holding her to calm her. It always worked when she was little. But she became hysterical and hit me and that's when I phoned you and... well, you know the rest. I'm not sure how I would have coped if you hadn't been here. I'm so grateful to you.'

They both stared at the spot where Marianne had collapsed, as if it would tell them more. Esther sobbed, not aware of the tears dripping down her face or her runny nose.

Steph pushed the tissue box towards her. 'The doctors will find out what's wrong with her.'

'I hope so. This was not my Marianne.' She paused. 'Well... she's been drunk a few times, but they all do that, don't they? She's been such a good girl. Doing so well at college.' She stared into the flames for a few moments, then her head jerked up. 'Oh – college! You won't tell them, will you? She can't lose her place because of this. I'm sure it was just too much vodka or what do they call it... Geiger bombs.'

'Jaeger bombs. Yes, they're vicious.'

'What do you think it could be?'

Steph had dreaded this question. Should she tell Esther what she suspected, or should she wait until the hospital found something? She'd always thought she was good at giving hard messages, but this one stuck in her throat. Perhaps it was because this woman appeared so unworldly or was a husband with MND enough stress? Esther let her off the hook by not waiting for her to reply.

'I've read about girls having their drinks – what's it called – spiked. And on the news they said girls were being injected with drugs. Maybe that's what happened?' Another pause while she gazed into the flames, lost in her thoughts. She turned to face Steph. 'Although she's been a little strange, different somehow, since she met Luke.'

'Luke?'

'Yes, at Latitude, you know the big festival up the road in July. I thought he was such a lovely man when I first met him. Said he went to St Andrew's. Utterly charming.'

Once again, Esther floated off, gazing into the flames. The whisky had made her sleepy. Sneaking a glance at her watch, Steph sighed inside as she counted the four hours' sleep she'd get. At least tomorrow, or today, was Friday.

'Marianne went to stay with Luke in the holidays. Darcy wasn't keen on him and said she shouldn't go, but Marianne always had more friends than Darcy. I think he was jealous of Luke, who lives in Canary Wharf, you know... Now I think Darcy may have been right.'

Esther's glass was empty so Steph took it from her hand then held it out, questioning. Esther nodded, so she poured in another decent measure but added a large dollop of water. At least this way, Esther would get a few hours' sleep before going back to the hospital. As Steph turned away to push the cork back into the bottle and return it to the tray, she heard an animal-like howl and realised it was Esther. Was it bad news from the hospital? She hadn't heard a phone ring. Esther was kneeling in front of the fire, sobbing and holding out her phone.

'Oh, will this never end?'

'Why? What is it?'

'Look. It's Darcy. On WhatsApp.' She handed over her phone, and in a pale green box on the screen Steph read,

Sorry Mother. This is all my fault. If I'd looked after M properly, she wouldn't have got herself into this mess. I'm going to sort it out with Luke. Don't worry, I can look after myself. Phone you later. Darcy XXX

Steph handed the phone back. 'What does 'looked after M properly' mean?'

Esther slumped in her chair. 'They came back together tonight and when I saw the state she was in, I blamed him, shouted at him. Told him he couldn't live here anymore. Never wanted to see him again.' She sobbed.

'When?' Steph was confused.

'After he came back with Marianne from the party. He was up in his room, but when he heard our row, he came down. I was so angry, I took it out on him. Now he's gone to find Luke. He thinks it's all his fault.'

Steph was getting lost in the torrent of words. 'Whose fault?'

'His, Darcy. Oh Steph! Now he's gone off to London to find Luke. He could get killed, couldn't he? Those gangs, they're so violent.' Where had gangs come from? Esther struggled to her feet and pressed the buttons on her phone to check if any other message had appeared. It hadn't. She sighed as she placed the phone on the table, face up.

'Darcy said there were bad drugs going around. I'm sure she'd never take drugs.' Esther fell back into her chair, exhausted.

Steph waited. Esther was like so many other parents she'd worked with. All they wanted was for their child to be normal and not in whatever trouble they'd found themselves and to pretend it wasn't happening.

'The message isn't being picked up!' They waited in

silence as a frantic Esther pressed the screen several times. 'His phone's off. I'm so worried.'

'Do you have any idea where he's gone?'

Esther's head sank, and she took her time, taking several sips. She raised her head as if she'd decided.

'You'll think me a dreadful mother, but I've put an app on their phones that tells me where they are. Is that so bad?' Esther winced.

Amazed, Steph said nothing and kept her face as non-judgemental as possible.

'It makes me feel safe if I know where they are. It gives me the place, shows me their texts and their photos.' She paused, looking sheepish. 'You must think I'm awful, spying on them like this, but I get so worried, and without Dickie I feel so alone and I don't want them to get into trouble.'

'Will your app show us where Darcy is now and where he's been?'

'Yes.'

With a sudden burst of energy, Esther leaped up and went to her bag, which she'd dumped on the sideboard beside the door. She rummaged around and pulled out a second phone. Steph was astonished to think that this woman, who presented herself as a Jane Austen figure, could be so tech-savvy. Esther fiddled with its screen and handed it to Steph. A green blob showed Darcy's location on a map with arrival time, a list of his texts, and his photo gallery. It appeared he was in London. Steph handed the mobile back.

Esther returned to her chair and stared at her first phone to see if Darcy had replied to her message. Giving up and putting it back on the table, she turned towards Steph and paused before saying, 'I don't know what to do. I can't leave Marianne to get him back, can I? He could get killed or – God forbid – kill someone.'

Esther's sobs shuddered through her, and she looked so lost and so tiny. Steph sat on the arm of her chair as Marianne had done that first night. Esther lifted her tearful face up to Steph.

'This is a big ask, but do you think you could use any of your contacts to see if you could find him before he does something silly?'

Steph's stomach tightened. How many years was it – fourteen since she'd left the Met? There was no one she'd stayed in contact with since then. Maybe Hale would have more contacts up there, but she knew how delicate these issues were. Best to avoid it. Before she could reply, Esther scrubbed at her eyes, blew her nose and looked up at Steph as if something had hit her. 'And suppose you find him? After everything I've done for him – he does this.'

Perplexed, Steph didn't know what Esther was going on about. 'Sorry?'

'You see, we adopted Darcy. After all I've done for him, he gets my daughter in a coma and she may die. How will I live with him again?'

Steph returned to her chair, feeling conflicted. On one hand, she admired Esther for having adopted and loved Darcy as her own child. On the other, she was surprised to hear the venom in Esther's voice as she blamed him for all that had happened. Was Darcy really to blame? And how had she got in so deeply and so quickly with this family? She tried to hide a yawn.

Esther pulled herself out of her chair and moved towards Steph. 'Look at the time. You should go. You've got college tomorrow.'

Surprised at this sudden change in Esther's tone, Steph felt dismissed, but also relieved that Esther now looked as if she could be left alone. Steph was shattered and reckoned she'd get nowhere near four hours' sleep before the alarm woke her.

'You're right. And you ought to get some sleep before you go back to the hospital.'

'Oh Steph, I don't know how to thank you. You've been wonderful.'

Steph stood a head taller than the fragile little woman, who leaned forward to kiss her cheek. As she stepped back, she held on to Steph's arms and searched her eyes. 'I know you've done so much already, but is there any way you think you might contact someone you know in London. Please?'

'I'll think of something. Don't worry. We'll get him back.' As she heard her words come out of her mouth, Steph's stomach somersaulted. How? She could hear Hale's voice now. Making such a stupid promise had put herself, and indeed Hale, in an impossible position.

10

SATURDAY 7TH OCTOBER: 5.00 AM

STEPH

'IT COULD HAVE BEEN WORSE, I s'pose. You could have promised her world peace.'

Steph sneaked a look at Hale, who was driving them to London. They were now fifty minutes into the journey and on the outskirts of Ipswich, driving on the A14, their headlights slicing through the dark with dawn a couple of hours away. Normally she enjoyed the view of the boats on the estuary as she peered over the high walls of the Orwell Bridge, but today she could only make out a few pin prick lights on the distant shore; she looked anyway. It gave her something to do. He'd hardly said a word since they'd set off. She heard him let out his breath noisily. Not a sigh, more an annoyed 'phew'!

'And as for bringing that dog!'

'You know Felicity doesn't do weekends, and it's too late to book a kennel. Anyway, he's no trouble, are you Derek?'

At his name, Derek's black-and-white head appeared over the back seat. He looked around the car and, presumably seeing a walk wasn't imminent, lay down again on his bed.

'He'd better not get in the way.' Hale's tone was grudging. He was not going to give way easily.

Since Mike had died and she'd lived alone, she'd forgotten the demands of a partnership. The cajoling out of bad moods, the compromises, and the silences when words made things worse.

As they drove up a deserted A12, Steph thought back to last night, when she'd told him about her conversation with Esther. He'd been silent and listened with a deep frown as the story unfolded. He ran his hands through his dark hair, a sure sign of irritation. They had sat for a long time with Hale's eyes fixed forward on the hearth before he pushed himself out of his chair and grabbed his mobile from his coat pocket.

Without saying anything to her, he called a contact, Jim, in the Met. She recognised the name as an Inspector in CID who'd also worked with Mike and her. Hale told him he was on speaker and that Steph was listening, no doubt a hint to moderate his language. She really had left the club!

After the initial pleasantries, Hale explained the situation and asked if he would object to them coming down early on Saturday to see if they could find Darcy at an address in Battersea, given to them by his mother. They discussed the identity of Luke and discovered that Jim had information on him. Of course he did.

The police thought Luke might be Antony Shaw and were keeping an eye on him, as they suspected he ran several lines to East Anglia, Essex and the Midlands. He was quite an operator, but so far, they hadn't been able to get anything on him to stick. He was clever and when they got close, he always disappeared. The one time they picked him up, he was clean.

Jim made it clear he didn't want Hale to trample all over his operation but said they could visit the house where they thought Darcy might be and take him back to Suffolk. He grumbled about it being his first weekend off for weeks yet agreed to meet them at eight o'clock opposite at The County Arms on the Trinity Road, the main road to Wandsworth Bridge, and he would join them to visit the house.

'Why did you agree to come?' she asked, rather scared of the answer.

'You want to help that family and I want more intel on the line up to us, but I don't want to piss off Jim.'

'Right.'

'Come on, you know the score. We'll need the cooperation of the Met further down the line when we've got some solid evidence. I only hope this isn't too early and going in to find Darcy doesn't compromise their op.'

'But he could be in trouble.'

'Yes, and he could also be running the line up to us.'

'Not Darcy. He seems such a good kid and his poor mother's been through so much. Her husband's dying, her daughter's in a coma and now she's convinced her adopted son is going to get involved in gang warfare.'

'Don't be so over-dramatic. You're too soft, that's your trouble. Anyway, I think Jim would have known if there'd been a murder on his patch.'

They passed Colchester football stadium on the left of an empty A12 dual carriageway, which wasn't surprising at five o'clock on a Saturday morning. Keeping quiet not to irritate him further, she was grateful he'd agreed to take her, and with any luck they would find Darcy and bring him back to Suffolk by nightfall. She understood his reluctance to interfere on the Met's patch, but the drugs originated from there, and when and if they found Darcy, he might give them some inside information.

At Chelmsford, the sky was greying-up a little and a few more cars joined them on the road to the M25. Two white vans appeared to be in a race and broke the speed limit as they overtook them. Hale tutted.

In the headlights and the lit sections of the road, Steph watched the landscape zoom by and noticed that the trees and hedges were further into autumn the closer they got to the outskirts of the city. The few leaves that clung on to the branches were a dirty brown, emptied of life and colour and the hedges were roped with the white fluff of 'Old Man's Beard'. Didn't that mean it was going to be a hard winter? How strange that hedges could predict the weather.

'OK, you're right. We had no choice. We have to get that lad back home.' Hale moved his left hand across to caress her thigh through her jeans. She placed her hand over his and squeezed it to acknowledge his almost apology. Say as little as possible and let him talk, she told herself.

'It's early in their op, but Jim thinks it won't do too much harm, and we may find more out from Darcy if he's been on the inside.' Was this a concession? She waited for him to continue. 'Let's hope he's done nothing stupid and got into even more trouble. We'll make an undercover visit to the house then get back home.'

'Is that why you put on that scruffy jacket and your red converses?'

'This jacket isn't scruffy! It's my favourite. Expensive leather!'

'Well once, perhaps. But you're right – you'll pass for a cool city dude, not a country yokel.'

She had also dressed down in her dog walking clothes, which were dark and devoid of bright colours, knowing how important it was not to be noticed.

Smiling across at him, she stroked his shoulder with her hand. 'I could kill a coffee.'

As they were approaching the roundabout on the slip road to the M25 Junction 28, Hale took a left and they drew up outside a small restaurant. 'Please let it be open,' Steph mouthed silently, looking at her watch.

A bit after six o'clock. They'd made good time, but was it too early for the restaurant?

'That's lucky. It's open. Thank goodness.' She climbed out into the early morning light, stretched her stiff back and, after letting Derek out of the car, they joined a few other travellers desperate for shots of caffeine.

A few minutes before eight they pulled up opposite The County Arms and parked in the entrance to the Fitzhugh Estate, a collection of concrete 1960s blocks of flats, surrounded by lawns with notices screaming 'No Ball Games'.

Opening the boot, Steph grabbed Derek's lead as he leaped down. 'Good boy.' To her relief he hadn't uttered so much as whimper on the journey, and after a walk around the edge of the grass square and lots of snuffling exciting fresh smells, he jumped back in the car.

As Steph climbed back beside Hale, he smiled at her. 'Derek OK?'

'Fine, thanks.'

She let her hand fall onto his thigh, and he squeezed it, then held it and winked. Good. He was becoming himself at last. She didn't enjoy his distant moods when he shut her out, but also knew she had to stand her ground and not give in all the time. In comfortable silence, they watched the cars zoom past towards Wandsworth Bridge.

The road into London from the M25 had changed little since she and Mike had moved to Suffolk almost fourteen years ago, but the amount of traffic had increased. The Victorian terraces and grander detached Edwardian houses around Wandsworth Common left little space for modern in-fill, so the main roads looked much as she remembered them. It was still too early for the daily queue of traffic to build up along the Trinity Road and anyway, there'd be fewer cars on a Saturday. She was pleased she no longer had to drive in London.

Over the road, the formidable walls of Wandsworth Prison provided a bizarre backdrop for Neil's Garden Centre. The bright leaves of the house plants she could see through the gigantic glass house stood out in stark contrast with the blackened bricks of the prison. She had often visited there to buy shrubs for the tiny garden in their terraced house a few streets away. She and Mike had got a kick out of growing salad vegetables in small troughs and always planted bright pink geraniums in pots over the summer. Lost in her old life, she jumped as the car door in the back opened and a shadow climbed in.

11

SATURDAY 7TH OCTOBER: 8.00 AM

STEPH

'HELLO HALE, Steph. Good to see you.'

They both turned and there sat a tired-looking Jim who smelt of sweaty socks with a whiff of bacon and polo mints. At that moment, Derek stuck his head over the back seat to lick the ear of the new passenger. 'What's this? A dog? Thought you couldn't stand them, Hale.'

'It's Steph's. No doggy day care today. He'll be fine. Down, Derek!'

Derek obeyed and disappeared. Hale looked pleased, clearly relishing his new dog trainer role while Steph was relieved he hadn't disowned Derek completely.

'Long night, Jim?' Steph swivelled round, smiling, and Jim patted her shoulder.

'We had a tip-off from a reliable source and sat outside a lock-up all night, but nothing. We thought we'd got a big one, but it wasn't to be. That's life.'

Squirming around further in her seat, Steph was amazed at how Jim Connolly had aged. He was about the same age as Hale, but looked at least a decade older. His grey hair, what there was of it, was combed over his head and his skin had an unhealthy yellowish pallor, but his eyes were still that bright penetrating blue. He'd also put on quite a bit of weight and his clothes could do with dry cleaning. Perhaps he needed a holiday.

'How's life in the outback, Steph? I heard you'd retired.'

'Not so you'd notice. I work in a sixth form college by day,' she nudged Hale, 'but seem to do quite a lot of work for my friend here in my free time as a Civilian Detective.'

'He's got you on that game, has he? Wise move, Hale.'

'How's Patrick?' asked Steph, changing the subject.

'Same old Patrick. Moans about my long hours, but he's always there for me. He's now set up his own practice and works from home.'

'That's great news! He always hated that snooty West End architect's office, didn't he? Couldn't stand the politics.'

Evidently, from the look Hale was giving her, he was surprised she knew so much about Jim's private life. But then, during the period they'd worked up here together, the attitude to gay men in the force had hardly been warm.

'Well, life in Suffolk certainly suits you both. Now, let's get down to business. Where do you think this lad might be?'

'On the edge of the Winstanley Estate, we think. Look.' Hale handed Jim two screen shots printed from the tracker on Esther's phone, showing a house on a London street and a map complete with a green dot. 'We enhanced it and it looks like a number ten on the side of the door. You might recognise that pub on the corner. We think he's down in the basement.'

Jim stared at the photo. 'Where did you get it from?'

Hale reached over behind the seat and grabbed his laptop. As he booted it up and fiddled with passwords to find the images, he half turned to Jim. 'Darcy, the boy we're after, was being tracked by his mother. We downloaded all the information that might help. I'll send you a copy – you might see someone there you recognise... Ah, at last – here.'

Hale handed the laptop over the back to Jim and watched him zip through it.

'Thanks. I've a pretty good idea of where it is. Let's go.'

'Right. Are you happy to come with us or will you go in your own car?' said Hale.

'Better for us to use yours. Less attention.'

'Good. You can navigate.'

With his head poked through the gap between the front seats, Jim directed them to turn right, then right again to Battersea. The traffic had increased a little, but it was still easy driving early Saturday morning.

Arriving at the edge of the Winstanley Estate, Jim looked at the photo again and said, 'Go past this road, then turn left. We'll park halfway down.'

Steph recognised the pub caught on the corner of the photo. She had remained quiet while the two men planned the action. What should she do? Stay in the car or go with them? More important, what would they expect her to do? The answer came from Jim, as they pulled into a residents' parking space alongside a rather smart house with white plantation shutters at the windows.

'If it's OK with you, Steph, I suggest you take the dog, walk past the house and suss it out, while Hale and I hang around outside that newsagent's on the other corner. You're less likely to be noticed.'

Pleased to be involved, she nodded and waited while they locked the car and walked to the newsagent's at the other end of the street to the pub.

Was she getting too old for this? She'd done this masses of

times, so why this sick feeling? There was no real danger, as she was simply a woman taking her dog for an early morning walk. A similar surveillance in Brockley about fifteen years earlier forced itself into her mind when a crazy man jumped out from behind some bins and attacked her with a machete. Saved from serious injury by two members of her team, she'd shrugged it off as 'shit happens'.

Reminding herself of the hundreds of times when nothing had happened, she decided this would be one of those times. She was out of practice, that was all. The stress of living through these operations had been tucked away in the past and forgotten, but now she must cope with it all once again. After all, it had been her idea, and she'd given her promise to Esther. Taking a deep breath, she got into role, a middle-aged lady walking her dog around the block. She stood taller, frowning, aware of both men watching as she took her first steps.

The street was a typical line of London Victorian terraces, many being 'Chelsea-fied'. A skip outside one of them over-flowed with hardboard doors featuring pretend brass handles, popular in the eighties. Strips of woodchip wallpaper were scattered among the remains of what previous owners had used to cover up the original features, which were now being resur-rected. She relaxed, feeling calmer. That was better. Keep thinking the thoughts of a local woman getting fed up with the constant stops made by Derek to pee, even when he'd got nothing left to pee with.

All the three-storey red brick houses had bay windows with steps in front of them leading down to basements. Designer wrought-iron gates on some created elegant entrances, and those were the houses with the pristine white lintels above the gleaming gloss on their window frames. Their sills held window boxes filled with bright purple and orange pansies, which stood out against the white shutters that so many had installed instead of curtains. She counted the houses with shutters – now nine – to distract her from the dread of failing. She couldn't let Hale down now.

In between these poshed-up houses were some no one had loved for decades, their basements littered with old crisp and cigarette packets, broken bike frames and a couple of rotting push chairs. No pansies decorated the grey concrete sills of grimy windows with curtains that didn't quite fit. Steph walked slowly, taking in the street's atmosphere. After all, she was meant to be old and invisible, but she was aware of Hale and Jim watching her closely from outside the newsagent's. They'd planned to buy a *Racing Post* and had agreed to debate the chances of horses at Kempton if anyone came close to them.

At last, she reached number ten, and she paused as Derek stopped to sniff the steps. She pulled the loop of his lead up her arm and bent down to adjust a buckle on her green ankle boots. They were decorative and adjusted nothing, but it allowed her to put her right foot on the step that led up to the house and fiddle with it, while she looked down the basement steps into the window beside the scruffy door, graffitied and with a kicked-in hole in the bottom panel. Derek cooperated and stood still, savouring the local canine perfumes.

A pathway had been cleared in the concrete area at the bottom of the steps to give access past a rusty bike frame and an overflowing black dustbin. Old take-away food trays cascaded out of the top of the bin, suggesting the people who lived there were not concerned about their fat intake. The filthy window was covered with a thin faded yellow sheet that had become unpinned from the top corner of the sash window and created an open triangle for her to glimpse into the flat.

Derek raised his head, his nose in the air, sniffing and

pulled her towards the steps. Ugh! She caught it too. The foul smell of decomposing rubbish. Was it cabbage or meat? Whatever it was rotting in that bin, was vile. Hand over her nose and mouth, she was moving to the left, to get a better look inside, when she felt she was being watched. Looking up, she saw a face peering at her from the bay windows of the room above the basement.

12

SATURDAY 7TH OCTOBER: 9.15 AM

STEPH

STEPPING BACK, Steph avoided falling over Derek, who had moved behind her to sniff the other concrete post. Trying to look as if she belonged, she pulled Derek's lead so she could pretend to finish adjusting the buckle on her ankle boot, stood upright, picked up her bag and turned, ready to walk back towards the newsagent's.

The door above her opened and a man with an enormous stomach, wearing a stained vest and pyjama bottoms, shouted down. 'Can I help you?'

'No... no thanks... just my boot. Need to fix it.'

A mumbled reply that sounded like 'Do it and fuck off then' was followed by the slamming of the door.

Feeling relieved that Derek hadn't made a fuss, she pulled him to face the way they'd come, and they walked back at the same steady pace to Hale and Jim. Had they noticed her initial hesitation? As she joined them, they moved around the corner, out of sight, and waited for her report.

Report? Sounding like her old self, she noticed her voice was lower, stronger. She told them about the entrance to the basement flat, the quick glimpse she'd had of the inside and the exchange with the man in the flat above. Hale stood silent, waiting for Jim, as it was his patch, so his decision.

'Right. I think we go in and take a look. Come on.'

The two men turned and strode down the street, with Steph and Derek trailing behind them. When they reached number ten, Jim led the way down the steps and gave them nitrile gloves. Gloved up, they stood outside the graffiti-tagged door, the bottom of which had a jagged hole where it had been kicked in. It wasn't locked and opened wide at the slightest push. Jim walked inside, and Hale and Steph climbed down the steps to stand behind him in the entrance to the dark room.

They hit the nauseating wall of smell as soon as the door opened. Steph gagged and put her hand over her mouth to stop herself throwing up. Hale rammed tissues up to cover his nose and handed some to Steph with the small tube of Vick he always carried with him. They both knew what the revolting stench meant. She dabbed some of the jelly under each nostril and returned it to Hale, who did the same.

Jim pulled up his scarf to cover the bottom half of his face. 'Stay here. I'll check it out.' Jim was in charge, so they did what he said. They watched as, creeping along the wall by the window, he stopped every few steps to listen for breathing or any movement further in the flat. He opened a door at the far end and they heard him exclaim, 'Ugh! Fuck! It's here. Open that window and turn the light on.'

Steph tied Derek's lead to the iron handrail at the bottom of the steps. 'Sit!' She held up her hand as the training lady had taught her and, for once, he sat. 'Good boy!' Gasping a breath of the slightly less fetid air, she returned to the doorway.

Hale arched behind Steph and, using the tip of his pen, flipped the light switch. The horror of the room was revealed.

Steph slid along the wall to the sash window, pulled up the bottom pane to allow air to dilute the rank smell, and the sheet, giving up its attempt to be a curtain, slipped to the ground.

As she stepped back from the window, her feet made a crunching sound on a swarm of dead flies. She shuddered. Scanning the room, she gasped in disgust. It was a long time since she'd been in one of these.

In the far corner was a stained brown mattress topped with a muddled heap of scrappy blankets. A pile of cigarette papers, roach stubs and ash beside the mattress suggested that whoever lived there found little use for ashtrays. The trail of old pill bottles, empty silver pill packets, used coke cans and water bottles led to a low table covered with further evidence of drugs use. Syringes, bent and brown stained spoons and a tea strainer were scattered across old newspapers. A roll of silver foil, the edges ripped away and ragged, lay beside another heap of old ash, stubs, scraps of cling film, little plastic bags and old water bottles. She felt filthy even though she'd touched nothing yet and was pleased that Derek was outside. If he'd come in with them, he'd have cut his paws on the needles and broken glass scattered across the floor.

Jim indicated they should stay where they were. Then he phoned it in. 'Yes, that's right, number ten. We need a full CSI crew here as soon as possible. Thanks.'

He returned to stand beside them. 'This is now a crime scene. You can stay there, but don't move any further. You know the drill.' They nodded. 'In there is one of the filthiest lavatories I've ever seen and, in the bath, a body.'

'Really? Not your after shave then!' said Hale.

'Piss off, Hale, and thanks for ruining my first free Saturday for a month. We now have what looks like an execution on our hands. He's been shot in the back of his head, with the exit wound at the top of his forehead – or what's left of it. Been there a few weeks.'

Steph shivered. 'Is it Darcy? The body, I mean?'

'Describe him.'

'Nigerian descent, white father, very good looking and about six foot three.'

'No, that's not him. He's white. Had dark hair, I think.'

Steph relaxed, relieved that the body in the bath was not Darcy. For a moment, she'd dreaded having to go back to Esther to tell her Darcy had been killed.

The door, which Hale had pushed to after they'd entered the flat, flew open. They swivelled round to face Darcy, looking as shocked as they were. Hale's swift move behind him cut off any chance of escape. He hadn't tried to move towards the door, but closer to Steph. 'Steph, what are you doing here?'

13

SATURDAY 7TH OCTOBER: 9.45 AM

STEPH

'I COULD SAY the same to you, Darcy. Your mother's worried sick. Where've you been and what are you doing here?'

At that moment, he took in the others. 'Why? What's happened?'

'That's what we'd like to ask you, son.' Jim invaded Darcy's personal space and came up to the top of his chest. Steph hadn't realised Jim was quite so short. Darcy appeared elegant, well-dressed and out of place in this dump of a room.

A van and a car drew up outside and, as the CSIs were putting on their white suits, Jim, followed by Hale, climbed up the steps to meet them. Taking advantage of the absence of the two men, Darcy moved closer and said in a whisper, 'What are you doing here with the police?'

Before she could answer, she heard her name called out by Hale and realised there was no way the CSI team could get into the room. Indicating that Darcy should go up the steps onto the pavement, she untied Derek and followed him.

'Is that your dog?' Darcy bent down to pat Derek as if he was out for a Saturday morning stroll, not visiting a drugs den.

Jim appeared and patted Darcy on the shoulder. 'Right son, let's all get in the car and have a little chat.'

Steph glanced at Hale and moved her eyes to the car. Did that include them? He shrugged his shoulders and nodded. Where else were they to go?

All four of them walked up the road towards Hale's car. Jim held open the back door for Darcy to get in. He slid across the back seat and folded his long legs in the small foot well, followed by Jim, who climbed in beside him. Steph, having loaded Derek into the boot, joined Hale in the front and they swivelled around.

'Now, when did you arrive here from Suffolk?' Jim pulled the car door shut.

'Last train, Thursday night. I think I've got the ticket here somewhere.' Darcy wriggled around and dipped into his jacket pocket, but his hand emerged without the ticket. He raised his eyes in apology and opened the inside of his jacket. Jim winced and jolted back in automatic reaction, but relaxed when a Greater Anglia rail ticket appeared. Jim squinted at it, took out his mobile phone and photographed it before handing it back.

'Right. That seems to fit. An open return. When did you intend to go back?'

'I wasn't sure. I'm still not. I want to find Luke first to tell him how he's put my sister in a coma.'

His eyes misted over as thoughts of Marianne clearly moved into his mind. He ran his hands under his nose and across his eyes. Steph felt in the side of the door but couldn't find any tissues, just the rustle of lots of chocolate bar papers.

'Tell him, eh? And then what? Where've you been since Thursday?'

Darcy sighed, lowered his head, and took a deep breath

before facing Jim again. 'I've been on Luke's trail. He told my mother he had a place in Canary Wharf, but I haven't found it.'

Jim made a note on his phone, lowered it and, with a quizzical look on his face, stared at Darcy. The silence became uncomfortable.

At last, Darcy gave in. 'This isn't the only place he dosses down, you know. He has loads of dens. I started off here first, but it was empty, so I left.'

'Then where did you go?'

Darcy recounted his travels across London. He'd stayed in a cheap Airbnb near Victoria station, as he thought it was central to his search, and he produced a receipt on his phone as proof. Darcy named four other addresses across London, in Camden, Brixton, Hoxton and The Oval, where he'd visited, hoping to find Luke. Apparently, Luke had been at all of them at some time, but Darcy hadn't found him.

Hale whispered beside her, 'Quite an empire.'

'Right, son. How do we know you didn't find him?' asked Jim.

Darcy looked across at Jim as if he had a very low IQ. 'If I'd found him, I wouldn't still be searching for him here, would I?'

'Less of the cocky answers, son. So why did you come back here?'

Darcy sighed. 'Last ditch effort, I suppose. I decided it was worth going round them all again before going back home.'

A knock at the window made them all jump. As they were steamed up, they couldn't see who it was, so Jim and Hale opened their doors and got out, allowing a blast of fresh air into the car. They stood outside and Steph could hear the female pathologist giving her initial findings to Jim. She could hear the speech, not the actual words, but felt she shouldn't get out of the car. She saw the pathologist hand something to Jim, which he showed to Hale who nodded towards the car. Relieved that Derek had been silent throughout the interrogation, she turned to check that he was lying down. Darcy caught her eye and broke the silence. 'How's Mother?'

'As you'd expect, devastated and not sure how to cope. She needs you at home, Darcy. Let's hope the police let you come back to Suffolk.'

'Why wouldn't they? I haven't done anything.'

'Yes, but they need to be confident of that—'

Hale poked his head through the open door. 'Could you two come out here for a moment?'

They both climbed out of the car and joined Hale on the pavement. Jim stood at the top of the steps as two of the techs carried out a stretcher on which lay a black body bag.

Darcy gasped. 'Is that a body?'

'Yes, it is, son. And it appears you're in the clear. The pathologist says he was killed well before you arrived on the scene. But I'd be grateful if you'd have a quick look at this and see if you know who it is.'

Jim held out a square of four small photographs, headshots of a man in his twenties, which Darcy examined through the transparent evidence bag. It was bizarre to see photos on old fashioned photographic paper instead of a phone. They appeared to have been taken in one of those photo booths, perhaps for a passport.

'That's Luke.' Darcy paused. Something in the tone of his voice made Steph search his face. He appeared calm. It could be the shock of seeing the body bag. After all, how many eighteen-year-olds have experience of murdered corpses?

He continued to look at Steph, telling her the story. She was aware of the men listening to him intently. 'We met at Latitude last July. Marianne fell in love with him, then stayed down here with him over the summer. Luke used her and now she's in a coma because of what he's done to her. I'm glad he's dead.'

'Thanks, son.'

The white-clad men finished pushing the stretcher into the van then closed the doors, nodding to Jim as they climbed in. The four stood in silence and watched until it reached the main road.

Jim turned to Hale. 'Well, that was an exciting morning. I need all three of you to come to the station with me to give statements and have your prints and DNA taken so I can exclude you from the investigation.' He turned to Darcy. 'I'm assuming you haven't been inside but only touched the outside of the door?'

'Yes. That's right.' Darcy replied in a subdued voice. Again, Steph felt uncomfortable and suspected there was something he wasn't saying. Since he'd identified Luke, it appeared as if all his energy had sapped away. Maybe it was because his mission had been completed by someone else.

'Let's get going. We should be finished with you by teatime then Hale here can drive you back to Suffolk. It would be best if you stayed up there, son, and didn't get involved with stuff that doesn't concern you.'

Walking back to Hale's car beside Darcy, once again Steph admired his composure. It had been no joke identifying the body, even on a photo, but, although subdued, he appeared to have coped well. At last, the smell of death was disappearing a little from her nose. She knew it would stay with her until she showered, using a massive amount of shower gel and perfume to drown it.

She looked across at Darcy. Once again she was struck by his good looks, perfect manners and soft voice. His clothes hung well – he could wear anything and it would look good on him. He caught her eyes, and she smiled. 'Sounds as if you've had quite an adventure.'

Darcy sighed. 'Don't know whether to be relieved or angry about it. Suppose it's good someone got there before me. Anyway, how did you know I was up here and come to look for me?'

His question forced her into a corner. Should she tell him about Esther's tracker app? How else could they have known where he was?

'Your mother told us.'

'How did she— Ah! The magic app! She threatened she'd put it on our phones but I thought she didn't know how to do it. How stupid of me – I never through to look. I'll get rid of it.' He pulled his phone out of his pocket.

Hoping to distract him, she changed the subject. 'Well, back to college on Monday.'

'Yeah. And you never told me why you're with the police.'

'Quite simple. I was a police officer before my job in the college and they asked for my help.'

'So, a sort of double agent, then?'

'No, not at all. I'm helping Hale take down the drugs line. Trying to stop the people who gave the corrupted drugs to Marianne that—'

'—may kill her.' he interrupted.

His voice, sharp and strong, made her turn her head towards him. He reached out and touched her arm. They stopped. He looked deep into her eyes, 'Then we're on the same side.'

14

SATURDAY 7TH OCTOBER: 8.00 PM

STEPH

AFTER THEIR STATEMENTS, prints and DNA were taken, and Derek had been fed and watered, they left London in the early evening and were soon driving through Essex. After the city's well-lit streets and the M25, it came as a shock to rely on the red lights of the car in front and the wavering beams of the headlights as they penetrated the driving rain.

Steph had never enjoyed driving at night and she was relieved that Hale, who was a good driver, was happy to take control, but in these conditions, she wished he would slow down. He patted her knee as she pushed her foot down hard on the non-existent brake once again. She couldn't help doing it, but clearly it was getting up Hale's nose, so she placed her foot flat on the floor to remove the temptation of pressing the phantom brakes.

The journey had been in silence for much of the way, apart from neutral comments about the traffic and the appalling driving skills of lorry drivers racing each other when neither HGV engine had sufficient power to compete. It was as if there had been a tacit agreement between the three of them not to talk about the momentous day they'd shared. It was not every day you found a body in a bath after all, but Darcy didn't appear to be phased by it.

Hale took a deep breath and said, 'Are you going to tell us about your visit, Darcy?'

'I told the policeman who took my statement.'

'Indeed, you did, but that stays with the Met. It would be helpful for us to know what you've found out, as I'm convinced the line in Suffolk originates there.'

Steph knew all Hale had to do was ask Jim for a copy of the statement and he'd email it over, but she waited for Darcy's answer. There was a pause and a slight rustle as Darcy made himself comfortable in the back seat. He cleared his throat.

'Well, as you know, I left Mother late Thursday night and went to London on the last train. I got the circle line to Victoria, where I'd booked an Airbnb on my way down, then caught the bus to Battersea.'

He went on to recite the list of houses he'd visited on his quest to find Luke – the same list she knew Jim had given Hale before they left. It sounded as if he was hoping they would accept his story as a tour of London on the tube and buses and stop there.

'Yes, you told us all that earlier. Now tell me what you learned about the line into Suffolk.'

'Not much.'

'Well, tell me what you did find out then. Surely you want to help us stop it after what's happened to your sister.'

It appeared that Hale had pressed the right button; Darcy's voice was much louder as he replied. 'Of course I do. That's what all this shit has been about. Why do you think I did it?'

'So, don't keep it a secret. Tell us what you know, and we

might be able to do something about it. You surely don't think you can sort it out alone like some caped crusader, do you?'

'I think I'd stand a better chance than the police. You lot haven't done such a great job so far, have you? If you'd done your job properly, then Marianne wouldn't be in a coma, would she?'

Steph looked across at Hale and knew he was taking a bit of a risk. Although Darcy was over eighteen, so technically an adult, suppose he came out with something incriminating that wasn't recorded? She decided to say nothing, knowing that Hale was desperate to stop the lines ruining kids' lives, like Marianne putting them in comas or worse, killing them.

Steph got in before Hale and Darcy started shouting at each other. 'Come on, this isn't going to solve anything. You both want the same thing after all.' She waited for the tension to dissipate before continuing. 'Tell me, Darcy, did you find out who'd been supplying the contaminated ecstasy that Marianne took?'

He sighed, paused, then said in a much calmer voice, 'Yes, I think I did. I told you I visited about four addresses where I thought I'd find Luke, or Antony, whatever he's called, and saw the extent of his empire. I must have seen over twenty kids working in those dumps, managed by his lieutenants. Luke runs it like one of the large companies we learn about in Business Studies. Each den has a group of kids, mostly chucked out of school or moved out of home, care homes, many of them.'

Darcy stopped as Hale hit the brakes and swerved when a BMW cut in front of him from a slip road on the left.

'Cor! That was close!' Steph couldn't stop herself from exclaiming and she shifted her knee, which ached from pressing her foot down so hard. 'Sorry, Darcy, go on.'

'It was like the gang had become their family. The boss

would come in with treats for them – sweets, pastries, MacDonald's, takeaways. One day one of them brought in a video game for their breaks.'

'Breaks? From what? What were they doing?' said Steph.

'Mostly sorting the food – you know the drugs – weighing and packing them into wraps. The stuff's brought in by the boss, then the kids, teenies they're called, weigh it into little amounts on scales, like they have in the science labs in college, and wrap them in bits of foil or little plastic bags.'

'Sounds like quite an operation.' Steph glanced at Hale, who gave a brief nod, as if to tell her to continue.

'It is. Massive. The kids work all day in the dens and then a few become runners. They deliver the wraps out to the dealers, on bikes mostly.'

'Bikes?'

'Who's going to suspect an eight-year-old kid on a bike?'

'Eight?' Steph was shocked. Why weren't these kids being looked after and missed? So much had changed since she'd left the Met.

'Yeah, I saw several about that age.'

'Don't they get scared and want out?'

'One of the lieutenants talked to me – I think he fancied me to run the line up here – he said they scared them stiff. Tell them they'll be put five feet under, or if they still care about their families, they'll get hurt.'

'Really?'

'Yeah, they go from a caring crew to vicious mobsters in a moment. One of the kids told me he carried the drugs in his... er... his inside... you know... up his bottom.'

Steph smiled at the use of the childish word, as if he didn't want to shock her by using worse. 'Oh?'

'They call it plugging so they can travel around and not be

found carrying stuff. The elders in the crew threaten to cut them... you know... there... so they can never plug it again. That terrifies them. They all say they know one kid where it's happened.'

Darcy was describing a world in the shadows most people didn't know existed. No wonder the police found it difficult to investigate this sophisticated underworld.

'And did you manage to find out who'd supplied that ecstasy to Marianne?'

'I'm convinced it was through Luke. He may not actually have handed it to her, but he made it happen.'

'Really?'

'I told Mr Connolly. One of his lieutenants running The Oval den said something about going up country beyond Ipswich.'

'Good, that's a start.'

Rain battered the windows. It was getting worse. Steph gasped as she felt the car aquaplaning. In the darkness, Hale obviously hadn't seen that the road was flooded. He got control of the car and joined the slow queue pushing through the deeper water. At last, the tarmac re-appeared, and they picked up speed. Derek had not emerged or made a whimper during the drama – good boy!

Darcy sat back from perching on the edge of the front seat. 'You know, I can't understand why she fell for him. He may be attractive, but he's a hard bastard underneath the charm. In the summer, we lost contact – I mean, we still texted and emailed but she was distant as if she was in a different world. I suppose she was.'

He paused and sounded pained. 'When she came back, she was troubled by something but wouldn't tell me what. It's my fault. I should have sussed him out and stopped her going with him.'

'You mustn't blame yourself. Marianne made her own choices, and it sounds as if you couldn't have stopped her.'

'No, but we can stop them bringing in the drugs to Suffolk.'

'Can we?' asked Hale. 'I tell you, it's a tough job. All those dealers you met in the dens are there to satisfy the cravings of their customers. There are thousands of them out there.'

Once again, Darcy leaned forward so his head was between them. 'Marianne got caught up in that world and couldn't get out. I want to help – stop others like her from getting trapped.'

Hale turned off the A12 towards Southwold.

15

SATURDAY 7TH OCTOBER: 11.00 PM

STEPH

THE PORCH LIGHT guided them down the lane to Esther's house. Darcy had become quieter the closer they got to Southwold and now sat silent as they drew up outside the house. Hale turned the engine off and lifted both arms up to the roof to stretch his back after the long drive and even longer day.

'Ooh! That's better! OK, Darcy?'

'Fine, thanks.' Still, he didn't move.

Steph climbed out and opened Darcy's door. 'Right, let's get you home, shall we?'

Darcy met her eyes and at last got out of the car. She pushed the porcelain bell and waited, with Darcy and Hale standing behind her. Footsteps tapped down the tiled hall before the door was opened by a pale and exhausted-looking Esther. No bright paisley shawl today, just the dark shades of mourning. Had Esther received news from the hospital? She gazed at the group as if she hadn't met them before.

Steph moved sideways, thinking the mother couldn't see her son. 'Home at last.'

'So I see – do come in.' Esther stood aside and made an

open gesture with her right arm, ushering them into the house. Esther said nothing to Darcy and didn't seem too pleased to see them either. Perhaps she was inhibited by Hale's presence? Steph took a step past Esther, then stopped. Hale crunched into her back.

'Sorry, Esther, this is Philip Hale. I think I told you we used to work together.'

'Pleased to meet you. Thank you so much for using your contacts in London. I'm so grateful.' They shook hands. He moved away so she could see Darcy, who hovered behind them and stepped in front of his mother.

'Darcy, at last.'

Surprised at the cool reception Darcy received, Steph recalled Esther's desperation when she'd received his text message and her pleading that they should rescue him. Now she was behaving as if they'd just brought him back from the shops. No hugs, kisses or even signs of relief that he was home and safe. What was going on?

The sitting room light threw a bright oblong on the black-and-white tiles. They trooped down the hall towards it and Esther waved her hand at the chairs, indicating they should sit. Esther turned off the TV – a snatch of Jane Austen frocks flickered before the screen went black. The room was chilly and felt uncomfortable, as the fire wasn't lit.

Steph noticed that as he had passed Esther, Darcy had moved towards his mother to embrace her, but she'd stepped back, changed direction and sat down, as if she wanted to avoid any physical contact. Hale's left eyebrow raised as he pulled a 'what's going on?' face to Steph, who responded with a tiny shrug of her shoulders.

Darcy sat beside Hale on the sofa. No one said anything, but all looked ahead. The silence became uncomfortable until

Darcy broke it. 'Steph and Hale did a great job in finding Luke, Mother. He's been killed. Good to know that scum is off the street.'

Esther sat upright. 'You didn't think that when you introduced them, did you?'

Darcy's head jolted back as if he'd been hit. Steph was taken aback by Esther's cold aggression to him. 'Look, Mother, it wasn't my fault. You can't blame me.'

'You took her to Latitude and let her get involved with that man when you should have been looking after her.'

'I can't help it if she fancied him and went off with him. Anyway, you didn't object when she disappeared to stay with him in those dumps in London, did you?'

Tears appeared on Esther's cheeks. She turned away and wiped her hand across her face.

Hale stood. 'It's late. I think it's time we got home.'

Steph joined him, not wanting to get involved in this domestic row, which could go round in circles. She was shocked at Esther's behaviour. After all, Darcy had been trying to help, and she appeared to be blaming him for the mess Marianne had got herself into. Maybe she was missing something?

Esther stood. 'Sorry. So rude. Thank you both so much for bringing Darcy home and I haven't even offered you a drink.'

'No need. Pleased we could help.' Hale moved to the hall door.

He was beaten to it by Darcy, who opened it for him and said, 'Thank you. If you hadn't been there, I'd probably still be in a cell under suspicion.'

'You're welcome.' Hale smiled but Steph felt him bristle at Darcy's comment.

'Good night.' Steph nudged Hale into the hall.

As they walked out of the front door, Esther rushed out to

stop them. 'I forgot to tell you, Marianne woke up and she should be home soon. They think she may recover.'

Steph smiled. 'That's wonderful news. I'm so pleased.' She hugged Esther and, stepping back, noticed Darcy watching from down the hallway, also hearing the news for the first time. She smiled over Esther's shoulder at him. 'Goodnight, Darcy, Esther. We'll leave you to celebrate the good news.'

Steph shivered as she shut the car door. Hale started the engine and moved the heater dial to full. 'Soon be warm.'

As they drove off, she could see Darcy standing alone on the porch. He raised his hand to wave them off before turning and closing the door. To go inside to what?

'Was it me or was that the weirdest homecoming ever?' Hale turned the heater fan down a little so he could hear her answer.

'You're right. Did you see Esther wouldn't go anywhere near him – wouldn't touch him?'

'Yeah. Obviously blames him for all that's happened.'

Steph held her hands to the air vents on the dashboard. 'And she didn't tell us about Marianne waking up until right at the end. She knew all the time but still had a go at Darcy.'

'Families, eh?' Hale sighed. 'Sunday tomorrow. Great. We can have a lie in, can't we?' He moved his hand over hers. 'Your hands are like ice. Not long and we'll be in the warm.'

Arriving in Oakwood, they drove along the deserted High Street, the shops in darkness, with a few people leaving The Leg of Mutton and Cauliflower as its restaurant closed. It felt so different back here in Suffolk after seeing her old stamping ground in London again. Recalling Jim's lined face and the dark bags under his eyes, she realised she was lucky to have moved away from the stress of working in the city.

'I was thinking about Jim. How he's aged. He looked so much younger and fitter the last time I saw him.'

'Don't we all?'

'Yes, but he looks deeply exhausted, as if he's gone well beyond sleep.'

Hale turned into Steph's road, pulled up outside her house, switched off the engine and turned to her. 'I bet he's cursing us, after thinking we were simply looking for Darcy, then finding that body. So much for his weekend off.'

Derek leaped out of the boot, and Steph waited while he relieved himself against the lamppost. Leading the way to open the door, she turned to Hale. 'Did you notice anything funny about Darcy's voice when he identified that body?'

'No. Why?'

'It's probably me, but I had the feeling he might be lying.

16

SUNDAY 8TH OCTOBER: 12.30 PM
STEPH

IT HAD BEEN after midnight when they got back from dropping Darcy home and collapsed into bed, pleased they could have a long lie in. Too exhausted for anything other than a gentle peck on the cheek, their early night had evaporated, but they certainly made up for it in the morning, if half-past noon could be described as morning.

Lying back, Hale continued to stroke Steph's breast and smiled. 'Umm. Let's stay here for the rest of the day. We'll take Derek out later. He also looks exhausted after his visit to the big city.'

Although Hale hadn't mentioned the 'W' word, Derek had heard his name, climbed out of his basket and poked his head into the bedroom. He knew he wasn't allowed to step over the threshold and they could hear his tail wagging as it bashed against the open door.

'OK, boy.' Steph sighed. 'I'll feed him and let him out. Coffee?'

As she waited for the kettle to boil, she stepped outside onto the flag-stoned terrace. watching Derek patrolling the edges of the lawn to check on night visitors. She breathed into the very bottom of her lungs, the tang of an autumn bonfire filling her nose. The lawn was scattered with artfully shaped humps created by Derek in his regular bone burying and hunting.

Below, the cows in the dip concentrated on synchronised munching as they all slid in slow motion across the field towards the wood. Still warm enough to leave the door open, so Derek could stay in the garden snuffling for bones, she returned to the kitchen.

'Coffee, sir.' She put the mug on Hale's bedside table, climbed in beside him, and sipped hers. Her feet were cold from the flagstones, and she rubbed them along his legs.

He jumped 'Oy! They're freezing!' She moved them back to her side. He caressed her thighs, and she giggled, wobbling her coffee. 'Careful!'

'Umm!' He hauled himself up on his elbows and sat against the padded headboard, enjoying the strong, nutty taste of the coffee. 'Good stuff, this.'

The thin sunlight pushed through the slats of the shutters and rippled across the duvet. Steph glanced sideways and smiled. A perfect Sunday. Hale, aware of her look, turned and winked. He had the most beautiful grey-blue eyes. She was so lucky. The lazy afternoon spread before them. Bliss!

The shriek of a mobile shattered their fantasy. They stared at it, willing it to stop. It did. Then it started again. No actual increase in the volume, but it sounded as if it had doubled.

'I'll get it.' Steph reached out to the bedside table and swapped her mug for the phone, still hoping it would stop. It didn't. 'Hello... Yes.' She turned on the loudspeaker.

'Steph, it's Esther. I have something important for you and

your – er – friend to see. It's urgent. May I bring it over to you? Today?'

'Sure. Say about four o'clock?'

'Thank you.'

Steph dumped the phone on the bed, lay back and groaned.

'We have a couple of hours...' Hale grinned, leaned across and caressed her, then moved down to arouse her with his tongue. He stopped and smiled up at her. He did look sexy. A ripple pulsed through her body. She pushed him back and climbed on top of him.

———

By the time Esther rang the doorbell, Steph and Hale were decent and sipping another coffee. After Derek performed his ritual greeting, he returned to his bed to devour the treats thrown there by Steph to distract him.

'Coffee?'

'No, thanks.'

Esther chose the armchair on the other side of the fireplace opposite Hale; Steph sat on the sofa between them. 'How's Marianne?'

'That's what I've come about. She's fine now and out of hospital.'

'That was quick – I mean, what fantastic news. You must be so relieved.'

'Yes, but... I went in first thing this morning to find her almost back to normal. Perhaps a little drowsy, otherwise fine. The doctor came on her rounds while I was there and said she thought Marianne could come home after another couple of days' observation.'

Esther fiddled with a large opal ring on her right hand, swallowed, then continued. 'Marianne got very angry, insisted on coming home with me. I was so embarrassed – she was so rude to the doctor.'

She glanced at Steph, who gave her what she hoped was a sympathetic look. 'That doesn't sound like Marianne.'

'Well, it didn't used to be. That's what worried me. But I couldn't do anything. They said she's eighteen, so can discharge herself.'

'Right.'

'Anyway, as I was waiting while they went off to sort out the paperwork, I noticed the doctor's notes were on the bed and I read them.'

'Oh?'

'I was so shocked.'

'Really?'

'They think she behaved as she did and collapsed because of taking corrupt MDMA – I looked it up – that's ecstasy. You knew all the time, didn't you?'

Steph felt herself blush. 'Well... I suspected, but didn't know for sure.'

Why should she feel so guilty? She was certain Esther had suspected it too and replayed their conversation after they took Marianne to hospital. Hadn't Esther used the phrase 'bad drugs' and blamed Darcy for getting her involved? Perhaps she shouldn't blame Esther for being confused. She must be so worried and all over the place with what she'd been through, and it sounded as if it wasn't over yet. Best to let it lie.

Before Esther could reply, Hale stood up. 'Let me get you a glass of water, Esther.' He filled a glass with water and handed it to her, and she gulped at it gratefully. 'Would you prefer me to go?' He remained standing beside her.

'No. I came because I want you to know – both of you.'

'If you're sure.' Hale returned to his chair.

Esther took another sip of water, placed the glass on the table beside her, adjusted her shawl around her shoulders and settled her hands in her lap before lifting her head to speak.

'All the way back from the hospital, she wouldn't say a word. I tried to talk to her in the car, but she either ignored me or told me to shut up. She walked through the front door, went upstairs, got changed and went out.'

'Where?' Evidently Hale hoped for an address.

'No idea.'

'But I thought you had trackers on their phones?' Hale looked puzzled.

'They seem to have disappeared. I've no idea where they are now.'

Steph got up to help herself to a glass of water, hoping Esther hadn't seen her guilty blush as she'd told Darcy about the app.

'I heard her talking to Darcy, then she grabbed her coat and they drove off. I've no idea where she is now.'

'Oh, Esther, you must be so worried.' Steph leaned towards Esther.

'I was furious when she'd gone, so I went to her laptop – she lives on it like they all do – to look at what she had on there, to see what she'd been doing. This is it.'

She picked up her red tapestry Gladstone bag, twisted the amber clasp and rummaged around in the bottom. Steph looked across at Hale, who raised his eyebrows. Clearly, he too was concerned what she might produce from the depths of her bag.

'Ah! Here it is.' Esther held out a data stick to Steph. 'I've downloaded several videos of when she was in London. I think it explains what's happened to her.'

Steph stared at the little piece of blue plastic. 'Are you sure you should be giving us this?'

'Absolutely. I sat for ages, ever since I found it, not knowing what to do. Then I thought of you two. I want it to stop. I want my Marianne back. I know you can help me.' She half stood and thrust the data stick towards Steph, who reluctantly took it.

Hale turned towards her and cleared his throat. 'You realise once we've seen it, we can't un-see it. Are you sure?'

Esther turned to him. 'Yes. I realise it's possibly illegal what I've done, but at least you'll know what's going on here, if you don't already. You can stop it.'

With that, Esther snapped her bag shut, stood, wrapped her maroon paisley shawl around her shoulders, and glided to the door. Steph followed and put her arm on Esther's shoulder. 'Keep going. If you need me, you know where I am.'

'Thanks, Steph. I know this is the right thing.'

Having shut the door, Steph leaned against it and sighed. 'Well, I'd never have predicted that when she phoned. What on earth is on this?' She held up the data stick.

'We'd better see, hadn't we?'

17

SUNDAY 8TH OCTOBER: 5.00 PM

STEPH

STEPH CARRIED her laptop to the table from her desk in the bay window and slotted in Esther's data stick. Hale pulled up a chair beside her. A column of files appeared on the left side of screen and Steph clicked on the top one. It was a video file.

Marianne's face appeared. It looked as if she was filming on her mobile, in a loo on a train. They could see the cramped space with a tiny metal wash basin and, as she moved the camera, her reflection in the mirror above it. The rhythmic sound of the travelling train dominated. The picture swung to a sports holdall on top of the sink before returning to her face.

'I'm filming this on a train from London to Oxford. The eleven ten on the sixteenth of August.' She paused. 'Not sure why I said that. It might be useful later? I've been staying with Luke in a house in The Oval. The reason I'm doing this now is I'm scared, really scared and need evidence in case it all goes wrong.'

She looked exhausted, with dark bags under her eyes, and her sunken cheeks suggested she'd lost weight. Her pale blue blouse was creased and needed a wash. Steph wouldn't have recognised this girl as Marianne if she'd passed her on a station platform. Her blonde hair was scraped back into a tight pony-tail and could also do with a wash. She had heavy black kohl outlining her eyes and dark red lipstick stained her lips. She reminded Steph of a child who'd smeared her lips with red Smarties, not the delicate, tasteful Marianne at college.

Steph gasped. 'What a transformation – doesn't look like our Marianne at all!'

'Shh! She's speaking again and the sound's not good.'

Marianne turned the camera towards the bag. A black sports bag in a shiny material. She unzipped it with one hand, pushed the opening apart and whispered, 'Honestly, I had no idea what was in this until I got on the train. Luke told me not to open it, but I heard something clank as I climbed up the step. When I was on the train, I opened it and saw this.'

She pushed the phone further into the bag and moved aside a grubby, blue-squared tea towel. Pushing the side of the bag down further to catch the light from the crazed pattern on the window, the contents were revealed. Steph gasped. A black handgun nestled in the material. Marianne moved the tea towel aside, being careful not to touch the metal of the gun, and a second one appeared.

'Freeze that a moment.' Hale leaned into the screen to get a closer look. 'That one at the top of the screen looks like a nine-millimetre pistol, and the one below it – wow! That's a semi-automatic. Serious pieces.' He nodded to Steph. She pressed play.

Marianne's hand could be seen going into the depths of the bag and shifting the tea towel to reveal a handful of gold-coloured bullets at the bottom. She wrapped up the guns, making sure she didn't touch them, zipped up the bag and turned the camera towards herself.

'I thought Luke loved me. If you love someone, you don't exploit them like this. When I met him at Latitude and first came down to London, he was so loving. Said I was the only thing that mattered to him, that we had a great future together. I thought we'd have a brilliant time going to clubs, art galleries, museums... That's what he said, and we did for a few days... about a week. Then he changed. Wanted us to stay in all the time, except when he told me to deliver packets to his friends. I travelled all over London, alone, with them stashed in my bag. He said if I loved him, I'd help him. I knew what was in them, but I thought I could—'

A hammering on the door interrupted her, and they heard a male voice. 'You in there, I need to see your ticket. I'll wait here.'

'Won't be a minute.'

The film stopped.

'What has that girl got herself into?' Steph closed the file and went down to the next icon. Another video.

Hale tutted, 'It's looking grim all right. I should have her arrested for possession of a firearm and conspiracy to supply drugs. No wonder Esther looked so scared.'

Once again, the screen was flooded with Marianne's face. This time in a darker place, outside, under some trees in full leaf. A line of oaks spread across the background and she crouched down in front of a bush spattered with white blossom. She appeared to be in the middle of the vegetation. Her voice was low, and she kept looking around to make sure she was alone.

'Now off the train in Oxford. In Botley Park. A few minutes from Oxford Station.'

The camera panned and a small brown river came into view with bushes on the edge of small promontories. It was deserted. 'Luke told me to take this bag to Oxford and not to open it, but hand it over to a man called Terry. Here by the river at one thirty. I assumed it was drugs. He runs the line here. Now I know it's more serious. I want to record it. I didn't know—'

The river somersaulted, and the screen went black. A rustling suggested she'd stepped out from the bushes. The muffled sound continued.

'You Tanya? Luke's nitty?'

'What's a nitty?' Steph whispered.

'Slang for girl. Now shh! I missed that – go back a bit.'

Steph slid her mouse back, and the conversation returned.

'—Luke's nitty?'

'Who are you?'

'Terry.' There was a pause. 'Here. You don't need to count – it's all there. Now hand over the food.'

Silence. The screen flashed alive and captured the back of a small man in jeans, black top, hoodie up, walking away through the trees in the distance. Marianne's face appeared, and she whispered, 'It's now one forty-five and he let me think it was drugs in that bag. Either Terry doesn't know or he put on a pretty good show. He gave me this.'

A picture of a well-used Jiffy-Bag swept onto the screen. Opened, it showed a pile of twenty and ten-pound notes. The screen went black.

'At least a thousand there,' said Hale.

'I wonder if he knew about the guns?'

'Probably. We'll never know. No way to identify him from that back view. Is there anything else on that stick?'

Steph returned to the first screen. There were two more files. The next one was sound only and again muffled. They strained to listen, heads down beside the computer, but it was difficult to make out.

'Can't you turn the volume up any further?' said Hale.

Steph did, and they could hear a distant Marianne and a male voice.

'Anyway, I've got to get back to do college work, so I'll have to go.'

'You can be useful to me up there. It's ripe. Set up another line.'

'I'm not sure, Luke... I think I want out.'

A pause.

'You looked in the bag, didn't you?'

'You told me not to.'

A pause.

'Ow!! That hurts!'

'Well – did you?'

'What?'

'Open it. Tell me or I'll cut you.'

A scream. 'OK! Stop! Yes, I did.'

A pause. A slap, then another, some shuffling and a scream. A chair or table scraped across the floor.

'I told you not to, didn't I?' His voice louder, nastier.

More slaps. Then loud sobbing.

'No way out now, sweetie.'

Another crash and loud crackles through the speakers, followed by his voice, quiet and menacing, close to the microphone.

'You thought you'd come down here and play the big girl for a few weeks, then go back? You're in it up to your neck, my love. No way can they tie those pieces to me. You'd be inside for years. Open your mouth and that's it.'

A gasp, 'Ow!'

Then silence.

Steph closed her eyes for a moment and breathed in slowly. 'What has she got herself into? It's like Marianne's being... being held hostage.'

'No signs of anything when you saw her in college?'

'No marks I can remember, but this must have happened weeks ago. And who'd guess she be involved in dealing? Marianne, the perfect student.'

'That's what makes Luke so clever. He must have spotted her potential when they met at Latitude. Bright, innocent little girl who knows the local area and the kids. Who'd suspect her?'

'He groomed her?'

Hale nodded, shifted his chair back. 'Ooh! Got a stiff back sitting crouched over for so long.' He stood and, holding on to the back of the chair, bent over, stretching and flexing his spine. 'Yes, he really wanted her to find the guns in the bag and then he'd have her. Some serious shit she's in.'

'Even with the film and sound recording?'

'Depends on what else we find out and what she's done since she came back to Suffolk. I wonder if she has been running a line?' He sat down, flexing his back and looking at the screen. 'Wasn't there one more?'

Steph wobbled the mouse, revealing the line of folders, and clicked on the remaining file. This time Marianne's face was in a room in sunlight. Steph moved in close to the screen. 'That could be her bedroom. I recognise the shutters.'

Shelves of books, some hardback but mostly paperback, were held upright by piles of ring binders at each end. Old oak shutters folded back from the window let in the light. Their brass hinges glinted in the sun.

Straight to camera, once again Marianne looked exhausted, her voice soft and weary. 'I was stupid, thinking I could control it. I checked on the internet and Luke's right, I'd go to prison if they found out about the... what was in the bag. I really thought I loved him. I did... I think I did. He was so grown-up and loving and so different from the pathetic lot up here. I'd never met anyone like him. It felt so exciting being with him in London. He knew how to live. He made me feel as if I was the most beautiful woman he'd ever met.'

'We'd lie in bed and make wonderful plans for our future together – travels across Europe after my A Levels. Florence, Amsterdam, Venice – all the great cities, and I'd be with him. I felt so safe and as if my life was beginning at last. Now this. No way out.'

She sighed and rubbed her eyes. 'I can't stand it for much longer. On Wednesday evenings, I pick up a bag from the car outside St Mary's Church or the station, ready for the weekend. Kids at college bump into me or they send their orders on a burner phone he gave me. I get invited to parties and pubs and pass it over.'

'I'm their dealer, their pusher, their pill lady, their source.' She stopped and wiped away the tears that spilled over onto her cheeks. 'I no longer know who I am. All I know is I can't stop. He won't let me. I owe him and have to work it off. I think the last lot he sent was cut with something – it wasn't good. I want it to stop. I want to go back to me, the me that was. Not sure how, but I want out.'

The screen went blank. They sat for several moments, transfixed by what they'd seen.

Steph sighed. 'How depressing. She's nothing more than a slave to that Luke. Have you any idea how she can get out? Surely now he's dead, she can escape?'

'No. She's right. She's trapped. One of his lieutenants will have taken over. If she comes in to us, she's likely to face prosecution, even if we take coercive control into account. If she tries to get out, the new man will punish her. Possibly kill her. She's setting up a valuable line here from the sound of it.'

Having got through the data stick, Steph felt contaminated by the vile drug world out there. Although Hale had his head stuck in the paper, she could see, as she made supper, that he wasn't really concentrating and suspected he too had been shocked by the mess Marianne was in.

Clearing up after their roast beef dinner, they were enjoying a quiet night in front of the box when Steph's phone rang, making them both jump. 'Who's this? It's after nine o'clock.' She grabbed her phone.

'Hello... Oh no!... Are you sure? ... We'll be over right away.'

'Who was that?'

'Marianne's in a coma again and Esther says she's not breathing!'

18

SUNDAY 8TH OCTOBER: 7.00 PM

DARCY

DARCY WAS RELIEVED when Marianne glanced at the door and signalled it was time for them to leave. They both had college the next day and needed to be up early. As ever, he envied Marianne's confidence as she worked her way round the room at this gathering. Too small for a party but big enough for the rap music pounding out of the gigantic speakers to vibrate the windows. Crammed in the front room, about fifteen or twenty bounced around to the beat. Through the sweet brown smoke, they looked like a single animal with a mass of heads.

He was still worried about her – she looked so pale and fragile. She said she felt fine, but she'd discharged herself from the hospital when the doctors had wanted her to stay there. Doctors don't want you to stay in hospital for fun, do they? She'd come home, had a row with Esther then pleaded with him to take her to Oakwood, to this party. As usual he did what she wanted.

Darcy scanned the room for Luke, as this was why she'd asked him to drive her there. It should be easy to spot him – tall, blond, floppy hair, always with a group of adoring girls clinging to him. They'd met Luke the first day at Latitude, the four-day festival up the road from Southwold. By day two Marianne had left their tent and moved down the field to Luke's, which was unusual for her, as she was always chased by boys and never committed herself. But this time it was different. Very different. She was entranced by him, as was their mother, when Marianne took him home on his way back to London.

His public-school accent and supreme confidence, along with his family connections and their large country house in Berkshire, convinced his mother that Luke could be exactly the right man for Marianne. He'd been to St. Andrew's. Another box ticked. He worked in the City at something he was vague about but which sounded impressive enough to re-assure their mother and to persuade her, despite the age gap, to let Marianne go to stay with him in London for a few weeks in the summer holidays.

'I'll take good care of her, Mrs Woodard, and you'd be welcome to visit my flat in Canary Wharf. You too, Darcy.' That speech clinched it. Off she went to London and came back a very different person.

Since she'd come home, Marianne had told him some of what she'd seen with Luke, but he sensed it wasn't everything. Nightmares now dominated her dreams. Some mornings he would wake to find her asleep on the rug beside his bed, wrapped up tight in her duvet. They had set up camps like this when they were kids. He thought, hoped, she'd stopped using as the further she got away from London, the calmer she became. If only he could have stopped her from going away and could now keep her from parties like this one. It was a total shit show. What was she doing with these people?

He watched her as she moved around the room, chatting to

one group, sharing a joke with another. She'd always been popular and had no trouble making friends. Standing with his back against the wall, Darcy was always the observer, on the outside of the action. While Marianne was in the middle of it all, she totally belonged.

Through the kitchen door, he could see her chatting to a man he hadn't seen before, who towered over her. He leaned against the wall. Darcy thought he looked like an older version of himself, but relaxed and oozing calm confidence. Marianne leaned into him so he could whisper something in her ear, draping his arm around her shoulders. She giggled, stood back, and playfully flipped her fingers across his chest.

Just as she was moving away, he pulled her back, said something that wiped her smile away and backed her against the wall. Most of her was hidden by the man's broad back, but Darcy saw him reach into his jacket and pass something to her, which she stuffed in her jeans pocket.

The man placed his hands on the wall, either side of her head, moved in closer and, locking her in, once again appeared to whisper something. She ducked under his left arm and emerged, trying to laugh. Darcy could see her mouth moving, then a smile, but underneath he sensed she was nervous as she made a direct line towards him, through the bodies moving as one to the relentless beat.

As she reached him, a piercing scream from the corner penetrated the ear-numbing sound from the beat box. Darcy stopped and turned round to see what was happening, but Marianne pushed him out of the door. 'Out, quick!'

'What's going on?'

'It's going to kick off. Go!'

They dashed out to the car and slammed the doors. Darcy didn't start the engine but stared across at Marianne, who, aware of his scrutiny, turned to face him. He looked her in the eyes as he spoke. 'What were you doing? Some of them were kids.'

'Only samples. If I didn't, someone else would've.'

'What?' He felt disgust flow through him and it must have reached his face as Marianne paused, looking out of her window before mumbling, 'Look, it's a business.'

'Listen to yourself! "It's a business" What the fuck does that mean?' He couldn't stand her when she was like this.

'They want it, we give it to them.' Why did she keep trying to justify the unjustifiable?

'You want to fuck them up like you were?' He was aware that he was shouting, as a couple passing in the middle of the road turned to see what was going on in the car.

'I was fine. I could cope.'

'Cope? You should have seen yourself. Totally fucked. And now, just when you're getting yourself sorted, you go back to it again. Why?'

Once again, she stared out of the window, and he was aware of her becoming tense and defensive. Desperate, he reached out for her hand, wanting to make contact with the real Marianne again, to cut through the crap. She wasn't having any, and pulled her hand out of his grasp. Clasping her hands on her lap, she picked at the skin at the corner of her thumb-nail. He lowered his voice and tried a different direction.

'But you said you wanted out.'

She didn't reply. He could feel her thinking about what to say next. They'd always been so close before she went to stay with Luke. Best friends who shared everything. Since she'd returned, the old Marianne had come back. Those weeks had been amazing.

A week ago, it all changed. She became distant and

worried all the time. Spent hours in her bedroom alone. Cut him off once again. Horrified by what he'd seen her do at the party, he didn't know what to say to this Marianne. As she reached out for his hand, she mumbled, 'I need to work it off.'

'Work what off?'

'My debt to Luke.'

He searched her face. What was she going on about? 'What debt? How much do you owe him?'

'Oh, Darcy. You don't understand. I should never have gone to stay with him. I owe him. A lot. That's all you need to know. This is the way I have to work it off. If I don't...'

She looked trapped and very, very frightened. He must be able to help her out of this mess.

'We need to tell someone about this. It's wrong... it's... blackmail or something... it must be illegal and you shouldn't have to do this.'

'Leave it Darcy, I know what I'm doing. It'll be over soon and anyway—'

A girl screamed as she ran out of the front door and was pushed over the garden wall by a boy, desperate to escape. He was chased by the tall boy from the kitchen and three others, shouting as they pursued their quarry out of sight around the corner.

'Darcy! Get going. Now! Before the feds arrive!'

He drove in the opposite direction to the chase. "Feds?" Where did that come from? Before London they were police.

'There's going to be trouble. Big trouble!'

Darcy turned off the main road towards Southwold. 'No shit! I can see that for myself.'

'Oh that? That was nothing. Dude, that guy in the kitchen warned me off. He works for Luke but said the other guy, the one he ran after, had turned and was running his own line up here and there's going to be a war.'

'Marianne, you're talking like some bad TV show. Stop it!'

'You've got no idea, have you? This is bad. I'm stuck in the middle of it and not sure how to escape.'

19

SUNDAY 8TH OCTOBER: 9.30 PM

STEPH

As they crossed Mights Bridge, they could see the flashing blue light magnified as it lit up the marsh. Steph drew up behind the ambulance. They dashed through the open door and into the sitting room. Empty. They stepped back into the hall. Steph called up the stairs, 'Esther!'

In the shadows on the landing above, the hem of a long skirt swished through the bannisters. Esther appeared at the top of the stairs and ran down, throwing her arms around Steph. 'Thank goodness you're here. It's not good. They're working on her before they take her to hospital.'

'Esther, I'm so sorry.' Steph hugged her. Esther stood back. Her mascara had run and left grey smudges down her cheeks. Her eyes darted between Steph and Hale in panic. 'It's different this time. They told me to leave. Do you think she'll be all right?'

Steph steered Esther to a hall chair and helped her to sit down before she collapsed. She knelt beside her and looked up into her face. 'We'll stay here so you can hear them when they call.'

Esther wiped her eyes with her sleeve. 'I phoned as soon as I found her on the floor in her room. Not like last time. Not like you saw. She was quiet, unconscious. I went to say good night and there she was. On the floor. I couldn't lift her onto the bed.'

Wringing her hands, she appealed to Hale. 'Phoned an ambulance as soon as I found her. I didn't hear a thing. Do you think if I'd found her sooner she might have been fine?'

'Don't say that. It's not your fault.' Her knees aching, Steph stood, Esther's eyes followed her. 'Anyway, we don't know what's happening up there. You did all you could.'

'But did I? Should I—'

Upstairs, a door opened, and a voice floated down the dark staircase. 'You can come up now.' A head appeared over the landing bannister, 'Would you like to come up?' This time louder.

Esther grabbed Steph's arm. 'Come with me, please.'

Steph helped Esther to stand and held onto her as she swayed. The head over the bannister disappeared as soon as they started to climb the stairs. At the top, they crossed the large landing through the open door of Marianne's bedroom. Steph recognised the shutters and bookcase from the video.

On the bed lay a beautiful Marianne. Her blonde hair fanned out around her delicate white face. Once again, Steph was reminded of the Victorian pictures of dying heroines.

The head over the bannisters belonged to a middle-aged bald man with deep smile lines etched into his face. He put his hand on Esther's shoulder. 'I'm sorry. We did everything we could. She—'

His words got drowned out by a scream so loud Steph's ears tingled. Esther flew across the room to Marianne, put her arms under her head, lifted her up, held her and kissed her over and over. 'No! Not my Marianne. No, look... she's warm. She's alive... You feel... she's not gone. Do something!'

The other paramedic stood at the end of the bed. Frozen. He looked about fourteen but was probably over twenty. The older man stood beside Esther. 'I'm sorry. We did everything we could. We couldn't save her. I'm so sorry.'

'But there must be more—'

'I'm so sorry. I'll call it in. They'll look after her.'

'No! She can't be – she'll come back like last time. Don't go!'

'I'm sorry, there's nothing else we can do.' With that, he picked up his bag, already packed with the defibrillator and the empty syringes of adrenaline they would have used while Esther was down in the hall. He glanced at the younger man, transfixed at the end of the bed. It took a couple of silent eye nudges from the senior of the two to get him to pick up his feet and leave the bedroom.

As he walked through the door, the young man looked over his shoulder and whispered, 'I'm so sorry.' If this was his first experience of death, it would have been grim whoever it was, but to see this beautiful girl, close to his age, emptied of life, clearly shocked him. She heard muffled voices in the hall as the paramedics spoke to Hale, the snap of the front door as it closed, then silence.

Esther sobbed, holding tight onto Marianne as if she could transfer energy to her through her skin and bring her back. At last, Esther laid Marianne's head on the pillow, tucked her arms under the duvet and smoothed her hair. Marianne lay as if asleep, but now there was no doubt she had gone. She was dead. Esther continued to stroke her hair, watching over her. Steph stood beside her, looking down at Marianne, not sure what to do.

'Would you like me to stay or would you like to be alone?'

'I'll stay with her. Here, alone. But don't go. Please wait.'

'We'll be downstairs. Can I get you anything?'

'No.'

Esther sat on the side of the bed. With her right hand, she leaned forward and rhythmically massaged the side of Marianne's temple as she would a restless child who couldn't sleep.

Steph crept out of the room, leaving the door open, and joined Hale, who stood in the hall. He opened his arms when she reached the bottom step and she fell into them, soaking up his warmth and life.

'Sorry, Steph. That must've been tough. I'm so sorry. I heard Esther.'

'She wants to stay with her and asked if we'd wait until...'

'That's fine. The paramedics called it in, and they'll be here soon. Let's put the kettle on. Where's the kitchen?'

His arm round her shoulder, she led Hale down the hall to the kitchen and together they made a pot of tea. Steph added two mugs and a milk jug to a tray and handed it to Hale. She was trembling and didn't trust herself to carry it.

She was grateful for the warm, sweet tea Hale handed her. He sat in Esther's chair and looked around the sitting room properly for the first time. 'Beautiful room.'

'It was her grandmother's, all these antiques and the books and the paintings.'

It felt wrong to be talking about such mundane things with Marianne's body lying still warm upstairs. Steph sighed, and they sipped their tea in silence. There was nothing to say. Such a grim, evil world where this beautiful girl, her life ahead of her, had been destroyed – for what? Money? Marianne was collateral damage in the big business of selling drugs.

There was a gentle knock on the stained glass panel of the

front door. Hale went through to the hall and she heard him open it then a whispered exchange before he stood at the door of the sitting room. 'They're ready. It would be a good idea to get Esther down here while they move Marianne. It's not something she should see. You OK to go up?'

'Yes, fine.'

Steph hauled herself up, aware of how tired she was, walked past the two men in dark suits waiting in the hall and climbed the stairs. It struck her as strange that the men should be in business suits with black ties on a Sunday night, but she supposed they'd hardly come in jeans, would they? She dreaded going into the bedroom again and seeing Esther's grief tearing at her.

A picture of Mike shunted into her head. She'd been working in the police station at Ipswich, down the corridor when Hale had found him, folded over his desk. It was too late. A massive heart attack. In professional mode, she hadn't cried and everyone said how strong she was. But having watched Esther express her grief, she wondered if she had loved him enough.

Esther was sitting on the bed where Steph had left her, but no longer touching Marianne. She wept and didn't appear to be aware of the wet tracks down her face or her runny nose. Steph pulled some tissues out of a box on the dressing table and handed them over.

'They're here. Downstairs. It's time, Esther. They'll look after Marianne. Why don't you come downstairs with me until they've gone?'

'She'd want me to stay.'

'No, she wouldn't. Come on.'

Too weak to resist, Esther allowed Steph to steer her towards the landing. As she was going through the door she stopped, turned, looked once more at Marianne, then, held up by Steph, walked downstairs.

In the sitting room, Hale, having vacated Esther's chair, stood to the side of the hearth. Steph held Esther's elbow and lowered her into it. Hale moved to the door and closed it.

While Steph had gone, he'd made another pot of tea and poured a mug for Esther, which she drank automatically. He'd also found some brandy, which he'd poured into a crystal glass and left on the table beside her. She appeared not to have noticed it, so Hale picked it up, held it out to her and took the empty mug off her.

Esther stared into the fire, which he'd lit to take the night chill off the room. Steph was impressed that he'd found the hidden gas tap and worked out how to turn it on. She chided herself for not crediting him with common sense. It was so good having him there with her.

No one spoke. They sat in silence, waiting for the muffled noises of the men carrying Marianne to disappear through the front door. At last, they heard the door pulled to, with a gentle click. The engine of the van sliced through the silence of the night and they tracked the noise as it disappeared up the road alongside the marsh.

Esther broke the silence. 'If only I'd gone up earlier, she'd still be here.'

'You shouldn't blame yourself,' said Hale.

'It was all my fault. You see – we'd had a row. A dreadful row. I was so angry with her. I told her I'd seen what she'd put on her computer.'

She held out her glass and Hale re-filled it from the brandy bottle. 'I shouted at her and told her she should be ashamed of what she'd been doing. She kept saying she couldn't escape, couldn't get away from it, but I didn't listen. All I could think of was how much damage she'd done to all those kids. I should have thought about her. I should have loved her, not shouted at her. It's my fault.'

They said nothing, letting Esther pour out her grief.

'She stood there—' Esther pointed to a spot on the carpet in front of the fire. 'She stood there, saying nothing. She listened to me screaming at her. She stopped arguing and wouldn't look at me. Then she said she was sorry for failing me and left.'

Pulling out a soggy tissue from up her sleeve, she blew her nose. 'I should have gone after her... but I was so angry. I should have gone after her, then she wouldn't have done it, would she? I should have known... that last bit on the computer. She couldn't live with what she'd done and she couldn't get out of it. I should have listened. I should have helped her, not made it worse. She's killed herself because of me.'

Vanquished, Esther slumped in her chair.

Steph stood in front of Esther. 'I don't think you should be here alone.' Looking around, for the first time she became aware someone was missing. 'Where's Darcy?'

Esther looked around the room as if registering his absence for the first time, too. Then shook her head. 'Oh, Darcy? He went to see Dickie. He dropped Marianne off, then left before... before our argument. He'll be back soon. Please don't wait. I'll be fine.'

'Are you sure?'

'Yes, I'm sure. Thank you both so much.'

On the drive home, neither spoke, unable to find any words to describe what they'd just witnessed. Steph felt hollowed out. What a tragedy and a waste of life. Marianne had been so talented and beautiful with a glittering future until she'd met that man. And there was Esther, riddled with guilt, convinced it was her fault. It hadn't taken long for that family who already had so much to cope with, to be torn apart. They pulled up outside Steph's flat and sat, not moving.

Steph turned to Hale. 'You know. There was something funny about that.'

'What do you mean?'

'Well, I assume she took contaminated ecstasy – pills – but I saw a puncture mark on her right arm, just inside her elbow.'

'She might have graduated to heroin. It happens.'

'Maybe that's it. But I think she's right-handed so, if she did inject herself, it would be on her left arm, wouldn't it?'

20

MONDAY 9TH OCTOBER: 8.00 AM
STEPH

STEPH CLOSED the door to Peter Bryant's office and returned to her post behind the reception desk. She'd spent the last fifteen minutes telling him about Marianne's death and her probable involvement in the local line. Shocked, he was unable to say much and found it difficult to believe that the beautiful Marianne, the outstanding student, his star college rep, could have been dealing drugs in his college.

It was helpful to share the news with someone, but she found it depressing. By talking about it, Marianne's death and the drama of the weekend became real again. The grey, over-cast day suited her mood. To see a young life ruined, taken away by a manipulative drug baron, made her furious. She imagined Luke, the controlling man in Marianne's recordings, not caring about how he'd ruined Marianne's life or how he'd enslaved her. Now they were both dead.

She hadn't told Peter about the detail of the videos and sound recordings Esther had given her, but tried to explain that Marianne had been entranced by an older drug dealer who'd pressured her to set up a line in Oakwood. He found it difficult to understand that, although Marianne was a dealer, she'd not chosen to do it but, like so many other kids, had been groomed and blackmailed into it. If only Hale and his team could break into this vicious cycle and get these kids out of the mess they'd stepped in.

Her thoughts were interrupted by Peter. 'Steph, could you come back in here for a moment, please?'

He beckoned her over to his desk, where he'd already set up a chair for her. He wiggled the mouse, and the screen lit up with the film from the security cameras in the canteen.

'It hasn't taken long to find her, has it?' He pointed to the jerky pictures of a girl with long blonde hair moving around the tables, greeting student after student with what appeared to be a friendly handshake. Both knew it was Marianne distributing drugs and accepting payment. So smooth. So simple.

'Do you know,' Peter continued, 'if I'd looked at that film last Friday without knowing the truth, I'd have suspected nothing. It's all too easy to con us, isn't it?'

'It's a different world out there now. If they didn't deal in here, they'd do it outside on the way home or in town where we couldn't see them.'

'You sound as if we should give up. As if there's no way to fight it.'

Steph was upset she'd created such a negative impression, but today it was how she felt. 'Sorry, Peter, but having seen the damage done to Marianne, I feel overwhelmed. It's like... it's like a... I don't know... a tsunami coming in and we can't stop it or protect our students against these bastards. Those at the top never get their hands dirty and make sure others get caught while they rake in the money. It's the Mariannes who suffer most.'

'Surely Hale and the police can do something? At the conference he sounded so confident.'

Aware she'd allowed her feelings and shock to dominate and contaminate Peter, she tried to pull it back. 'He and his team are working really hard to piece together the network that runs the line here. Whenever they find the runners, the kids on the ground, they add names and information to what they know and work with the Met to set up surveillance to stop the drugs from leaving London.'

'That's what he said at the conference, but it hasn't saved Marianne, has it?'

She sighed. 'No, you're right, it hasn't, but it's early days.'

Switching off the film, Peter took out a notebook from his desk drawer. 'Now, how do we tell the staff and students about Marianne?'

He couldn't have been listening when they spoke earlier. She repeated what she'd said. 'Hale suggests we keep it quiet for a day or so. Now, the only person who knows in college is Darcy and I don't expect he'll be in today.'

Hale planned to see him, to find out what he knew about the drugs line. When they'd brought him back, they'd assumed he wasn't involved in supplying Oakwood. Now they weren't so sure. Peter didn't look convinced, so she continued, trying to re-assure him.

'If we have a word with him, we may be able to keep it quiet for a couple of days. That'll give Hale a chance to follow up leads on some of the kids involved in a party over the weekend.'

Peter drummed his fingers on his desk, always a sign of his impatience. 'Not more of our students, surely?'

'Well, a few, I think. Jake Martin's—'

'Not our Jake! Jake can't possibly be involved in drugs!'

'No, not him but his neighbours, our students, might be.'

He sighed and collapsed into an armchair. 'What? This is dreadful!'

Steph sat opposite and stared into his eyes. Peter, usually so controlled and calm, was now panicking.

'Yes, it is appalling, but if we sit here and do nothing, it'll get worse. We can try to find out as much as possible about what's happened to Marianne. She'll have used other students to help her. We need to watch the CCTV pictures and walk around campus at break and lunch to spot anyone who's dealing. It's the wrong end of the week, I know – Thursday and Friday are the best days, but we have no choice.'

'But you know what will happen. As soon as you or I appear they'll cover it up.' Peter slapped his notebook on the table, clearly frustrated that he couldn't take decisive action.

At that moment, the door flew open to reveal Paul Field, who stepped inside the room without knocking. Somehow his smart grey suit always kept its knife-sharp creases and the bright red silk handkerchief matched his tie perfectly. He looked the part – a pity he couldn't play it. Steph pulled herself out of her chair, about to go, but Peter waved at her to sit down again.

'Could you give us a few minutes? I'll phone when we've finished.'

'Of course.' Deflated, Paul Field shot a poison glance at Steph, made a dramatic turn and shut the door rather loudly.

'Now, where were we? We need to move forward and try to find a solution or a way in, but I'm damned if I can think of one.'

She paused. She knew what Hale wanted, and he'd planned to come in himself later to approach Peter. But this moment felt just right. She took a deep breath. She knew she was going against what she and Hale had discussed but, trusting her instinct, plunged in. 'Hale's thought of that. He said if you agree, he'll send someone – a girl who looks as if she's their age, to go undercover as a new student and see if she can find out what's going on.'

Peter stared out of the window for a few moments, clearly weighing up his options. He sighed, sat up straight and looked across at Steph.

'I don't have much choice, do I? If I say no, it'll carry on anyway. At least if we have an uncover cop here, we might find out what's happening and try to stop another student dying. We've had enough death in this college after last year.'

He moved to the window and appeared to be fascinated by a student trying to park his car in an impossible space before giving up and driving off. She waited. He turned, picked up his notebook and went to his desk. 'Undercover cop? Listen to me – sounds like a bad crime novel. Please tell Hale to send her in. I'll interview her, as I would any new student. I presume she'll need a timetable and tutor group?'

Steph was relieved. For a moment, she'd thought he was going to refuse. He was right; he didn't have much choice, but it had been an enormous step for him to accept Hale's suggestion.

'I think Hale may want her in the same sets as some of the students he suspects. She'll tell you the names when she arrives.'

'And when's that?'

'After I phone him.' From the look on Peter's face, her confident reply was convincing, but inside she shuddered. She knew the extensive arrangements, paperwork and authorisations needed before an uncover officer could become part of an investigation but also knew Peter. He was only happy when he could solve problems, act, make decisions, and wasn't great at waiting on the edge of events.

She hoped Hale wouldn't be furious with her pre-empting him and knew he'd spent many hours climbing the necessary mountain of bureaucracy. Steph's mobile rang, and she looked at the screen. 'It's Hale. Do you mind if I take it?'

'No, carry on.'

Steph walked out of Peter's office and across to the corner of reception, where she couldn't be heard.

'Sorry for the delay, I was with Peter. I hope it's all right, Hale, but I mentioned the idea of a new student to him...' She held the phone a little way from her ear and checked that no one could hear Hale's fury at full volume. She decided not to interrupt his explosion.

'Yes, you're right, of course you're right. It was stupid to say anything before you'd fixed everything. I'm sorry.'

Listening patiently as Hale reminded her of all the hoops he'd jumped through to arrange the undercover officer in a college and to have Peter aware, she stared out of the window and winced as the same student car attempted to edge into a tiny space, the only one left in the car park before giving up and driving round the back. Didn't they ever learn?

'Yes, I am listening, and I do know how long it's taken to develop her backstory and build her legend... I can always tell Peter to hold on for a few more days... Oh, you're that close? ... What?... You're sure? Not another one. I'll tell him to expect you later.'

Peter looked up as she returned to his study and stood behind an armchair.

'When can I expect her?'

'Hale will be coming in at the end of the day to go through the details.'

'Fine, the sooner the better.'

'That wasn't why he phoned. They've found a body hidden under rubble on the waste ground at the end of Jake's road. He had an Oakwood College student card in his jeans.'

21

THURSDAY 12TH OCTOBER: 7.30 PM
STEPH

STEPH CLOSED THE FRONT DOOR, leaned on it with her shoulder, checked it was locked and climbed into Hale's car idling by the kerb. She could feel the electric tension, confirmed by the grim expression on his face. No idle chat, no kiss, nothing.

'Good day?'

'What do you think? A mass more paperwork, meetings and phone calls to get the necessary authorisations for tonight's little jolly.'

'Oh.'

'This had better get results or I'm in for it. And as for your Peter—'

'He's not—'

'Peter had better behave. We can do without his prima donna act.'

'That's not fair. It's his college. He's the one held to account if his students are harmed in all this. He has to protect them and his staff; that's his job.'

'We'll park here and walk the rest. I hope you told Peter to do the same.'

Deciding not to provoke any further moaning about Peter, Steph didn't reply but strode out beside him until they reached the second block of flats on the left after the Co-op on the Norwich Road. The anonymous slab of 1960s concrete was an excellent choice for a safe house. Nothing about it was memorable. Hale pushed in the four number code and the scuffed door buzzed open.

In silence they edged past two bicycles leaning against the pale blue wall, scarred with black marks and chunks of plaster crumbling where the handlebars and pedals rested, and climbed the concrete stairs to the second floor. Two flats on each floor were separated by a tiny landing lit by the half-light from the stairwell, but as they stepped further into the gloom, a security light flashed on and they could see the dark blue door of number five. Hale used a key to open the door into a well-lit sitting room.

Steph looked over his shoulder and could see two women sitting on a sofa beside a gas fire, Viv, she recognised from college but not the other one. Both women stood as Hale walked towards them, and the taller of them stepped forward and held out her hand to him.

'Hale, good to see you again. This is Viv, your Under Cover Officer. Viv, Chief Inspector Hale.' Viv stepped around the other woman, shook hands and smiled at Hale.

Hale made way for them to see Steph. 'And this is Steph Grant, our Civilian Detective, who also works at Oakwood College. Steph, Elizabeth Day, Suffolk Cover Officer and Viv, you'll know.' Steph leaned forward; grinned at Viv and shook hands with Elizabeth. When she was in the force, Elizabeth would have been known as a 'handler' but she supposed it didn't sound as important as this new title.

'We're expecting the Principal, Peter Bryant?' Elizabeth indicated they should sit at the light oak dining table inside a bay with floor-to-ceiling dark green curtains drawn to ensure total privacy. It had taken a great effort to get the authorities to allow Peter to be fully involved, but, as Steph pointed out, he had to interview and enrol Viv as a new student to create her timetable and do all the college admin necessary. She couldn't simply walk in off the street.

While they were waiting, she scanned the room. It would be quite a challenge to design a more boring interior. The dark grey solid sofa and single armchair either side the stained gas fire looked as if they'd been lifted from a dentist's waiting room. No pictures decorated the white walls, which reflected the single pendant light wearing a plain beige shade to make it feel more like home. It failed. No doubt the kitchen and bedroom, which she assumed were behind the two closed doors opposite, were the same depressing style. Imagine having to live in this sterile, colour-free place. Safe perhaps. But that would be good enough if you feared for your life.

Elizabeth also appeared to be designed as the ideal cover officer, instantly forgettable. In her late thirties, average height, wearing plain navy trousers, navy pullover and black shoes. There was nothing Steph could pick out to distinguish her. She wasn't wearing any jewellery except a simple watch, and her dark hair was pulled back in a tight ponytail. Even her face was devoid of expression – she hadn't smiled once – but after all, she was responsible for Viv's safety while she was in Suffolk, which was a serious job.

The buzzer by the front door interrupted her thoughts and an image of Peter appeared on the tiny video screen. Elizabeth turned to Hale. 'That him?' Hale nodded and took a seat with his back to the window beside Steph.

This meeting had been a big ask. An awfully big ask, but Hale, and later they discovered Viv, had felt it was essential to the operation. The normal procedures in which the Under Cover Officer only communicated to the investigating team through her Cover Officer had been amended, so that all those involved in the sensitive environment of the college could discuss progress and tactics and ensure that the students were protected during the surveillance.

Having been introduced to Elizabeth, Peter sat opposite Steph and Hale while Elizabeth took her seat facing Viv. In a flat tone of voice, Elizabeth spelt out the procedures they should follow in supporting Viv's undercover role. She asked if they had any questions, but they hadn't. Elizabeth sat back, her notebook open, waiting for Viv to tell them what she'd discovered in her first few days at Oakwood College.

Viv was at the opposite end of the pole to Elizabeth. She was twenty-two but looked about seventeen and wore the same uniform as the rest of the students – jeans, hoodie and designer trainers. A diamond stud on the left side of her nose twinkled in the light, and a line of gold earrings climbed up the side of her ears. As she pulled off her hoodie, she revealed a Banksy navy tee shirt with a cheeky bright yellow cartoon bear about to throw a Molotov cocktail. The orange and red flame matched her short red dyed hair. She certainly looked the part.

Peter appeared to be mesmerised by the image on her chest, but he had also taken in the interior of the flat. Steph had caught him as he sneaked a look around. Their eyes had met, and he'd smiled at her. She knew it was fascinating but at the same time disappointing to see the inside of a bland 'safe house' – like being in a le Carré novel or a film.

Hale took control. 'Thanks, Elizabeth, for agreeing to this meeting. After a couple of days, I suspect it's going to be a short one, but let's see what we have. Viv, over to you.'

Viv's voice was that of an actor. Deep, warm and right on the spot of received pronunciation, which was at odds with her appearance. Steph had listened to her chatting to students in the canteen and from her accent had assumed she'd come from east London or Essex. Her story was that she'd been sent up to Suffolk to live with an aunt to get her away from the local gangs. She was convincing, especially as she'd come from Dorset, far away from the lines Luke had established across London and the Midlands.

'Pretty good for two days, Sir.'

'Hale will do, thanks.'

Viv told them about her experience in Art, Sociology and Business Studies getting to know the group Hale had named as likely users and runners. She turned to Steph. 'Of course, Caroline had sussed me out in that first lesson, but you sorted it out brilliantly.'

'Who the fuck is Caroline?' Alarmed, Elizabeth also stared at Steph.

'Sorry, I didn't know what else to do,' said Steph, stammering like a pathetic schoolgirl being told off. 'She nobbled me having seen Viv's first drawings, which were nowhere near A Level standard – sorry, Viv – and insisted she should move to photography. I had no alternative but to explain.' She glanced at Hale searching for his support. 'Sorry, I did agree it with Hale before I told her. We decided there was no alternative. She'll never open her mouth.'

'This is becoming a total shit show!' Peter and Steph jumped as Elizabeth slammed her hand on the table and glared at Hale.

Before Hale could reply, Viv interrupted. 'Caroline's been amazing! She's saved me. Gave me a sketch book where she'd made loads of fine pencil sketches, which I can draw over and paint, so I'm as good as the others. Anyone looking at it would think I'd been working at home and brought them in to finish. The advantage of art is that she has music on all the time and the students chat. I hear all sorts of fascinating gossip.'

'Like?' prompted Hale, who appeared to be desperate to find out what she knew. Elizabeth sat back and listened to Viv's account, with a rather grumpy, unconvinced look on her face.

'Like when Dude's coming in.' Viv looked pleased that she could provide information so quickly after being planted in the college.

'Dude?' Hale and Elizabeth both wrote in their notebooks.

'From what you said, Steph, I think he's the guy you saw delivering drugs to Fred Castle, who, incidentally, is Dude's principal contact.' Viv paused and searched for something in her tiny, scuffed notebook. 'Yes, here we are. Dude, AKA Henderson Green. They've got quite a little business going on in college.'

Until then Peter had been quiet, but at this he groaned. 'On no! Really? How many do you think are involved, Viv?'

'Between twenty and thirty, I think, which isn't bad for a college your size. Dude arrives just before break Wednesday and Friday – but the big drop is Friday – meets Fred, makes his delivery, then gets out quick. The drop takes minutes.'

'Do we have him on CCTV?' Hale looked up at Peter.

'You won't,' Viv interjected. 'He's clever, that guy. Comes up the back pedestrian path and avoids all cameras. I watched him. If he comes near one, he pulls up his hood. You might catch his walk or his back, but no way will you see his face.'

'How disappointing. Surely you need to get a few more

cameras installed to ensure the safety of your students?' Elizabeth raised her eyebrows and looked at Peter.

'No need. I've got him on my phone.' Viv couldn't resist a little smile as she dropped in this surprise. Steph knew only too well the warm feeling of satisfaction where she'd shared the tiny nugget that made all the difference. She noticed the way Viv pulled out her phone, like a skilled magician, enjoying every second of her reveal. Even Elizabeth looked impressed. Viv fiddled with the app and held out the screen so they could all see the mini video. It appeared to be the same boy Steph had seen doing exactly the same thing.

'How did you get that?' Hale was impressed.

'Fred was showing off and told me when it was going to happen, so I went into the resource centre and found a window that overlooked the back of the drama studio and waited. Sorry it's a bit small.'

Hale held his hand out for the phone and Elizabeth peered over his shoulder while he played the video again, stopping it when he could see the boy's face. He enlarged it with his fingers, paused it and stared at it before handing it to Peter.

'Anyone you know?'

Peter squinted at the tiny, blurred image. 'At first sight, it looks a bit like Darcy – Darcy Woodard, Marianne's brother – but no, it's not him. He's not one of ours.' He looked round the table, relieved. Steph noticed that the police officers stared at him, clearly impressed by his detailed knowledge of the students.

Steph held out her hand for the phone. Peter was right. He looked a bit like Darcy, but now she could view the image close-up, it was definitely the man she'd seen.

'We'll get that downloaded and enhanced and see if we can identify him.'

'Will you be there on Friday to arrest him?' said Peter, his voice showing his desperation to stem the tide of drugs into the college.

'We'll be there, but not to arrest him.' Clearly, Hale was trying to appear calm but in charge, not wanting to be rushed into too much action too soon. 'No, he's still a relatively small fish, as was Marianne. We need the guys at the top of the food chain. If we move too soon, they'll close it down and we'll never get them. I'll get him followed after the next drop and keep an eye on him for a few days to see if we can trace his contacts.'

She noticed Hale assessing how his words had affected Peter, who now looked even more desperate, elbows on the table, head in hands. Hale's tone became warmer and more re-assuring. 'We will get him and stop him, I promise, Peter, but we need to be patient.'

Hale glanced at Steph. Both knew what he didn't say was that when they caught this dealer, he would quickly be replaced by another. Elizabeth looked down at her notes. Clearly, she had decided to stay out of the internal issues. Her job was to ensure Viv was safe, and it appeared she'd been re-assured.

Peter raised his head and sighed. 'Well, you know what you're doing. My priority is to keep my college as clean as possible and to protect my students from getting involved.'

Hale nodded in sympathy. 'You're right. It's good to work with you on this.' He looked down at his notes and checked off a few bullet points before he continued.

'The pathologist came to see me about Marianne today and she thinks her death may be suspicious. They found some unexpected results in her blood samples, so they'll be doing further tests. We'll know in a day or so. And as you know, that's not the only suspicious death we have on our hands.'

Hale turned over a few pages in his notebook before continuing. Steph now realised why the unconventional under-cover arrangements had been made so quickly. Not only were they attempting to close county lines, but three deaths were linked to them. 'Moving on to the body found on the waste ground at the end of Renshaw Road. The pathologist said he'd been beaten, or rather kicked, to death. He had massive internal injuries and his face was well mangled. Did you manage to identify him from the ID card?'

Peter sat up and took a photocopy of a student card out of his file, which he placed on the table.

'Sorry, no. It's a forgery. Whoever he was got hold of an old student card, added his photo and laminated it. We're trying to trace its original owner, but the ID number is pretty well scuffed out.' Peter pointed to a blurred series of numbers and bar code below the fuzzy photo. 'Is the original any clearer?'

'No, afraid not. Never that easy, is it? Then we'll have to hope we've got his DNA on our records to identify him. We're sure he's involved with Luke. In his pockets he had similar packets to those we found in Marianne's room and we suspect he gave her the contaminated drugs.'

Viv cleared her throat. 'The students have been talking about some other boss coming in to take over Luke's line or set up his own. I wonder if this guy is one of Luke's crew and he's been killed by the other gang?'

'Could be, Viv. Of course, we think the body we found in London was Luke, but we're still waiting for a firm identifica-tion. If he's dead, I expect his lieutenant will have taken over his empire.'

'This all sounds so complicated and so organised.' Peter had been drawing a family tree to show the links between the people named so far while listening to Hale and Viv, but now he threw down his pen in frustration. Elizabeth stared at him but said nothing.

Hale nodded across at him. 'You're right. They are highly organised. These kids run the lines like a business.'

He turned to Viv. 'It'd be good to know a bit more about the other crew trying to takeover. See if you can find out anything from the kids who may've been at the parties near Renshaw Road.'

Steph sighed. 'It's all happened so quickly, hasn't it? I'm sure there were drugs in Oakwood before, but not on this scale. With other suppliers moving in to fight over the territory, we now have two deaths linked with drugs in Oakwood in less than a week. It feels as if we've moved into a new world.'

'And it's a pretty grim world, isn't it?' Peter closed his notebook.

'I'm afraid it is, Peter, and your kids are on the front line.' Hale pulled back his chair, signalling the end of the meeting.

22

FRIDAY 13TH OCTOBER: 10.00 AM

STEPH

IN HER FLOWING claret velvet dress and shawl, Esther was more suited to the older building than the modern glass sliding door that swooshed open as she floated into the college reception.

'Good morning, Steph.' Esther's voice was low and dull, every word an effort. The shadows under her eyes told of nights with little sleep. The numb, automatic getting on with the routines of life was familiar to Steph, who knew words made little difference.

'Hello, Esther. I'll tell Mr Bryant you're here.'

As she spoke, Peter's door opened and he emerged, hand extended to Esther. 'This is such a tragedy, Mrs Woodard. Please be assured you have our deepest sympathy. Marianne was an outstanding student and we'll all miss her. If we can help in any way, you only have to ask.'

Esther's gentle smile met the required social reaction to his words, but it didn't stretch to her eyes. 'Thank you. I'd like to discuss the arrangements for the funeral, if you have time?'

'Of course. Do come in. Would you be happy for Steph to

join us, as she'll be making the arrangements with the members of staff and students?'

'Yes, of course.'

They sat around the dark oak coffee table in front of the copper fire surround in Peter's study. It was appropriately sombre and suited their discussion.

'Following the advice of the police, I booked the date for her funeral even before they gave her back to me, and now they have. It will take place next Tuesday at St Mary's Church. She used to help in the youth club there, for her Duke of Edinburgh... Gold... you know.'

They waited while she reached into her bag and pulled out a piece of paper and a small packet of tissues. She dabbed at her eyes.

'Sorry.' She paused, swallowed, sat up straight. Steph was impressed by her strength at this dreadful time. 'I wonder if some of the students would like to be there... her friends... you know. I have this poem... by Charlotte Bronte, one of Marianne's favourite writers. Could you ask one of her friends to read it, please, and let me know their name?' She handed over a folded piece of paper with some verses printed on it.

'I'm sure one of her friends will be honoured to read it.' Peter scanned it and placed it on the table in front of him.

'And here somewhere are some hymns... Your choir...' She rooted around in the depths of the Gladstone bag until she pulled out another piece of paper. 'Or perhaps, I don't know, if your music department would like to play something?'

As Peter took the list of hymns, he leaned towards her. 'I'm sure they will. I'll contact you later today to let you know.'

Steph became aware of Esther looking uncomfortable and wanting to say something, but holding back.

'Is there something else?' asked Steph.

'Well, yes, there is. Marianne told me that last year when one of your students died, there was an enormous shrine of flowers in the Old Building. Now I know children of this age need to do something, but Marianne wouldn't want to see so much waste. And in the circumstances... you know.'

She paused, and Steph could see Peter was thinking the same thing she was. Marianne's death differed from the accidents or illnesses that were usual at this age. But was it really?

Esther continued. 'She would want something positive. If you agree, I wonder if you could talk to the students about planting a small garden somewhere in the grounds, with a bench or seating, as a memorial for her. I'm happy to pay for it.'

'What a good idea. I'll talk to the college reps at break.'

It was surprising that, with the efficiency of social media, news of Marianne's death hadn't spread through college. Perhaps most people thought she was still in hospital.

'Thank you so much. I'd better be going.' With what appeared to be a superhuman effort, Esther stood and held out her hand to Peter.

'Anything... Let me know if there is anything we can do, Mrs Woodard.'

Steph opened the door and accompanied Esther to the sliding doors.

'And you know you have only to ask.'

Esther turned and placed her right hand on Steph's arm. 'You and Hale have already done so much. Thank you.'

Steph watched as she trudged out into the car park and drove off. All hope appeared to have dissolved with Marianne's death. Beside her, Peter sighed. 'What a desperate state she must be in. Such a tragedy. Marianne had a glittering future before her – she'd already achieved so much. It's a real crime to see such a promising young life destroyed. I hope we can stop other parents from having to go through this.'

He returned to his office and left Steph to her routines. She didn't feel much like doing anything after seeing Esther so devastated. It all felt so pointless. But she smiled anyway and got on with it. She was taken aback when Darcy's shadow fell over her desk.

'Hi, Steph. I see Mother's been in.'

'She left a few minutes ago. How are you doing?'

He too looked exhausted and, for him, rather dishevelled; not his usual sharp appearance.

'I'm doing good, I s'pose. It's difficult being at home and not being able to do anything – I mean not stop it or try to make someone pay for what's happened to her.'

Reception was empty for once and the phones were quiet. 'But someone has paid, haven't they? It may not have been you that pulled the trigger, but Luke is dead. Isn't that enough?'

Darcy picked up the signing-in pen on its chain and fiddled around with it as if not sure how to continue. She reached out, took it from him and placed it back in the penholder. Worth a risk. 'That body you identified – it wasn't Luke, was it?'

'What do you mean?'

'What I say. When you looked at those photos, you said it was Luke but it wasn't, was it?'

His head drooped, but when he looked up, it appeared relief had washed over him. 'How did you know?'

'The way you looked and the tone of voice when you said his name. It didn't ring true, so who was it?'

'Mother always says I'm not a good liar. Does Hale know?'

'Don't worry about Hale. Who was it?'

'I don't know who he was. I think he lived in that basement

and worked for Luke. That's all I know. Honest. I think I met him when I first went there.'

'Why did you say it was Luke?'

'So I could continue trying to find him and kill him for what he did to Marianne.'

Four students Steph recognised as college reps approached the desk, and Darcy moved aside for them. 'Won't be a minute, Darcy. Hello, what can I do for you?'

'Mr Bryant asked to see us at break.'

'Oh, yes. Come this way. He's expecting you.'

After ushering in the students to Peter's office, she returned to her desk and was surprised to see Darcy still there. She thought he'd take the opportunity to disappear and was impressed he hadn't.

'You do understand, don't you?' Darcy's voice sounded like a child's pleading for forgiveness.

'It's not up to me to understand anything. You could be in big trouble wasting police time with what you've said, and you've put more people in danger if Luke's still on the loose supplying them with contaminated drugs.'

For a moment, she felt sorry for Darcy, who appeared to have become a small boy before her eyes.

'I hadn't thought of that.'

'Well, you think on it now and let me think how we can get you out of this mess.' Was she really suggesting this? She should phone Hale, tell him at once and let Darcy face the consequences of his actions, but she hesitated. He was a good lad really and had been through so much. Having seen the rejection he faced when they brought him back to Esther on Saturday night, her heart went out to him. All he'd wanted to do was to protect his sister and do something, even if what he'd done was stupid. He stood dumb, with a miserable look on his face.

'Look, suppose we say now you've had time to think, you realise you made a mistake and it wasn't Luke but someone who looked like him? Did he?'

'Yeah, similar. I suppose. But you're right, I panicked. It was horrible.'

'I'll talk to Hale and he can contact the Met. Anyway, they'll have taken steps to confirm his identity and probably found out it isn't Luke by now, but we ought to let them know you made a mistake. You'll probably need to change your statement.'

And was she to tell Hale the truth or go along with this rather thin story she'd invented to save Darcy? Why did she get herself in these messes? Grasping the desk as the waves of panic swept over her, she pushed the thought of Hale out of her mind and tried to concentrate on what Darcy was saying.

'Would you do that for me? Thank you so much. I've been really worried ever since I said it. I knew it was wrong but thought I'd have a better chance of finding him if everyone thought he was dead.' It was obvious a great weight had been lifted from him and she felt justified in what she'd suggested. Thank goodness she wasn't actually in the police force but a side-kick.

'Right. I'll do it on one condition. 'She gave him her most penetrating 'don't mess with me' look.

'Anything.'

'You do *not* attempt to find Luke or do anything to him, do you hear me? The last thing you want is to be in prison for years because you've killed that low life. Even though you'll have done the world a favour, the jury will still have to convict you of murder. Murder! Do you understand?'

'Yes. Thank you.'

He left reception with a bounce that had been missing for some time. It was the right thing to do, she tried to tell herself, and she'd think about how she would explain it to Hale later.

As she stood, staring out at the heavy lead clouds so low they appeared to be pushing in the glass walls, she replayed the conversation with Darcy. Had he complied too quickly? Given her a polite agreement to get her off his case? Now he'd admitted Luke was not the body, but very much alive, would he try to avenge his sister's death? Darcy's lie had kept the police from searching for Luke so he could find him. Suppose he did. What would he do to him?

23

SATURDAY 14TH OCTOBER: 9.00 PM

DARCY

DARCY DIDN'T NEED an address to find the house party as the wall of sound hit him halfway up the road. As he walked towards the house, he recognised 'Unknown T' followed by 'DigDat'. Pretty hard stuff. He wondered if the people living in the neighbouring houses had asked them to turn it down. Probably thought it was best to put up with it, scared of what might happen if they complained.

The party had erupted outside, to the front of the house. Kids were sitting on the brick wall, smoking and drinking from cans and bottles. Two others sat astride an upended supermarket trolley, its single remaining wheel rotating uselessly, the rubbish it had contained scattered around the garden. As he shifted the wooden gate, now hanging by its top hinge, to rest by the crumbling wall, Darcy breathed in the sweet smell of weed – boy, that was strong shit those kids were puffing. Through the haze, he recognised two of the kids from Marianne's youth club who must've been about fourteen, and their mates looked about the same age.

The front door was wide open, and he pushed his way into

the hallway, littered with tab ends and cans. Two boys he knew from college were standing opposite each other and appeared to be having a row. But as he pushed past, he could hear them shouting about Saturday's match at the top volume necessary to be heard over the blast of the relentless beat flowing into the hallway.

The front room had been stripped of furniture and the bare floorboards magnified the sound of four box speakers stacked up to the ceiling, which belted out the sound of the discs being played on the decks against the far wall. The powerful sound had become physical, making the black fabric in front of the speakers breathe in and out in time to the drumbeat.

He felt uncomfortable. He didn't belong with this group, or to think of it anywhere, since Marianne's death. It was all Luke's fault. Darcy had searched London, desperate to find him, but he'd always arrived too late; he'd moved on. Luke had taken Marianne away from him. If only they hadn't gone to Latitude.

The thought that he could... should have done something to save her gnawed at him. When he managed to sleep, his dreams were full of basements and bodies. He had to keep moving, doing something, anything, to distract him from the pain. His mother ignored him. He no longer existed in her mind. She no longer wanted him in her house. Most evenings he sat in the hospice with Dad, where he felt safe and wanted. He had to find Luke.

Darcy pushed his way through the crowd, moving as one to the hypnotic rhythm, the words distorted by the high volume, which defeated the point of Drill. He squirmed past the pulsating bodies, heads down, nodding as the sound travelled through them. At last! Success! In the corner he spotted Luke, surrounded by adoring girls, one from Marianne's tutor group. The other two looked younger – fifteen or sixteen.

Luke caught Darcy's eye, nodded towards the door and went out into the hallway. Darcy followed him into the kitchen, where a woman was slumped across the small table, her hands outstretched, her head on one side, out of it. A trickle of saliva made a pool below the side of her mouth on the filthy yellow Formica. Her mascara had run and got stuck in the wrinkles around her eyes. Not a great look. Not that she noticed. Luke led the way into the air outside. Darcy followed and shut the kitchen door behind him so they could talk without shouting.

Luke's black leather jacket over the dark tee shirt and jeans made him look cool. Darcy saw him again at Latitude, where he'd moved around the festival as if he owned it and where he was, was the place to be. Darcy envied the ease he'd shown, his ability to belong everywhere. He was desirable and knew it.

With his deep, confident voice, he exerted control in an understated way. Darcy knew from the guys he'd met in London, and the number of houses and flats he'd visited, that Luke ran a vast empire of drugs' runners, foot soldiers and crack houses. He was the boss, no argument. Despite his burning anger, Darcy envied him a little. He was a natural and didn't have to try.

'Heard you were looking for me.' Luke leaned against the brick wall, relaxed, in charge.

'Went round your London dens.'

'Have to keep moving in this business. Where's Marianne? Inside?'

Darcy pulled himself up as tall as possible and looked straight into Luke's eyes. 'No, she's not. She's dead.'

'What?'

'She's dead.'

'Marianne? No!'

Darcy stared him out, and for a moment, he saw the briefest flash of panic cross Luke's face.

'She's dead? Not Marianne! She was beautiful, brilliant. My crew, anyone who met her, respected her. She was building up a solid line. Had a great future. Can't believe it. Dead?'

Darcy moved in closer, not sure where he was finding the strength to challenge this supreme being. 'She had some bad shit from you or one of your crew. It messed her up so bad she was in a coma in hospital. Then it killed her.'

'Watch it. I never do bad gear. The stuff I do is fucking excellent. She must've got the shit food up here. Maybe she jumped to another line – got contaminated stuff.'

'No, she didn't jump. She got it from you.' Darcy refused to move, impressed by the sound of his calm voice, but inside he was terrified. Even if he hadn't handed the drugs to her, he knew Luke had given them to her, but having got this far, he wasn't sure what he wanted next. Then there was the debt. What did he want? An apology, a confession?

Luke must have sensed his confusion, and without warning, his arms flew out and pushed Darcy away, causing him to fall back over a small wall. Down on the ground, he was vulnerable and felt angry, stupid and scared all at once. He hadn't prepared himself enough. Luke now had the upper hand. Would he walk away having humiliated him or—

The kitchen door flew open and an oblong of light smashed onto the concrete followed by a dark figure, which hurled itself at Luke.

Surprised, Luke stepped back and held up his arms to defend his head as the boy started battering him. Darcy recognised him as

David, who lived in the house. He barrelled at Luke, who lost his balance and stumbled back a couple of steps. 'Hey kid, what's wrong?' Luke held onto the back wall of the house and straightened himself, so he was upright and towered over the furious David.

'My mum's what's wrong!'

'But mate—'

'I'm not your mate! You come here, get your gang to use our house, feed her that stuff – look what you've done to her! There!' He pointed back to the kitchen where the collapsed woman hadn't moved.

'Yeah but—'

David was fizzing. 'You think by buying us trainers and KFC and other stuff, you're buying us. But I've had it. I've had enough. Get your gang out and leave me and my mum alone. You're destroying her.'

As he pulled himself up from the ground, Darcy could see that Luke had regained his smooth confidence. 'My little Julie always wants the purest. She's happy to have all the dosh and stuff I give her. She wants it, she asks for it, and I give her more than just a bottle of Grey Goose. Always pleased to see me upstairs, know what I mean, kid?'

Once again, David launched himself at Luke, who was taken by surprise and stumbled. Then, as he stood upright, he flicked out a blade. He stood for a moment, knife held in front of him, tense and ready to pounce. Surely, he was just scaring the younger boy off?

Luke and David froze for a moment, ignoring the surrounding mayhem. In total control, Luke made a deliberate move, flashing the knife through the air towards David, who saw the glint of the blade and stepped back.

At that moment the noise of police sirens screamed

through the night, followed by a sudden stop to the music and a load of kids rushing past them, fleeing the party.

Panicked, David turned and ran down the alley at the side of the house. Luke burst into life and raced after him, along with about twenty other kids running from the police. David would stand no chance against Luke. Darcy chased after them up the passageway and out into the road.

24

SATURDAY 14TH OCTOBER: 10.00 PM

STEPH

THE FISH and chips had been superb. They'd walked Derek along Southwold beach and, as the sun set, found a cosy corner in The Harbour Inn where they'd eaten far too much. They pushed their empty plates away, relishing the warmth of the log fire after the sandblasting wind on their faces.

'Let's finish these, get home and—' Hale's phone rang. He listened intently. 'I'll be right there.'

He grabbed his coat from the seat. 'Come on! A party's turned violent and they think Luke's there!'

Blue lights flashing in the front grill and on the edge of the side mirrors, Hale made it back to Oakwood in record time. Pulling up opposite Debby and Jake's house, they were hit by the boom beat before they could open the car doors.

Three uniformed officers had beaten them to it and rushed into the house. The music cut out. Shouts and screams from the kids took over as they panicked and tried to escape through the windows and over the back garden fence. Steph checked that Derek's lead was fastened to the seat belt so he couldn't get involved in the mayhem and climbed out of the car.

A boy rammed into her as he fled from the house and she fell back against the edge of the car door. Her spine throbbed with pain and she screamed out loud in an automatic reaction. 'Shit! Oww!'

The boy streaked down the road, an officer close behind. Two lads spilled out onto the road, fighting and screaming. Arms and legs tangled as they aimed fists and feet, desperate to hurt whatever they could reach. A fist connected with bone, but the crack didn't stop them. Rolling around on the tarmac, the smaller one pushed the bigger boy into the gutter, where he hit his head on the kerb.

'Fuck off, you little runt!' The taller boy struggled to his feet, swooshed his hair out of his eyes, swayed and picked up something he'd dropped. He faced down the small boy who stood in front of him. The small boy hesitated. It was a mistake. Metal glinted silver in the streetlight. The tall boy lunged. The small boy saw the threat but too late. The tall boy embraced the small boy in an awkward hug, turned and ran up the hill.

Steph, who'd been running towards the fight, threw herself at the heap on the ground and knelt in the wet patch already seeping from under his hoodie. She took off her jacket, rammed it onto his stomach and pushed down. He moaned and lay back. It was David Richardson, the boy Jake's mother had mentioned, and it must be his house where the party was being held. A figure knelt beside her and she recognised Darcy.

Using her knee to keep up the pressure, she found her phone in her jacket pocket, and handed it to Darcy. 'Call an ambulance. Tell them there's been a stabbing and they need to get here quick!'

Darcy moved away. She could hear his desperate tone as he called it in. When he'd finished, he knelt down beside her again. Terrified, David realised he'd been stabbed and squirmed, trying to get up. Darcy gently pushed him back down. 'Don't move, David. It'll be all right.'

'They'll be here in a couple of minutes.' She lied, hoping it would be true.

Even in the fluttering light from the streetlamp, she could see the scratches and cuts around his cheek and chin, vivid against his pale face. Where was the ambulance? No Hale. Must be inside with the other officers. Shouts and screams cut through the dark. No one from the neighbouring houses emerged at the noise and chaos. Too scared to be involved. The house party must be a dreaded routine. David coughed, and she felt her soggy jacket getting wetter. Come on! Where had they got to?

'Nearly here. Hang on, David. Keep still. Try not to cough.' Darcy had taken off his tee shirt, and she grabbed it to replace her soaked jacket. He sat on the road, David's head in his lap, and stroked his forehead, trying to comfort him.

She couldn't feel her leg. Steph squirmed and adjusted her position, making sure she kept up the pressure on David's stomach. 'Who stabbed him?'

'Don't know. Didn't see it happen. Just saw David in the gutter.'

Steph pushed down harder with Darcy's top, and David moaned. 'Sorry. You've been in the wars, all right. You'll have a few stories to tell the other students on Monday.' She tried to make light of this tragedy, hoping that wasn't what it would become. 'Was he the one living with you?'

David's eyes rolled back, and his eyelids flickered. He was going. Steph felt sick. She could do nothing but push down and hope. His breathing was getting shallow.

'They'll be here soon, David.' Darcy's soft voice appeared to reassure David, and he smiled up at him before sighing and closing his eyes. At last, a siren and blue lights. The ambulance screeched up beside them.

'Quick! He's been stabbed in his stomach. Massive bleeding – now losing consciousness.'

'Right, we've got him.' Steph crawled back to make space for the young female paramedic, and Darcy released David's head to her male colleague, who fixed an oxygen mask over his face. 'What's his name?'

'David.' Steph stood up beside Darcy.

'David, can you open your eyes?' The girl spoke with the confident authority of someone who knows what she's doing. Her blonde hair pulled back in a business-like ponytail, she smelt of antiseptic. David's eyelids fluttered and opened, slits above the oxygen mask. 'That's good. Well done. We'll get you cleaned up and off to the hospital. Hang on in there, David.'

'Breathing is fine. No damage to his lungs. Here.' The man, about the same age as Hale, passed a package to the girl and went back to the ambulance, where he pulled out a stretcher.

Pulling open the package, the girl looked up at Steph. 'Could you point your phone torch at the wound please?'

Steph did as she was told, amazed at the amount of blood that had escaped through such a small gash. Expertly, the girl plugged the hole with gauze, fixed a large dressing over the wound and pulled down David's hoodie.

'Well done, David, not long now. I've put a dressing over the wound, which should help to stop the bleeding, and we'll get you in the ambulance.'

Her colleague positioned the stretcher beside David on the road, and they eased him onto it. He groaned as the movement pulled on his stomach. He was covered with a red blanket, then hoisted up and into the ambulance.

'Do you want to come with him?' the girl asked Steph.

'No. I'll come on later.'

'Right. It looks as if he's been lucky. Good job you were here.'

'Thanks.'

Hale arrived by her side. 'What's been going on here? What's happened to your jacket?' The night was chilly, but in the panic of the fight and David's stabbing she hadn't noticed. She shivered. Hale took off his jacket and placed it around her shoulders.

'Come on. Let's get you home and changed. Have a hot drink before we go to the hospital to see how that poor lad is faring. Who did it? Do you know?' His eyes were questioning Darcy.

'No, I didn't see who did it.'

'Was Luke there?'

'Yes. Don't know where he is now.'

'We all thought he was in the morgue, thanks to you.'

Clearly, Darcy was not going into details. His face was hidden as he bent down to pick up his bloody tee shirt from the road. Steph and Hale had discussed Darcy's lie, and she knew he wouldn't be let off so easily.

'If we weren't going to the hospital, you'd be coming down to the station to tell me why you've been perverting the course of justice. It'll wait. Don't worry.'

Darcy's head drooped, and he walked away from the house, bare chested, holding the bloodied tee shirt in his hand. He must be freezing. Steph felt sorry for him. 'Thanks for your help, Darcy.'

'No trouble.' He turned and raised his hand, holding the tee shirt. 'Hope David will be OK.'

Hale guided her back towards the car. Derek leaped up as far as his lead would allow to greet her. He stopped mid-pounce when he smelt Hale, not her, and whined.

'Good boy. Sit.'

Derek did as he was told as Steph belted herself into the passenger seat. Her trousers had wet patches that had spread from both knees up to her thighs and the skin of her right knee poked out through a hole.

'Who was that lad again?'

'David Richardson. You know, Debby's neighbour.'

'Oh him! Poor kid. They're sending another ambulance for his mum. She's in a right state.' Hale drove off, past the police van, now being loaded with teenagers, some looking sheepish, others furious.

Steph shook her head. 'That family's had enough to put up with over the last few months without losing him. The paramedic said it had missed his lungs but there was a lot of blood.'

'So I can see.' He looked down at her trousers and the crumpled, blood-stained beige jacket on her lap.

Pulling up outside her flat, she released Derek from the back seat and they trooped indoors. Now she'd calmed down, she felt exhausted, and as she changed, she looked longingly at her bed. Not quite yet. She could opt out of going to the hospital with Hale, but wanted to see for herself if David was all right, and she might find out how Julie was doing. She pulled on a clean pair of black trousers and a camel-coloured pullover, grabbed her black jacket and walked into the sitting room.

'All set? Let's go.'

'You don't have to, you know.' Hale looked as if he too wished he could stay there in the warm and catch up on some sleep.

'No, I want to. Be a good boy, Derek. Back soon.'

25

SUNDAY 15TH OCTOBER: 1.30 AM

STEPH

STEPH PUSHED the button to open the sliding doors of the Accident and Emergency department. 'Maybe I should get a season ticket. Seems only a few days since I was here last.'

'At least at this time of night there's no trouble getting a parking space.' Hale followed her in and held out his ID card to the nurse sitting behind the reception desk, looking as if she too wished she was fast asleep in her bed.

'We're here to follow up on David Richardson. He was brought in by ambulance from Oakwood?'

The nurse unhooked a clipboard from underneath the counter and ran her finger down the list. 'Ah, yes. David is now on Gurney ward. If you go in the lift along there,' she pointed to her left, 'it's on the third floor. I'll phone to warn the sister you'll be coming up.'

'Hospitals at night are spooky, aren't they?' Steph shivered as they arrived at the third floor.

'You've been watching too many psycho films.'

In the silent corridor, the squeak from Hale's shoes was so loud he tiptoed in an attempt to reduce the noise. Steph giggled at his cartoon character moves, and he frowned to rebuke her. As they were rubbing sanitising gel into their hands, the door opened and a male nurse came out to meet them.

'You've come to see David Richardson?'

'That's right. How is he?' Hale took the lead.

'He's one lucky boy. Lost a lot of blood; we're giving him a transfusion. We've sewn him up and we'll keep him here for a couple of days until he recovers. He's awake, if you'd like to see him but don't be long – he needs some sleep.'

'Don't we all!' whispered Hale.

They crept through the double doors and into a side room where a very pale David was lying elevated on a pile of pillows. He smiled as he recognised her. 'Hi, Steph, how are you?'

'More to the point, how are you? They told us you should be out of here in a few days.'

'Yes. They keep telling me I've been lucky, and the blade missed my vital organs and arteries, but made a bit of a mess. Sorry, I think it got all over your clothes.'

'Don't worry about that. The important thing is that you'll be fine. I'm so pleased.'

Hale took over. 'Are you up to answering a few questions, David? We want to catch whoever stabbed you and it helps if we can get going as soon as possible.'

'Sure.'

'Take us through what happened at the party.'

David described the argument he had with Luke in the garden, the arrival of the police, the chase, then the fight on the road. He claimed he wasn't sure who'd stabbed him and said it several times, as if he was trying to convince himself. It was too dark. It might have been Luke or one of his crew. He could recall Steph talking to him before the ambulance came, but everything else was a blank.

'Thanks. We'll need to take a statement from you. Was there anyone else who witnessed your argument with Luke?'

'Darcy was there, I think. It all happened so fast.'

'Darcy Woodard?'

'Yeah, that's him.'

Hale sneaked a glance at Steph and raised his left eyebrow as if to say 'interesting'. Darcy always seemed to be there. Obviously, Steph was aware he'd helped David after he was stabbed, but she had no idea he'd been with Luke and seen the argument with David. She thought back to their conversation outside Tate Britain and wondered if he'd stopped caring about his future or it was, what was it he said, FOMO? And there had been that racial bullying on his phone. Becoming involved in the drugs scene could be a way of getting accepted by his peers, couldn't it?

'And what was Darcy doing at the party?' asked Hale.

'Talking or sort of fighting with Luke. Darcy was on the ground outside the kitchen when I got to them. Luke's a fighter. Darcy stood no chance.'

Amazed, Steph wondered why, if David had worked that out, he had attacked the bigger, more experienced man. 'Do you know what they were arguing about?'

'No, I couldn't hear. Too busy getting my own back on him.'

'What for?'

'For what he's done to Mum. You saw her. They said she's here somewhere. Drying out, or whatever they call it. Ever since Luke's come on the scene, she's been different – not our mum.'

David gasped and frowned. Looking uncomfortable, he tried to move up the pillows, but winced as he pulled at his wound. Steph held out her arm so he could grab on to it to ease himself up and she re-arranged his pillows to give him more support. He needed one of those acrobat swings to pull himself up. She spotted it tidied away to the side of his bed and fished it round so he could reach it.

Hale waited until David relaxed back, and his breathing settled before continuing. 'How long has Luke been around?'

'About a month. Comes and goes. London mostly, but he mentions other places too. Essex and Birmingham I think he said. Leaves his crew here all the time. Not our house anymore.' He sniffed and wriggled to flex his back. Steph darted a glance at Hale to warn him that David might be getting too tired to go on much longer.

Before Hale could react, David continued in a breathy monotone. 'When he's there, we live the high life all right. Take-aways, bills paid, big TV, new bits of furniture. He even bought a posh new bed for Mum's room but that's... that's only because he... you know... wanted to use it with her.' He looked shocked at what he'd just heard himself say, but clearly he'd decided to tell it as it was, or perhaps it was the painkillers freeing him up. 'Mum's got taken in by him. She was happy at first. So happy. But then he got her hooked on that stuff.'

'What stuff?' asked Hale.

'Crack cocaine mostly, but she'd take anything he gave her and he gave her the lot. Every time he went, she was desperate for him to come back to give her more. Josie and me hated it. We spent most of our time at Jake's.'

'I'm sure they'll sort her out here, David. She's safe here. It's important you recover and get back to us.' Steph was aware he was struggling to keep his eyes open.

'They said I could come out on Tuesday. Lucky it didn't go in deep.'

'That's great news.' Hale put away his notebook but

stopped himself. 'Before we go, do you know how your mother contacts Luke? Phone? WhatsApp? Anything?'

'Luke uses burners a lot, but there's a number where you can get him or get a message to him. I don't remember it but Mum has it... Oh, and I think Darcy does.'

'Darcy?'

'Yeah. I think he has.'

'Thanks, David.' Steph nudged Hale towards the door as she could see David was struggling to stay awake.

'Yes, thanks. You've been really helpful. I'll send in an officer to take your statement and we'll keep an eye on your mum, don't worry.'

As they reached the door, Steph glanced back. David's eyes were closed.

'So pleased he'll be fine.' Steph yawned. 'Not too good at these late nights now.'

'Interesting how we keep bumping into Darcy, isn't it? I wonder how deep he is in all this.'

26

TUESDAY 17TH OCTOBER: 11.00 AM
STEPH

'SHUFFLE ALONG, you two. Standing room only soon.' Caroline stood at the end of the back pew where Steph and Hale sat so they could see everything that was going on. Dressed in a long black coat, topped by a wide-brimmed black hat and wearing dark glasses, Caroline resembled a film star, incognito. The pews gradually filled with hushed and subdued students, punctuated by adults or friends of the family. Peter had given permission for any students and members of staff who wanted to go to take the morning off college and twenty minutes before the service began, most of the seats were filled.

As each group walked down the aisle, the heavy, exotic perfume of the large arrangements of white lilies fixed to the end of every pew wafted through the air. Peter arrived with Paul Field, who stood at the end of their pew but a little way back, to avoid staining his suit with the yellow pollen from the waxy trumpets of the lilies. Caroline caught Steph's eye and grinned. Evidently, she'd thought the same.

Peter leaned around Paul Field to shake hands with Hale, who had to stand to reach him. 'Thank you for coming, Hale,

Steph.' His eyes, puffy and red, suggested he hadn't slept well. 'There have been too many of these occasions.'

Steph nodded in agreement, recalling the funeral of the talented music student murdered in the college the previous year.

'I'm sure Mrs Woodard will appreciate all this support. See you later?'

'Certainly.' Hale resumed his seat.

Caroline leaned in and whispered, 'That silly little man really gets to me. He's such an interfering busybody and thinks he's so important!'

'Who? Peter?' Hale appeared to be taken aback by her criticism.

'No! Field. No wonder he's been a VP for so long – no chance of him ever leaving to become a Principal. Only three brain cells, and that's on a good day!'

Steph loved Caroline's outspoken approach to everything, especially the weaselly Paul Field, who resented the way Peter took her into his confidence and her involvement with the police. Paul Field made it clear he thought he should be at the centre of everything going on in the college.

She watched as he moved down the aisle. Where Peter had acknowledged the students and members of staff with dignity as he walked to his reserved seat behind the family pews, Paul Field made a point of stopping at each pew and talking at length to show off how well he knew everyone. Just as he lowered himself into his seat beside Peter, he jumped up again as if he'd sat on something and scanned the church, looking worried.

Steph wondered what the emergency was and looked towards the open double doors. She could see nothing wrong. The church was packed and about fifty students stood along the walls as all the seats were taken. Ignoring the appointed ushers, Paul Field bobbed about, ordering students to push up and telling those standing to squeeze into the spaces he'd created. What he was doing was fine, but she felt irritated by the way he was doing it. So showy.

Caroline reflected her thoughts, 'Now look. He has to be bossy and important. Can't sit still and leave it to the people who should be doing it. I'm sure they're capable. But no, he has to show how thoughtful and responsible he is in a crisis.' Steph was prevented from replying as the organ began to play and the congregation stood as Marianne's coffin was carried in.

If a coffin could ever be beautiful, then this was it. Ivory wicker-work, the sides woven with wild flowers and white ribbons, felt more appropriate for a May Day celebration than a grim death, which must have been the effect Esther had hoped to create. Dressed in a long black velvet coat with a veil over her face, she followed the coffin with Darcy beside her.

He towered over her and, as they passed Steph's pew, reached out to hold his mother's hand. Was it an attempt to comfort her, or did he need support? At that moment, Esther lifted her left hand to adjust her veil. Subtle, but Steph was convinced it was a rejection. He stepped a little further away from Esther, letting a shaft of sunlight through a stained-glass window come between them. Elegant, in a well-fitting black suit, his eyes were red and swollen and he appeared to be unable to stop weeping. Why had Esther refused to give him the love he needed to get through this?

The funeral service was beautiful, or as good as it could be. Gentle and re-assuring in a sad way. Faure's 'In Paradisum' was a perfect choice for the pure young voices of the college choir and gave a calm, reflective tone to the service.

Steph leaned into Caroline. 'That was magnificent. So touching.'

'Yes, Margaret will be pleased. She's got it together in a few days.' Caroline smiled down the aisle at her partner, Margaret Durrant, a part-time music teacher who ran the choir and had done Marianne and the college proud.

Ahead of Steph, in the rows of black clothed students, several were sobbing, and they clung onto each other in desperation. For some, this would be the first time they'd faced death and while the moment of crashing into mortality was difficult at any age, for them, it was brutal. They believed they were immortal and were stunned that their friend had been taken from them. Tissues were passed along rows to mop up tears as the reality hit them that they too might die. Several of them grasped little bunches of flowers, their bright colours florescent against the black, to throw into the grave. Jo, a friend of Marianne's, read the poem that Esther wanted to hear, *Life* by Charlotte Bronte.

Life, believe, is not a dream
So dark as sages say;
Oft a little morning rain
Foretells a pleasant day.
Sometimes there are clouds of gloom,
But these are transient all
If the shower will make the roses bloom,
O why lament its fall?

Rapidly, merrily,
Life's sunny hours flit by,
Gratefully, cheerily,
Enjoy them as they fly!

What though Death at times steps in
And calls our Best away?
What though sorrow seems to win,
O'er hope, a heavy sway?
Yet hope again elastic springs,
Unconquered, though she fell;
Still buoyant are her golden wings,
Still strong to bear us well.
Manfully, fearlessly,
The day of trial bear,
For gloriously, victoriously,
Can courage quell despair!

As Jo returned to her seat, a loud howl of distress from one of the girls in the row behind her stabbed the silence. Jo came out of her pew, took the girl's hand and led her outside into the autumn sunlight. The deep anguish of the girl spread through the students and several more started to cry. The loud opening chords of the organ playing the Twenty-Third Psalm interrupted them and they stood, trying to sing the words with stuttering voices. Towards the end of the hymn, very few people in the pews were able to sing. Only the choir managed to ensure the words reached the angels carved into the rafters.

Steph sighed. It was miserable to think this beautiful girl's life had been cut short after the traumatic experience she'd endured at the hands of that bastard Luke, or whatever he was called. Marianne had loved him, or thought she did, and he'd exploited and destroyed her. She must have been desperate.

Catching her breath, Steph shuddered as she tried to control herself. Hale put his arm around her waist, pulling her towards him, and she welcomed the warmth of his body. She had been to many funerals in her life, but Marianne's had whipped her back to Mike's. She wept for them both.

The service continued with a positive eulogy by the vicar, who knew Marianne well as she'd helped at his youth club. The authenticity of his words, with the lack of clichés or platitudes or reasons why it happened, made the tragedy of Marianne's death sharper. Although this was a celebration of her life, Steph felt it took away all sense of hope. It was difficult to find anything positive about what had happened to Marianne.

At last it was over and they could leave, walking behind Marianne and Esther and Darcy out into the shocking, bright sunshine of the autumn morning. They blinked as their eyes adjusted to the light. The empty blue sky created the wrong backdrop. Instead of raising spirits, it mocked the sombre group around the open grave. It should have been grey murk that blanketed them, as they waited for the final words to be said and Marianne to be lowered into the deep hole in the earth.

Groups of students processed past the grave, on the opposite side to Esther and Darcy, and dropped their flowers on top of the coffin, which was soon smothered in a multicoloured mass of blooms. Steph found it difficult to think of that vibrant young girl being left in the cold, deep grave. Would cremation be better? No, she didn't want either – who did?

Esther held herself tall and straight, acknowledging the tributes of Marianne's friends with amazing self-control and dignity. It was difficult to penetrate behind the veil that hid her face, and it had been a sensible move to wear it.

'Let's go somewhere. I need to be among living people who aren't tainted with this horrible waste of life.' Steph squeezed her hand around Hale's arm, relishing the firm muscle her fingers explored.

'No, sorry. We need to go back to Esther's. She invited us

and we might find out something. Peter's going and that awful man. Sorry Steph. Duty first.'

She knew it was the right thing to do and that would be his answer. She shouldn't have bothered making the comment and felt ashamed that she wanted to run away from it all.

'Of course, you're right. We'll go back to Esther's and see if we find out anything more.'

27

TUESDAY 17TH OCTOBER: 12.45 PM

DARCY

DARCY WAS on duty at the front door, welcoming guests and taking coats, which he passed to a girl from the catering team hired in to help. She hung them up on a clothes rail, further down the hall, which his mother had found in the loft and he'd spent ages cleaning. He handed out small schooners of sherry from a tray on the hall table, filled by the girl while they'd been at the funeral.

'Please go through to the sitting room, first door on the right.' He waved his right arm in the direction of the door and moved to greet the next pair.

'I am so sorry, Darcy.' Mr Field cut across Mr Bryant before he could speak. 'You must come to talk to me if you need any help. My door is always open.'

He took the glass and Darcy watched him as he walked down the hall to the sitting room, stopping to examine the row of pictures. Impeccable, in a solid black suit and tie with a floppy black silk handkerchief, he stopped to pick off a small piece of cotton or something attached to the bottom of his lapel. Looking around to see who had ruined his appearance, he caught Darcy's eye, smiled, and tutted. What a dickhead! He really was up himself!

Mr Bryant had stood back to let Mr Field pass and stepped towards Darcy.

'Please accept my deepest sympathy, Darcy. You know you have only to ask. We're all on your side and will do anything we can to help you through this difficult time.'

'Thank you, Mr Bryant.' He liked the Principal who always seemed to say the right thing and didn't need to show off like Field.

He was pleased to see the next guests, Steph and Hale with Caroline and Miss Durrant. 'It's good of you to come. Thank you so much for that beautiful music, Miss Durrant.'

'My pleasure, Darcy.'

As he could see no one else arriving, he walked with them into the sitting room. The autumn sun was still shining and the French windows opened onto the garden. It hit him, as he tuned into the chatter and even some laughter, that it felt more like a lunch party than a sad farewell to Marianne.

'Do help yourselves, please.' He felt more comfortable with the quartet than Esther's friends, and as he handed plates and white linen napkins to them, he gestured to the feast spread over every inch of the table. Prawns, lobster, vol-au-vents, tiny blinis loaded with smoked salmon and caviar, mini-Yorkshire puddings with rolled up pieces of rare beef, bowls of celery and carrot sticks and tiny tomatoes. Must have cost a fortune. He felt nauseous just looking at it. How could anyone eat after leaving Marianne in that dark, cold hole?

'There's wine, water and fruit juice over there on that table.' Continuing to do his job, he pointed to the bay window and the bar the catering company had set up.

'Thanks, Darcy. Can we get you anything?' Caroline

nodded towards the drinks table. 'You look as if you could do with one.'

'I've had my orders: family hold back! I'll have one later.'

He watched as they scooped food onto their plates, picked up glasses of wine and stepped out into the sunshine. His mother arrived from the garden. She'd had a gardening company out there for days. Weeding the beds, manicuring the lawn, which now had crisp edges to show off rows of rust and white chrysanthemums, which he was sure hadn't been there the week before. Would the company dig them up and take them away to the next funeral tomorrow?

She walked towards him and hissed, 'Take a red and a white bottle round and fill glasses.' Not a question, an order. He turned, picked up the bottles and worked the room, topping up glasses and noting that the talk was becoming even louder as relaxed social chat was released by the alcohol.

Paul Field, who'd drunk several glasses of red wine, toured the room as if it was one of the National Trust houses Darcy's parents had dragged him round when he was younger. Fascinated, Darcy watched as he pulled out a few books to read the inscriptions or check on the edition. He looked less impressed by the collection of DVDs, but nodded his approval at the oil and water-colour paintings of Suffolk landscapes. Definitely his style. He'd never cope with Darcy's heroine, Marlene Dumas – far too shocking! Darcy felt invaded by this nosy little man, so he went over to him as he reached the collection of miniatures by the bay window.

'Everything all right, Sir?'

'Oh! It's you, Darcy! Yes, jolly good, thank you. Just admiring your parents' collection of paintings. So evocative, don't you think?'

'Umm, they give a good idea of nineteenth-century Suffolk,

but I prefer something more contemporary. Do help yourself to some lunch. Some more wine? Sorry, bottle's empty. I'll get another one.'

'Don't worry, I'll help myself, thank you.'

Darcy had no doubt about that. Laughter from the garden floated into the dark room, tempting another group out into the bright sunshine. What were they laughing at? How could they laugh?

He necked three glasses of red, then picking up two bottles walked outside and saw a small group he recognised as Dickie's old work colleagues exchanging anecdotes. They'd visited a couple of times before his dad became ill, and he wondered why his mother had made a special effort to invite them. He'd never seen them at the hospice and they hardly knew Marianne. What were all these strangers doing here? He'd had enough. Caroline was right. He needed a drink.

He walked up the garden to the old apple tree, the boughs crammed and drooping with red and green fruit asking to be picked, and sat on the slatted wooden seat that encircled its trunk. Making sure the guests couldn't see him, he gulped from the bottle. Good stuff! Esther had pushed the boat out all right. He felt better as the alcohol touched his nerves and made him relax. He finished the bottle of white and was starting on the red when he became aware of someone sitting down beside him. It was Steph.

'You've had a tough time, Darcy. You certainly look better for that.' She nodded at the empty bottle on the grass at his feet.

Fascinated, he stared at three wasps grazing on a rotting windfall then buzzing into the neck of the bottle. He wanted to drink until he slept and get out of this shit show. He heard

Steph speaking to him and turned to her. 'Sorry. Did you say something?'

'Can I get you some lunch?'

'No thanks. Not hungry. I'll eat later.'

'Might be a good idea to soak up the wine.'

He took another swig of red wine, not noticing that it dribbled down his white shirt. 'Has Hale found Luke yet?'

'No. They've been looking, but he keeps on the move. Don't worry, they'll catch him.'

He felt his anger erupting. 'It's all his fucking fault! He gave her that contaminated stuff deliberately to kill her. She knew too much. He had to take her out. Hale and that Met man must catch him and make him pay.'

His voice got louder as he screamed out the words. Without warning, someone grabbed the bottle, then slapped him around the back of his head. His mother had come round the other side of the tree.

'What do you think you're doing?' she spat at him. 'Look at you. You're drunk and at a time like this.' She glanced over her shoulder to make sure no one apart from Steph could hear her. Seizing his arms, she dragged him up to his feet and shook him hard. 'You should be helping me, not making things worse. Look at you!' She jabbed his chest, his white shirt now sporting a large red wine stain, and followed it up with a hefty shove. He fell back onto the seat and hit his head on the tree trunk.

'I'll get him something to eat.'

He heard Steph speaking through a haze and wasn't sure if it was the wine or the blow to his head. He was getting a hell of a headache. Before Steph could move, his mother continued scolding him in her quiet, venomous voice. Darcy had never heard her go on like this in front of other people before and could only sit, shocked, while she banged on at Steph.

'This is typical of him. Selfish boy. Useless – no use to anyone. Getting drunk at his sister's funeral – disgusting! How could he have done this? Showing me up in front of all these people – you, the Principal, Dickie's friends!' She hit him hard, this time on the side of his head. It hurt. She'd never hit him before. Not even as a child. What was wrong with her? He saw Steph stand up and hold her back.

'Esther, stop. I know this is difficult, but this isn't the way to make it better—'

'What do you know?' She squared up to Steph. Was Esther was going to hit her too?

'Come on, Darcy, let's go for a walk.'

He felt Steph grab his arm and propel him through the garden gate out into the lane. He turned to see his mother glaring after him, furious.

28

TUESDAY 17TH OCTOBER: 2.00 PM

DARCY

DARCY LET STEPH take his arm and walk him down the unmade lane to the main road. Just before they reached it, she stopped, took off her black wrap and put it over his shoulders, covering the red wine stain.

'That's better. Don't want to get arrested for being in charge of a drunk student.' She adjusted it so it looked like a large scarf and less like a woman's pashmina. 'And you look very arty – so appropriate.' He let her get on with it. He didn't care about anything anymore. Where he was. What happened to him. None of it mattered.

He was steered over the road, past a gate and onto the pier. His feet felt as if they were going in different directions and, when he looked down to the sea flowing backwards and forwards in the gaps between the pier decking, he thought he was going to throw up.

'Right, let's get you something to eat and soak up some of that wine. Sit there and do not move.'

He obeyed and sat on a grey metal bench halfway up the pier, facing back towards the coast. He took deep breaths, trying not to be sick. Turning back to the pier, he concentrated on the small crowd gathered around the grey metal water clock, about to chime the hour. The water filling up the bath overflowed and watered the tulips, which grew up tall and the children laughed at the metal man peeing. Marianne had loved to watch it when they were younger, never tiring of the complex water sculpture.

Two packets of sandwiches appeared in front of his face. 'Sorry, all they had. Which do you want first? Egg or tuna? Not quite up to the banquet we left, but they'll do.' He felt the bread pushed into his hand. 'Now eat.'

He chewed through the soft bread sandwiches, not tasting what was in them. She was right. It did make him feel better. The coastline stopped moving up and down and came into focus.

Sitting beside him, Steph handed him the next sandwich. 'You have to understand, your mother's under a great deal of stress and I'm sure she didn't mean it.'

'She did. She hates me.'

'That's not true.'

Deep in his anger, rejection and hurt, he found it difficult to find words to say how he felt, so he said nothing but concentrated on swallowing the soggy bread. He needed Steph's company, but he also wished she'd piss off so he could be left alone to sink further into total misery. He'd never felt so low. For several minutes, he nibbled the sandwiches, hoping he could keep them down. The coastline wobbled, but not as violently as before. Steph took the cellophane packets from him and put them in the bin between the grey metal tables and benches.

'Happy to stay here for a bit?'

'Please.'

Sipping the mineral water she'd given him, he hadn't realised how thirsty he was. He started to feel better.

'I've never belonged here.'

'What do you mean?'

'Isn't it obvious?'

He turned to her, and she looked at the coastline, clearly not sure what to say.

'I came over here as a baby and was bought up as their child, but I know I'm not and Mother has never loved me, not really. Since Dad got ill it was only Marianne who made me feel I mattered. Now I haven't got her I'm lost. I don't belong in that house anymore.'

'Esther will calm down. She's had so much to cope with. Your father's illness, worrying about Marianne and the drugs and her death.'

'She said it was all my fault.'

'I told you she didn't mean it. Anyway, you know it isn't.'

'She said Marianne would be here now if it wasn't for me.'

He watched a boy of about four holding hands with his parents and being swung high into the air as they walked to the end of the pier. Darcy smiled at the boy's delight and his giggles. He looked safe and loved. Had it ever been like that for him? Yes, before Dad was ill, he'd enjoyed lots of days by the sea and maybe even Mother had loved him then. What had gone wrong?

'Think it through, Darcy. What have you done? It wasn't your fault Marianne fell for Luke and went to London. She made up her own mind. It was her choice. Could you have stopped her going?'

'No, I suppose not.'

'And when she was there, did you make her take the drugs and get involved with Luke's gang?'

'No.'

'And after she came back, did you encourage her to take drugs?'

He stared at the waves bashing up the beach, taking more of it with each wave. The tide had turned and was rushing in. The sunbathers packed up their camps.

'Well, have you?'

'Not exactly.' He sighed. 'I did take her to that party.'

'Which party?'

'The one where Luke's dealer gave her the bad drugs.'

'So, you can identify the man who killed her?'

The beach was now disappearing as the waves reached out to the concrete prom. The sandcastles had been swept away and the children who'd made them fled from the beach to play in front of the beach huts. Darcy was tired and wanted to sleep and switch off for a bit. He wished Steph would shut up and leave him alone.

'Look, Darcy, Marianne has gone. You know the man who gave her the drugs. You need to tell us so we can catch him. It's too late to protect Marianne now.'

The waves smashed up against the concrete wall, leaving big splurges on the top. Three children playing chicken ran towards the edge of the prom, daring the sea to wet them, then screaming back as it did.

'Darcy, are you listening to me?' Why couldn't she shut the fuck up and stop going on? 'You could help Hale catch this man and punish him for what he did to Marianne. You could get your revenge on Luke by breaking up his empire. That's what you wanted. The reason you went to London, isn't it?'

He was hypnotised by the rhythm of the waves. How did the concrete walls survive this every day? One day they wouldn't and the sea would claim the land and the beach huts.

The brightly painted sheds got craned away each winter and parked in the pier car park to protect them from destruction in the storms. One day, the sea would trick them and pull them in before the crane arrived.

He felt his eyes sting and his eyelids closing. Why couldn't Steph fuck off and let him sleep? But where? He couldn't go back until all those people had left. He couldn't face them, and then there was his mother. He'd have to face his mother.

'This is your chance. Your chance to get him stopped. You owe it to Marianne. What happened wasn't your fault, but in the future it will be if you don't help us stop it. If other Mariannes die because you didn't tell us everything, then, yes, that will be your fault. We both know Luke as good as killed her because she wanted to get out of it all.'

She was right. Marianne was doomed the moment she told Luke she wanted out. The prom had emptied as the splashes hit the far edge and even some of the bright blue and yellow boards on the bottoms of the huts. A painting of these blocks of colour against the clear, impossible blue sky would make a good starting point for a picture.

Darcy dragged his mind back to what Steph was saying. She was right, of course she was. He hadn't told them everything; hardly anything, in fact. Another four addresses at least, a long list of names in a notebook Marianne had given to him and there was her email to him in case it all went wrong. He wanted them to know about the blackmail and the way she was forced to work for that bastard, like a slave. Could he trust Steph? She'd helped him so far, and she was right. If he was to help Marianne and get his own back on Luke, he had no choice.

He decided and turned to face her. 'You're right Steph. I haven't told you everything. I was scared of Marianne getting in trouble up here but now... now she's not here... I'll give you her book.'

'Her book?'

'She wrote it all in a small notebook. Names. Addresses. She gave it to me to keep safe in case anything happened to her. She knew, didn't she?' He would keep the email. It wasn't the right time yet.

'Is the book at home?'

'No, here. I carry it with me. Safer than at home.'

'Right, I suggest we go back to mine and you can tell Hale and me everything you know and all Marianne told you. I'll take you home later and make sure it's all right with Esther. She'll have calmed down by then.'

'I wouldn't bet on it.'

29

TUESDAY 17TH OCTOBER: 7.00 PM
STEPH

'I'M afraid we're now dealing with the murder of David Richardson, who was stabbed after a party on Saturday.' Hale paused to let his words sink in. He had managed to organise another debrief with Viv and Elizabeth in the flat, freezing cold this time. The two women sat side by side, with Steph, Hale and Peter on the other three sides of the table.

'Oh no! What a tragedy! I thought David was recovering. At least, he was when I visited him.' Clearly shocked, Peter stared at Hale. 'Wasn't he meant to come home today? What on earth happened?'

'The knife must have gone in deeper than they thought. They stopped the haemorrhaging, and he appeared to be doing well until late yesterday when he developed sepsis, which, despite massive doses of antibiotics, killed him. The knife was probably infected.' Hale summarised the notes he held from the hospital and returned the sheet to his file. Elizabeth added to the notes she had made.

'We now have a major crime team investigating the stabbing. We've got several vague statements, but we suspect Luke, also known as Antony Shaw, was responsible, although no one has confirmed it and we don't have any real evidence. We're working with the Met, as we think he's back in London. Unfortunately, we didn't get a signed statement from David before he died.'

Hale had already told Steph the grim news, but she didn't want to let the others know, so she lowered her head as if she'd just heard it. She also knew Hale was pretty pissed off he'd missed getting a statement. Someone would get it in the neck. For a few moments, all five sat glumly staring at nothing, as the futile loss of this young life hit them.

Viv cut into the silence. 'The kids at college will be shocked. Several of them visited him too and said he was doing fine.'

'Yes,' said Peter. 'That's what I saw. David was a good student who was doing well, despite all he had to cope with at home. I think he'd got a place at Imperial College to study physics.' He paused, and no one jumped in as they reflected on this sad news. The silence stretched.

Peter glanced at Hale. 'How's his mother taking it? She's back home, I understand. I'll visit her tomorrow.'

'Will you take Steph with you, please?' Hale made a note in the file. 'She might recognise someone from the night of the stabbing.'

Peter looked a little taken aback. 'I didn't know you were there, Steph. You didn't tell me.'

Steph felt uncomfortable. She sensed Elizabeth staring at her, trying to work out what was going on. Hale had told her not to discuss the party at college but to listen and pick up anything she heard on her tours around the campus. She'd been aware for some time of the tension developing between Peter and Hale and worried a lot about which of them should get the greater loyalty, as it was proving impossible to share it out equally. Now it appeared this was to become evident to Viv and Elizabeth.

'Sorry Peter. I thought I had. I'm sure I told you about the party and the drugs yesterday.' She covered her discomfort by fiddling around in her bag on the floor looking for something, she wasn't sure what.

'You did but didn't mention you were there and saw the stabbing.' Peter would not let it drop.

'There wasn't a lot to tell. It was over so quickly. It was dark, and I was concentrating on staunching David's wound.' Her fingers found Derek's bone and she pulled it out.

Thankfully, she was distracted by Derek, who whined when he saw what was in her hand. Not wanting to be late, they'd collected him from doggy day-care on the way to the flat and hadn't had time to drop him home. He'd revelled in the fuss Viv and Peter had made of him and he'd been almost good after the initial 'Get down boy' cries when they'd arrived. Elizabeth had pushed him away impatiently when he'd growled at her, causing Steph to smile at Derek's excellent taste in humans.

Steph gave him the large chicken-filled bone – she always carried one with her, in case. He wagged his tail and set about licking out the meat, which would occupy him for about forty-five minutes – hopefully until the end of the meeting. Elizabeth, who had frowned at Steph throughout her rescue operation, now cleared her throat and tapped her pen on the table, looking at Hale expectantly.

Clearly, Hale was irritated they had gone off track and riffled through his papers for no real reason Steph could see. She sat up straight, paying attention and he continued. 'Now, where were we? Peter and Steph will visit Julie Richardson and see what's happening there.'

Peter groaned. 'Oh! That's two funerals in as many weeks. Those poor young people and their parents. This is all so depressing.'

'Actually, we have some good news for a change. Steph spent some time with Darcy after the funeral, and he's given her a book where Marianne recorded all the dens, the lines and those running them. We now have several more leads to follow up – it'll keep us and my colleagues in the Met busy all right.'

Aware of Peter scrutinising her, Steph remained silent and thought she'd keep her mouth firmly shut for a while. She was relieved when Viv spoke. 'And Darcy also gave Steph a detailed description of the guy who passed the contaminated drugs to Marianne. Luke may not have handed them to her, but we know they came from him. He wanted her out of the way.'

Now it was Hale's turn to glare at Steph, evidently confused because she wasn't telling the story herself and gaining credit for her achievements. But she was happy that the attention had been deflected away from her and concentrated on making some notes on her pad. Steph noticed that Elizabeth appeared to be fascinated by the exchanges, clearly enjoying her discomfort.

Peter turned to Hale. 'So, we can say he murdered her then?'

'We've a long way to go before we can prove that.'

Peter tutted and sighed. Hale ignored him.

'Viv, anything from inside the college?'

'Dude's been in again. I saw him in the distance by the drama studio and he scarpered as soon as I went towards him. I wonder if he might be on your CCTV tapes, Peter?'

'Let me know the time and I'll get the tapes for you.' Peter made some notes on his phone.

'Here, I've written them down.' Viv passed a folded piece of paper to him. Peter opened it, looked at it, took time to read it, folded it again, then slipped it inside his pocket.

'I'll have a look with Steph and she can take them to Hale if we find anything.' Peter spoke to Viv, obviously pleased that he could play a part once again. Then he turned to Hale. 'Have you had any luck tracing him from the picture Viv took?'

'We've enhanced the photo but can't identify him. I've sent it to my contact in the Met but have heard nothing yet.'

'It's vital we identify him as he appears to be at the centre of all this.' Peter looked directly at Hale, who sat up and met Peter's stare, clearly feeling he was being challenged.

'We've hardly been sitting on our backsides, Peter, but like you, working hard to get these guys. As soon as we get a lead on the source, we'll follow it up.'

'I have something else that I think may help.' Viv looked pleased that she could offer something to wave the flag for the police. 'Fred Castle has asked me if I would like to be one of his dealers. He believes I have a different network to him outside college. I've been sitting next to him in Art and texting and WhatsApp-ing my home phone for much of the lesson, when Caroline isn't on the prowl, so he sees that I have masses of contacts. I think he wants promotion up the line and having me will gild his reputation.'

'Shouldn't we pull him in?' asked Peter. 'At least we know who he is and that he's involved.'

Elizabeth tutted and shook her head. Oh, how rude was that? Peter ignored her and continued to stare at Hale, who took a deep breath and was clearly trying hard to keep his patience. What made it worse was that this was being played out in front of Elizabeth. Hale ran his hand through his hair and spoke slowly and calmly. 'I understand exactly how you're feeling, Peter. You want to safeguard your students and get your college as clean as possible but pulling in Fred won't solve this.'

Initially Hale had held Peter's gaze, but now he appeared to avert his eyes more often in what Steph recognised was a tactic to defuse the tension between them. Lifting his head and this time meeting Peter's stare, he continued speaking. 'All that will happen is the dealer will find another foot soldier to take over Fred's patch in college. No, we need to be patient and continue with Viv in place so she can discover where this stuff is coming from. I suspect when we find the identity of Dude, we may close down the line.'

'OK, Hale, if you think that's best, that's what we'll do. Now if you'll excuse me, I've a pile of paperwork to get through before bed. Good night, all.'

Peter stood up, walked to the door and opened it. Steph leaped up, grabbed his coat off the back of the sofa and followed him. 'Peter, your coat.'

He took it without smiling. 'Perhaps we could have a word in the morning, Steph.'

It wasn't a question. She smiled and nodded, trying to respond as if his authoritative tone was normal. 'Of course. I'll see you when I get in.'

Shutting the door behind him, she returned to the table, where Hale was checking Viv's 'to do' list, closely monitored by Elizabeth, who also made notes. Steph felt her cheeks burning and, head down, pretended to add some more notes to the list she'd written so she could concentrate on returning her breathing and her galloping pulse to normal. She felt Elizabeth's eyes on her. Derek had been right.

'Steph... Steph!' Hale waved his hand in front of her eyes, and she jerked out of her panic control.

'Sorry, I was miles away.'

'We noticed. Viv was saying she'll pop over to reception for a chat with you and pass on any information she picks up. She's noticed several students have regular conversations with you. OK?'

'That's fine. Yes, good idea. Lots of students visit for a chat so that wouldn't attract attention.'

'Good. I suspect this may get dramatic very quickly once we move in.' He shoved papers in his folder. 'And before you go, we picked up something interesting when we visited David. He told us that Darcy has a phone number to contact Luke directly or to leave a message. Rather than approaching him officially, see if you can find out anything, will you?' He nodded at Viv, who added another bullet point to her list.

'Thanks Viv, Elizabeth. Good luck. I'll contact you to arrange our next meeting – that OK with you, Elizabeth?'

Elizabeth nodded.

Hale continued, 'Viv, let me know via Elizabeth if you need anything. Thanks for all you're doing.'

Hale indicated to Steph that he would see Viv out. 'Bye, Viv. See you later.' Steph smiled at Viv, who grinned back. Had Viv noticed her panic? She was a sharp cookie and there wasn't much she didn't see.

Elizabeth grabbed her bag and coat and rushed out after Viv. 'Hang on, Viv. I want a word! Thanks, Hale, I'll be in touch.' As she passed Derek he stopped working on his bone and gave a low growl, watching her close the door.

'What the hell was wrong with Peter?' Hale stormed across the room and threw himself into the seat opposite Steph.

'Wasn't it obvious? He feels you and I are in control and

know everything and he's been left out of what's going on in his own college. It hasn't helped when you tell me not to tell him things. I'm stuck in the middle, not knowing what to say or who to listen to.' Her voice rose as her stress was released at last. Hale stared at her.

'Calm down. We need to sort this out. We need him onside.'

She felt nauseous but wanted to continue talking and attempting to de-fuse the problem before it got any worse. 'I suspect he's going to have a go at me tomorrow. I could see he was livid tonight when he realised he hadn't been fully involved.'

The tension crackled in the silence between them. She would not give way.

At last, Hale sighed. 'What's your solution, then?'

'I suggest we agree what I can tell him, without compromising your op, and then each day I have a formal meeting with him to let him know what's going on, so he feels included.'

'That's one way forward, I suppose.' His voice was grudging and oozed annoyance.

'Have you got any better suggestions?' She was losing patience with him. What did he expect of her? Was it so difficult to see how she was being pulled in two directions?

Hale took a deep breath and gathered his papers into a neat pile. He paused, reached out and held both of Steph's hands in his; she looked up to meet his eyes. He squeezed her hands. 'You're right. I haven't been very sensitive to your position, have I? Let's try it.'

All chicken licked out from the bone, Derek came over and sat by her side, nudging her until she stroked him. 'Good boy. We'll be going home any minute now.'

'Before we do, I've a favour to ask you.'

'Yes?'

'I have the initial PM report here. It seems to have taken ages. Cuts I s'pose. I'd like you to visit Esther to give her a copy. I thought it might be better coming from you rather than me.'

'Right.'

Steph took the plastic wallet but didn't pull out the printed report. She'd had enough and was desperate to switch off. No doubt he was about to lob in another revelation he'd decided not to share with Peter.

'They're still testing the bloods, where there were a few anomalies, but the difficult news is that Marianne was pregnant, in the very early stages. I wouldn't have thought she was the type to get pregnant.'

'And what's the type?' Irritated, she picked up her coat from the sofa and pulled it on, wanting to get away from this depressing place.

'What I mean is she was a mature, sensible girl and I would have thought she'd have taken precautions.'

She stood in silence for a moment as she pondered this latest bombshell. Hale didn't move but continued flicking through his copy of the report. Derek gave a soft whine. 'What else did it show?'

'That she had a massive amount of MDMA in her bloodstream and her blood sugar levels were very low.'

'Esther will be shocked.'

'About the blood test?'

'No, the pregnancy.' She returned to stand beside him and held out her hand. 'Come on. Time to go home.'

He looked up at her, took her hand and squeezed it. 'I wonder if she already knew? Perhaps you could find that out when you show her this.'

'Oh, so I do have some uses then!'

He stood and stroked her shoulder as he passed her. 'Then there's the inquest to get through.'

'Esther's had such rough ride. She'll be mortified if Marianne's drug use comes out in public as well as her being pregnant.'

'Well, it's bound to be reported in the local press and in this town will make quite stir.'

'Poor Esther. I'll go and see her.'

30

WEDNESDAY 18TH OCTOBER: 9.30 AM
STEPH

STEPH FOLLOWED Peter out of reception to his Audi, in the Principal's parking space to the right of the sliding doors. He didn't appear to worry about status much, but his parking space was sacrosanct and, however full the car park, everyone knew not to use it. He once told her it reduced his stress to know he didn't have to worry about wasting time looking for a parking space when he dashed in and out of college. She knew these minor points made a great difference to his daily life. Mike had always fumed if anyone took his space.

She wasn't looking forward to the drive following the tension in the previous night's meeting. When she'd arrived in Peter's office first thing, he hadn't looked up from his screen but said not to worry they could talk later, in the car. She left, feeling like a student with a telling-off hanging over her.

She was aware that Peter was upset by his loss of control and it was her, not Hale, who would take the flack. She was still cross with Hale, who, despite realising what was going on, had done nothing to de-fuse the tension. Men! If only they behaved openly, more like Derek, who, when challenged by another male, postured, growled and threatened until one of them lay on his back in submission. The picture of Hale or Peter lying down submitting, dog-like, made her smile.

'Something funny?' Peter's voice smashed the image. She felt as if she'd been caught out once again.

'Not really, just thinking about something stupid Derek did on our walk this morning.' Not a big lie, was it?

'Derek's important to you, isn't he?'

'Well, when you live alone, he's great company, and it's good to have a guard dog to bark loudly if anyone's around.'

'But you're not always alone now, are you?'

'Hale you mean?' She'd walked into that one! 'We've become closer since we met up again, but he has his own flat—'

Peter's phone came to her rescue. 'Excuse me.' He fiddled with a button on the steering wheel.

'Hello.'

Paul Field's nasal tone boomed through the speaker, filling the car. 'Peter, it's Paul Field here. I wondered if I could have a word when you get back?'

'Of course.'

'That would be when?'

'About an hour's time.' He paused. They both knew what Paul Field was after. 'Steph and I are visiting Julie Richardson. You know, David's mother.'

'Steph? Ah! That's where she is. Sorry to bother you – there was nothing in the central diary, so I thought I'd check. Hope you don't mind.'

'Of course not. I'll see you when we get back.'

Peter disconnected the phone and smiled at Steph. 'Good to know we're missed, isn't it?'

They drove down the High Street, the shops just opening up, the lights switched on inside the dark interiors to combat the dull morning.

'You know, I'm pleased with all the work Hale does on our behalf and it's a help to have you in college.'

'That's good.'

'It's a shame it's necessary though, isn't it? This is such a difficult time for young people – social media, the internet, all that technology – complicates life rather than simplifying it for them. What is it they say? Information is the new economy?'

'You're right. It all moves so fast now.'

'And I know things move fast in Hale's world, but when it's to do with my college, I'd appreciate knowing about it as soon as it happens.'

'Yes, I do understand that.'

They were about to turn left into David's road when they got stuck behind a learner driver, who was reluctant to move forward until convinced the road was deserted.

Peter looked across at her. Trying to keep a blush from running up from her neck to her face was useless. She felt told off and, worse, she knew he was right. It was becoming irritating always having to defend one or other of them. Now it was Hale's turn.

'You're right, Peter. All this has been moving fast. Hale is frantically busy. It's not that he doesn't want to tell us, but he doesn't have the time. But you're right. I suggest I come in first thing each morning to give you any updates.'

'Sounds like a plan. Ah! I think this is it.'

They drew up outside the Richardson house. Curtains closed. No lights on from what she could see. They sat, taking in the garden, which was an even bigger rubbish dump than when she was last there. Beer cans, plastic bags, and old take-away food containers overflowed the broken shopping trolley, and empty wine and spirits' bottles piled up all around it. Searching the road ahead, she tried to find the place where there had been so much blood but couldn't see it.

A dark shape appeared by her window and, climbing out of the car, she was surprised to find Debby waiting for her, standing in the road. 'Hi, Steph.'

Steph smiled back. 'Hi, Debby.'

Peter came round to join them.

'Hello, Mr Bryant.'

'Good to see you, Mrs Martin.' He leaned across to shake her hand.

'Dreadful news about David, isn't it? Josie, his sister, is staying with me at the moment.'

A concerned expression flashed across Peter's face.

'Don't worry, it's all fine with Social Services. They've agreed she can stay while her mum is in hospital,' Debby re-assured him.

'But I thought she was out?' Steph gestured that they should move to the pavement to get out of the way of a familiar custard-coloured Fiat Uno, as it parked on the opposite side of the road. Stepping onto the pavement, Steph made sure she could keep an eye on the car while continuing the conversation. 'Sorry, you were saying that Mrs Richardson is back in hospital?'

'Yes, I'm afraid she was so upset about David's death, she... well, last night... had a relapse. Josie was worried, so I went over and saw that Julie was in a really bad way. I called an ambulance and they've kept her in. The paramedics said it might be contaminated drugs or an overdose. Josie's at school and I'll take her to see her mum after work, if she's well enough.'

'It's good we caught you.' Once again, Steph was impressed by the calm, caring Debby.

'Thank you, Mrs Martin.' Peter turned to get back in his car and bumped into Darcy. 'Good heavens! Darcy! Shouldn't you be in college?'

'My first lesson is Art, after break. This is my free period.'

'What are you doing here?'

He held out an enormous bunch of flowers, dark pink and ivory lilies, still in tight buds. 'I've brought these for Mrs Richardson. Is she in?'

'No, she's back in hospital, I'm afraid.' Peter opened his car door.

Darcy made eye contact with Steph, who guessed that he would arrive at reception later on. Debby moved towards him and reached out for the flowers. 'What a kind thought. Shall I put them in water until Julie returns and then I can give them to her?'

'Thank you.' He handed the flowers to her. 'Right, well, I'd better be getting back to college.'

They watched as he got back in his car and drove off.

'Look at the time! I'm going to be late for work! I'll take these in the house, then be off. Sorry you've had a wasted journey.'

Driving back to college, they sat in silence for a mile or so. Peter broke it. 'You don't think it was a wasted journey, do you?'

'No. On several counts. It appears Julie Richardson got the drugs she used last night from somewhere. We know she hardly ever leaves the house, so Luke's back or one of his runners supplied her. It sounds similar to the stuff that Marianne took when she went into that coma.'

'What will you do?'

'Tell Hale and he'll probably put a watch on the house to see if he can get Luke.'

They started up the hill towards college, slowing down for a crocodile of children, carrying clipboards, heading from Oakwood Primary School to the common.

'That's looks like nature study, although I bet they don't call it that anymore. And look— 'She pointed at two girls chatting at the end of the group. 'There's Helen, Jake's sister, and Josie walking together. That's good. At least she's safe.' She turned back to Peter. 'Debby Martin is a good person.'

'Yes, she is. You said there were some other things you noticed?'

'Darcy Woodard. He seems to pop up all over the place. When we were at the hospital, David told us Darcy had a phone number where he could contact Luke, which suggests he may also be up to his neck in this mess.'

'Surely not? He's such a good kid. Talented. Bright too, I hear, and off to Oxford. He wouldn't risk all of that, would he?'

Pleased that Peter also had faith in Darcy's innocence, and was talking to her in the old, relaxed way, she sighed. 'You'd hope not, wouldn't you? He's had such a tough time recently. When I was on that visit to Tate Britain, I caught sight of his phone and he's been getting the most appalling racial abuse.'

'Really? I'll send for him when we get back and see what we can do.'

'No! Please don't. He begged me not to tell anyone. He's got enough on his plate with Marianne's death and he won't trust me if he thinks I've told you.' How stupid was that? Why did she always have to think with her mouth?

'I'll take your advice, but it's good to know.'

They drove to the college in companionable silence. She

thought of Darcy. Images of Esther's rejection of him flashed into her head – when they brought him back from London, at the funeral and at the wake. Could he be desperate enough to turn to drugs and Luke's crew?

31

WEDNESDAY 18TH OCTOBER: 11.00 AM

DARCY

DARCY STOOD silent beside the growing mountain of flowers in the old entrance hall. News of David's death had spread through the college before lessons. The mood was subdued, and the volume of the chat turned down. Well over fifty students stood in silence, needing to be close to each other but beyond speech. He recognised several who'd been at Marianne's funeral and like him, they'd faced a second hit.

Two girls from his Art group, red eyed and grasping soggy tissues, held on to each other as if making sure they were safe. He saw the Principal and Steph standing, backs against the old doors that no longer worked, watching the students. What were they looking for?

He caught Steph's eye, and she smiled at him. The Principal looked worried and continued whispering to her. Darcy moved around the group and heard 'meeting... no choice... next year's funding.' The Principal left, reluctantly it seemed to Darcy. When he was out of sight up the corridor, Darcy shuffled sideways through the group to stand beside Steph.

'You all right?' she said.

'Yeah, thanks. You?'

'Devastating that after your sister, we're here again. This must be dreadful for you.'

'Not great. I thought David was going to be fine. I went to see him in hospital, and he was getting better and then...'

He saw her hand coming towards him, but she pulled it back and didn't touch him. He wished she would. It might have helped to get rid of the sick feeling.

'Luke's got a lot to answer for,' Steph said. 'Don't suppose you've seen or heard from him?'

Even now she was looking for information and not too subtly either. 'No, no sign of him. Think he's gone back to London. He knows they'll be looking for him here.'

Caroline swept up beside them. Once again, she was wearing her crimson cloak. The students started calling her Red Riding Hood but, as most of them thought she was cool, it hadn't lasted long. Hardly imaginative anyway, was it?

'Darcy, dear boy, how are you? Are you sure you should be here after all you've been through?' Caroline put her arm around his shoulder and pulled him to her. Other teachers were careful not to touch students ever, but Caroline broke all the rules and got away with it. No one would ever dob her in. They all loved her.

'Thanks Caroline, but it's better here with everyone else than at home.' He was aware of Steph's penetrating gaze as if she was trying to read below his words. What had he said that she'd found so interesting?

'Well, come along then, if you're coming. If you want to get to Ruskin, you need to get on with your portfolio. Actually, I marked your sketch book last night and was most impressed by some of your latest studies. They've caught the tone of Marlene Dumas so cleverly, yet you've blended yourself in there too.'

Walking along the corridor and up the stairs to the art studio, Darcy felt as if he'd been given a superpower as she continued to praise his work. He belonged in Caroline's room, in her lessons. So often in the canteen or wandering around campus, he felt lost, as if he shouldn't be there. Not belonging to any tribe. Marianne had given him credibility, and he'd spent break and lunch times with her. They'd meet by the quad and walk through that door to the canteen together. That door he'd never open alone, but he'd have to face it now, now she'd gone. Everyone looked so cool and belonged to a group, except him.

Marianne had tried to make him feel better and told him everyone felt like he did, and they were pretending they didn't by being so loud and making lots of noise. He didn't believe her and anyway, how could she know what it was like? She fitted in with both groups, but he was stuck in the middle and didn't feel right with either. But in Art he was a star. Caroline kept telling him so and he always got top grades. There he felt safe and the better he did, the better he did – success was contagious.

He pulled his portfolio out of the rack and, as he was opening it, Caroline came up with his sketchbook. 'Here, see what I mean?'

She opened the book at the first few pages and flicked through them. 'Great stuff. Now where are you going next with that piece?'

Darcy was about to open his mouth when the room fell silent. Caroline always played music while they were working – Jazz, rap, even classical sometimes – but someone had ordered Alexa to turn it off. The atmosphere became tense, and Caroline stood upright and turned to the door to see who had interrupted her lesson.

It was Paul Field, who pulled himself up to his full five feet seven inches and puffed out his chest. He reminded Darcy of a robin. He stood at the front, waiting for everyone to give him their attention. Most of them hadn't noticed his arrival, so carried on with their work. Some had and carried on anyway.

Annoyed, he bounced up and down as he clapped his hands and scanned the room. 'Quiet everyone. I said quiet. *Quiet!*' A few students rolled their eyes and grinned. He really was a prize pratt, and the students took the piss mercilessly behind his back.

'That's better. Now put you crayons down, that's right, and look this way.' Why did he have to speak to them as if they were six? 'That's right. You boy, take that silly hat off. We don't wear hats indoors, do we?'

The boy scowled and looked to Caroline, who shook her head, and with an enormous sigh, dragged his beanie off his head and made a performance of folding it up and placing it on the table in front of him.

'Miss – er – Jones, do you think you and your students could all sit down on their stools as I have a rather important message to convey?'

'Of course, Mr Field. Students, please sit on your stools.' As Caroline spoke, her eyebrow raised, a few students giggled. She floated over to her desk and sat in her traditional oak captain's chair, arranging her hands in front of her and making a steeple with them. She shifted her head to one side and gave a little nod, as if giving him permission to speak.

The students grinned and followed her example, scraping the wooden stools as much as possible before sitting on them, arms folded, waiting for Mr Field's earth-shattering announcement.

'Well done. That's better. Now students, you're probably

aware of the er... passing of David Richardson. It has come to my attention that several of you were at the party where he was stabbed. If you were there, I want you to look on your phones, and if you have any photographs of that party, I would like you to send them to me to help with my investigations.'

The hush became solid. What was he asking? He must be joking! Caroline sliced through their disbelief. 'Mr Field, is that quite legal, I wonder?'

A deep frown showed his extreme annoyance at this challenge. Caroline continued, 'I mean the Data Protection Act. Don't you have to get permission before sending photographs of other people? You never know where they'll end up. I thought it was in the college Code of Conduct?'

Darcy appreciated the clever way in which Caroline had stuck a pin in the pompous pratt. Flushed and looking uncomfortable, Paul Field cleared his throat. Then, apparently having thought of a response, he grinned at her.

'Actually, Miss Jones, when the students signed the college contract on enrolment they gave that permission, so we're absolutely tickety-boo where that is concerned.'

He paused, evidently pleased with his smart rebuttal, and his frown went even deeper into his forehead. 'I mean, when you think of all the photographs that our students routinely post on their social media sites for public consumption, this would hardly be an issue.'

Like a crowd watching Wimbledon tennis, all the students turned their heads to see if Caroline would have something to lob back over to him. She did.

'But, Mr Field, that's their choice and they choose who will see them.' Caroline bristled a little and sat up straight, showing she meant business. Darcy wanted to cheer her on but was beaten to it.

'Right on, Caroline!' A voice floated from the far corner of the room.

Paul Field's head shot around so he could see who had spoken. 'Ah! Fred Castle. That was you, wasn't it?' Paul Field tottered towards the back of the room. Darcy thought of the bird image again as he fluttered across the floor with his fussy steps. All heads followed him as he tried to tower over Fred. It didn't work well.

'Now, let's see what you've been up to, young man.' He flipped the pages of Fred's sketchbook. Fred looked furious and stood up. Caroline always asked if she could have a look, but this silly little man assumed it was his right to pry, uninvited, into Fred's work. Caroline caught Fred's eye and shook her head. It wasn't worth it. Darcy knew Caroline could get away with it, but Fred would come off worse.

Paul Field stared him out. 'I've been hearing all sorts of things about you.' Fred met his gaze and said nothing.

'Yes, rumour has it you've been dealing drugs and that you run one of these countryside lines in Oakwood and in this college. What have you got to say to that?'

Defiantly, Fred continued to stare into Paul Field's eyes, but a red rash grew up around his collar. Darcy looked at the faces of his classmates, who were clearly entertained by the exchange, but like him, some looked surprised that it should happen in this full classroom.

'Nothing to say, eh, sonny-Jim? Well, let me tell you we have daily contact with the police, who are determined to stamp it out of my college. In fact, they have you in their sights at this very moment.' Paul Field scanned the room as if checking that the hidden cameras were switched on. Fred followed his eyes and looked shaken.

Clearly, Paul Field noticed that his words were having an

impact, and he puffed his chest out further. What a pathetic dickhead! 'Yes, the police are keeping an eye on you wherever you go and whoever you speak to and whoever you have dealings with.'

He smiled, but a couple of students groaned at his impromptu pun. He frowned, clearly puzzled by their reaction. Then the penny dropped. 'Ah! Dealings. Indeed, that's about right, isn't it, Fred? Dealings? Fancy a few years in prison rather than university, do you?'

At last, Fred averted his gaze and appeared to find his sketch book fascinating.

Paul Field continued rubbing it in, 'What will your mother say when you're convicted of dealing drugs? A town councillor, isn't she? How will that go down in the local papers? Ex-mayor's son guilty of drug dealing – I can see the headline now. Not only your life ruined but your family's reputation too.'

Fred fiddled around in his pocket and pulled out a well-used tissue to wipe his nose and get something out of his eye. His head dropped to avoid Paul Field's gaze.

'If you want to have a chat with me, my door is always open and we can sort this out before it gets any worse.' Paul Field bobbed down, so he was under Fred's eyes. 'Do you hear me, son?'

Head still down, Fred nodded and grunted something that sounded like 'Yes.'

Viv must have moved and attracted his attention as Paul Field went towards her and picked up her sketchbook, again without asking. 'I don't think we've met. You are?'

'Vivienne Brown,' said Viv, looking at her sketchbook over his shoulder as if she was in charge.

'Ah! So, you're Vivienne Brown. You've just transferred

here, haven't you? Settling in well, I hope?' He slapped the open sketch book back on the bench.

Viv shrugged her shoulders and mumbled, 'Yeah, fine thanks.' She looked away, picked up her pencil as if eager to continue drawing, and added some pencil lines to her sketch of an apple in the still-life. He put a hand over her sketch, so she stopped drawing. How rude was that? He flipped over a few pages and, holding several in his hand, pointed to something towards the back of the book.

'You've almost filled this book with scribbles and then you go back to work on earlier ones. That's a strange technique, isn't it, Miss Jones?'

Before Caroline could answer, Viv said, 'Having missed so much, I wanted to make sure I've caught up with the rest of the group.'

'I like to see our students planning, but why don't you do it with stronger strokes? All these faint pencil lines are not effective, don't you agree?' He raised his head and sniffed. 'What an interesting perfume you're wearing. In my day that was called Patchouli oil; quite takes me back, the sort of people who used it—'

Darcy interrupted. 'Mr Field, I've been exploring the style of a female artist called Dumas. I wonder if you think this picture's good enough for the cover of your magazine?'

Paul Field was the editor and chief contributor of the college magazine, which looked as if it was published in the mid-twentieth century. No one read it. Mentioning the magazine was attractive bait. At once, his head snapped around and he moved away from Viv, tempted by the piece of artwork Darcy held out for his inspection.

'Umm. Not the usual style we go for, but... umm... could do something with it. What's your name, Duncan?'

'No, Darcy.'

'Of course it is. I was at your sister's... of course it is, Darcy. Yes, why don't you come with me now and we can discuss how we could adapt it.' Darcy picked up his sketch book and started to follow Paul Field, who, without warning, stood still. Darcy almost crashed into him. Paul Field ignored him and swung around. 'And I expect as many photographs of the party as possible sent to my account by the end of the day, please.'

With that, he minced out of the studio, Darcy trailing behind him. As he passed Viv, Darcy winked and grinned.

32

WEDNESDAY 18TH OCTOBER: 12.30 PM

DARCY

DARCY FOUND Viv hanging outside the canteen on a bench, playing with her phone. He plonked down beside her, feeling confident.

'Hi, I thought you were with that silly little man, whatshisname? Fielding?'

'Mr Field. No, I've finished. He's keeping the picture and will think about it. Don't think he understood it or liked it.'

Viv put her phone away. 'Fancy a coffee?'

He nodded. They stood and walked towards the double doors of the canteen. It was the first time Darcy had gone through them since Marianne had been in hospital. He couldn't remember what he'd had for lunch in the past week, but then, he hadn't been hungry. No way was he going in there alone.

The wall of noise hit him, and the doors closed behind him. As usual, he felt everyone was looking at him, but this time, with Viv beside him, he could turn to her and chat and not notice so much.

They both picked up a coffee and a toasted bacon and

cheese panini from the heated display, found an empty table, shoved the debris littering it to one side and sat down opposite each other. For a few moments, they didn't talk as they bit into the crusty bread and tried to stop the melted cheese from dripping out of the side of the crunchy rolls. When they'd finished, Viv spoke first. 'You're good at art, aren't you?'

'Yeah, about the only thing. Hope to go to Ruskin College, Oxford. Caroline thinks I'm good enough.'

'She's a brilliant teacher and the stuff she wears – so cool. When I grow up, I want to be like her.'

'Sorry you had to move college. Where did you come from?'

'Essex, near Epping Forest. My parents moved me up here – you know, to get away from the East London gangs. Some of my friends got into trouble, so they thought I'd be better out of it. Staying with my aunt. Anyway, this place is good.'

Darcy gulped at his coffee. Now it had cooled and wouldn't strip his lips. 'You must've been pleased that all the exam boards fitted, and you didn't have to start again.'

Viv paused and took a sip of her coffee before replying. 'One didn't, Sociology. They did OCR; you do Edexcel, but I'm having extra lessons to catch up.'

A slice of pizza splattered in front of his mug. Darcy's head jerked around to see who'd chucked it. A boy on the table opposite raised his hand in apology. It had overshot its target. Darcy was relieved that it hadn't been aimed at him.

'Sad to hear about that boy being stabbed.' Viv pushed away the pizza gunge with her paper serviette and left it at the edge of the table.

'Yes, it was grim. I was there.'

She said nothing but waited.

'Yeah, I saw it.'

'Thought this sort of thing didn't happen up here. Where I was, it happened lots.'

'Stabbings?'

'Yeah, well, it's got bad on some estates – postcodes, you know.'

'Yeah. Here too.' Darcy shoved his serviette inside his empty coffee mug and watched the paper soaking up the dregs. Lifting his eyes, he caught Viv staring at him. Their eyes locked, and he turned away.

'I think David attacked some London dealer who was cuck-ooing his Mum.' Darcy pushed the plastic spoon inside his mug.

'You know a lot.'

'Get around.'

'Yeah?' Viv glanced at the boys from one of the pizza-throwing tables, who got up to leave. He saw her frowning at the revolting mess they left behind them. Strange she should notice it.

'Dickheads!'

As he spoke, Viv turned to him. 'Sorry, you were saying.'

'Saw him in hospital. Thought he'd be good, but he got some infection and didn't make it.' Darcy took a tissue out of his pocket and wiped a few pieces of escaped pizza from the table before squashing the tissue in the coffee mug.

'A real shock for his mates. They got who did it?' Viv took a final swig of coffee.

'It was dark. Couldn't be sure who it was.' He paused, feeling a little thrown by her questions. She knew a lot for someone who had just arrived. 'I think I saw you with Steph the other evening. Sure it was you.'

Darcy scrutinised Viv's face to see how she took this sudden change of subject. She frowned and looked puzzled.

'Steph?'

'Yeah, you know, Steph, in reception.'

'When was this?'

'Last week. I went past the Co-op and saw you with her. How do you know her?'

Viv looked across at the table next door where the food fight had moved and was getting serious. 'I think we should go before we get pelted with more of their crap.'

She stood, picked up her cup and went towards the bins at the side of the doors. Darcy followed and decided to push his question when he caught up with her, walking back towards the art studio.

'You've not told me how you know Steph Grant.'

'Oh, that's her name, is it? I know her as Mrs Grant. She was in the police when I knew her. Youth Offending Team. She was good to me a few years ago, when I got in with the wrong lot and was in trouble. Didn't know she'd moved here. Bumped into her outside the Co-op. That's all.'

It sounded too neat, and he suspected she was lying or at least not telling the whole truth. They walked side by side across the quad, which was full of groups of students sharing images on phones or laughing at a meme or Gif. He felt good being seen with her around college. Not as much as Marianne, but she was bright, and he felt relaxed beside her.

He lowered his voice. 'I'm helping the police, you know.'

'Sorry?' Viv hesitated and turned sideways to look at him. He noticed her surprise at this sudden news.

'I'm helping them to find out who gave my sister bad drugs. She died because of it.'

'Yeah, I heard. Sorry, Darcy.'

'Not a great time. But if I can help the police get the bastard put away, then I'll feel I've done something.'

Viv didn't reply, but continued walking towards the art studio.

'Perhaps we could work together,' said Darcy.

Viv stopped and stared at him. 'What are you going on about? Work on what together?'

'Helping the police.'

'Don't be fucking crazy! I'm not "working" for anybody, as you put it, and certainly not the police.'

'OK. Have it your way.'

'See you later.'

Viv strode away across the quad. However much she protested, he was convinced she was a plant.

33

WEDNESDAY 18TH OCTOBER: 1.00 PM

STEPH

STEPH PULLED up outside Esther's house. She stared at two gulls fighting over a few chips in a paper bag, a little way up the lane. They made a dreadful din. She dreaded having to break the news to Esther but, instead of going to the canteen, had dashed off to spend her lunch break in Southwold. Fewer calories anyway.

Esther opened the door and appeared to have shrunk since the funeral. Looking over Esther's shoulder, it seemed to Steph that everything from the wake had been cleared away and the house returned to normal. Esther looked exhausted.

The day after a funeral was the pits. Dashing around to do the admin and making the arrangements took up so much time after a death and made a great distraction. The day after the funeral, the beginning of the rest of time started. There couldn't be a worse time to give her the news about Marianne. Although would there ever be a good time?

'Steph. So good of you to call.' Esther stepped out onto the porch and kissed Steph on both cheeks.

'How are you, Esther?'

'Oh, you know, coping – just. Thanks for dealing with Darcy yesterday. It must have been his strange way of grieving, but when I saw him with the wine and getting drunk, I saw red. It was so helpful for you to take him out of the way.'

'How is he today?'

'Fine, I think. He'd gone to college before I got up, so I assume he's getting on with his life.' She paused, her attention caught by the screaming of the gulls. 'They're so noisy and greedy, aren't they?'

Steph waited. In slow motion, Esther turned and, confused, stared at Steph as if she had asked something. Steph was not sure what to say next.

'Shouldn't you be at college?'

'It's my lunch break. Wanted to see how you're doing.'

Esther scanned the lane, down towards the sea. The sound of the waves swooshed towards them. 'Have you got time to go for a walk with me? Walking by the sea would be... good. I need some air.'

'Yes, of course.'

'Thanks. I'll get my coat.'

Waiting in the large porch, Steph glanced at her watch, worried about being back late. But after the morning's peace talks in the car, Peter had readily agreed to her visit and sympathised with her role as the messenger. It helped that she'd shared the news of Marianne's pregnancy. If a walk by the sea was what Esther wanted, it was the right thing to do.

The click of the door as Esther closed it made Steph jump out of her dithering and take action. 'Which way would you like to go?'

'Towards Cove Hythe? We'll get away from other people and I like seeing the tree roots in the cliffs. It feels as if dinosaurs walked there, prehistoric somehow. So dramatic.'

They turned left at the end of the lane, past the bright neon lights of the pier entrance and through the tempting smell of fish and chips, and then walked in front of the vivid beach huts. Most of them were closed up this late in the season and almost ready for their move to the car park for the winter. A sharp wind blew off the sea and forced tiny white puffs of cloud to race across the blue sky that stretched out to the horizon. The perfect autumn day, and she hadn't brought Derek.

Surprised by the speed at which Esther walked, Steph hurried to keep up with her. They moved from the prom to the beach and, as Esther predicted, left others huddled behind their windbreak beach camps. The wild sea, whipped up by the wind, smashed up onto the sand and made her feel alive and energised. Esther appeared to experience the same lift and picked up a pebble to skim into the sea. Not bad, three bounces.

They tramped along the deserted beach, easy walking on the band of firm sand a little way above the foaming edge of the waves. To their left, the encroaching sea had undercut the sandstone cliffs and dangerous looking overhangs waited to topple into the caves carved out below. They didn't talk much, both locked in their own thoughts. Steph recognised the need for silent companionship, which she'd missed so badly until Hale arrived.

In the distance she made out the bleached tree trunk she'd noticed last time she was here with Derek, and knew she had to face telling Esther soon. As they reached it, she turned to Esther. 'Shall we sit down here for a few moments?'

'Why not? As good as anywhere.'

They perched on the trunk, at an angle to the sea, taking in the shifting seascape to their right and the fields inland to their left. From the red earthed cliffs, a constant trickle of sand measured time to their inevitable return to the sea. The previous year, nets had been stretched along the cliffs to hold back the erosion, but when the nesting sand martins became trapped, the nets were removed and the flow of the sand grains continued. Each time she and Derek walked along the cliff top, more land had disappeared. These days they picked their way well into the field to avoid the crumbling edge, as the path had been swept into the sea about a year ago.

The time had come. She could no longer avoid it. 'Esther, I'm not sure how to tell you this.'

'Tell me what?' Esther, as bright as she'd been that first night after the cinema, sounded strong. The walk had been good for her. Now Steph would smash her down again. She knew there was no way of prettying up sad news and had learned to say it straight and cope with the consequences.

Steph took a deep breath. 'The initial post mortem report has come back. It has shown that Marianne was in the early stages of pregnancy.'

'Sorry? I was miles away. Look – is that a marsh harrier over those fields?' Esther pointed up into the endless blue above the fields in the dip to the left of them where an enormous bird floated, dignified and powerful. 'Strange, isn't it? Whenever you see those birds, there's an eerie silence somehow, as if time holds back, waiting for them to dive to earth.'

Inside, Steph cursed the magnificent bird that had ruined her announcement.

'Esther, I'm so sorry to have to tell you this, but the post-mortem has shown that Marianne was pregnant. A few weeks, apparently.'

Esther's mouth dropped open a little as she searched Steph's face. 'Did you just say Marianne was pregnant?'

'Yes, I'm afraid so.'

'But she can't have been. I mean... not my Marianne.'

Steph gave Esther space to take in the shocking news and moved her hand to touch her arm.

'We always talked about that sort of thing. I mean... she would have told me, wouldn't she?'

'Maybe she didn't know? It was very early.'

Esther took several deep breaths and Steph was scared she might faint as the colour acquired on the walk slipped away from her face. She tightened her grip on Esther's arm, ready to hold her back if she collapsed.

'I knew how she felt about Luke, her first love. She told me. And of course they... you know... slept together... but she was a bright girl, she'd planned her future... she wouldn't have risked it... so how did it happen?'

'These things often happen whatever we do to prevent them, don't they?' Steph tried to reassure her.

'Maybe. But not Marianne. Are you sure?'

'That's what it said in the report.'

'It could be a mistake, couldn't it?'

'I don't think it was a mistake. Pathologists know what they're doing.'

Steph could see from Esther's face that the harsh reality had started to soak in. She swivelled to look at the sea and cut Steph out. Several long, very long, minutes passed. Steph let her hand drop to her lap as the danger of Esther fainting appeared to be over. The best thing to do was to sit and wait and just be there for her.

The wispy white clouds were getting thicker, merging into wide bands swathed across the sky and covering the sun. A shadow crept across the beach, turning the sea grey and the exposed tree roots at the top of the cliff dark and menacing.

Steph sneaked a look at her watch. Well past lunch time.

No doubt they'd cope, but she'd told Peter she would be gone an hour at most. She didn't think she'd be this long and she ought to phone him, but now was definitely not the time. Esther's back was solid, and she hadn't moved for ages.

A grey-haired man with a large brown dog, a Rottweiler, strode towards them. He must have come the other way down the beach from Cove Hythe. They should go back.

Steph touched Esther's arm. 'Sorry Esther. I think we should go. I ought to get back to work.'

Esther stood and took a step in front of Steph. 'You're right. We should go.'

'I'm so sorry.'

'Don't be. It wasn't your fault. You couldn't help it. I'd rather hear it from you than the police.' She sighed.

Steph got up, realising how cold she was now the sun had been swamped by the thickening clouds, which were also turning dark grey. The wind had changed direction, and she hoped they'd get back before it rained.

Esther noticed the dense grey above her and looked out to the horizon, where already dark streaks emptied into the sea. 'We'd better get back before we get soaked.'

Steph was relieved as they hurried home in front of the threatening rain clouds that it appeared they'd left the pregnancy at the tree trunk. Esther chose the topics of conversation and they chatted about Steph's job at college, how kind Marianne's teachers had been and how pleased she was with the many thoughtful and touching cards from students and staff.

They beat the rain. As Steph searched in her bag for her car keys, Esther moved to the driver's door, apparently wanting to say something. Now what? They stood facing each other.

'That was a really tough thing Hale asked you to do.'

Steph gave a weak smile, not sure what was coming next.

Esther placed a hand on Steph's arm. 'Thank you, Steph. I really appreciate how difficult it was and know that you're a real friend. Thank you.'

'As long as you're OK? Sorry, I'd stay with you but I need to get back to college.'

'No. I'm fine. Thank you. See you soon, I hope.'

She leaned forward and kissed Steph on both cheeks, squeezing her arm as if to re-assure her it was all right. Before Steph could say anything else, Esther went through her gate and up the path and she must have had her key ready, as in one movement she opened and disappeared through the door.

Left alone on the lane, Steph reflected on the last stressful couple of hours. A fluttering made her turn. The empty chip bag flapped in the wind, the gulls long gone. She picked it up and stuffed it in her car door to throw in the bin when she got back to college.

34

WEDNESDAY 18TH OCTOBER: 5.30 PM

STEPH

STEPH LET Derek off his lead, and he chased Marlene towards the waves. She dodged to the left to pose by the foaming edge, superior and dry, as he dashed through the waves after the ball thrown by Caroline. Marlene was a pretty, white bundle of fluff, and Caroline adored her, but she always relished the more boisterous ball play with Derek on their sea walks.

As usual, Caroline looked the part in navy-striped Bretton fisherman's pullover and jeans, topped by a yellow waterproof jacket, just in case. A whiff of her perfume reached Steph, musky and spicy, no doubt sprayed on for the walk. Steph felt dowdy beside her in her dog walking suit – jeans, old Fair Isle pullover and wrinkled green Barbour – and stepped back as Derek shook sea water over her, waiting for the ball to be thrown into the waves once again.

They'd chosen to walk on the beach by Southwold harbour, where dogs could still roam freely off their leads, away from the candy-striped beach huts and sedate promenade. The tide was going out, uncovering a soggy margin of water-logged sand that sucked at their feet. Moving a little further up the beach, they paused once again to watch an ecstatic Derek bouncing around in the waves while Marlene, who avoided getting her feet wet, observed him.

'Darling, it's centuries since we've done this, isn't it?' Caroline swooshed some sand off an enormous piece of driftwood thrown up the beach in a recent storm and sat down, patting the space beside her for Steph.

She loved the way Caroline turned her environment into a work of art. If someone took a photograph of them sitting on the sculptured driftwood, against the backdrop of the marram grass on the dunes and the delicate white clouds, the composition would be perfect.

'Yes, it's been ages. Not sure why.' Steph settled down in the prescribed position.

'I'll tell you why. You've been so busy with the college drugs squad.'

'Well, Hale—'

'No, not Hale. I was talking about that silly little man, Paul Field. I'd have thought Hale had more sense than to involve him.'

Taken aback, Steph turned to face Caroline. 'He hasn't.'

'Well, he seemed to know a lot about it all today when he invaded my lesson.'

'I can assure you he isn't involved. Field knows nothing. Hale insists that I only talk about it to Peter.'

'I had noticed, my dear. I could be mortally offended, you know.' Caroline threw the ball for Derek who bounced into the foam to fetch it.

'You're putting me in a very difficult position, Caroline.'

'Am I?'

'Yes, you are. You're a great friend, but I can't share it. Hale would go ape!'

'Oh! Well, at least now I know you aren't betraying me by revealing all to that pompous little man. So up himself, as the students would say.'

Steph had learned that Oakwood was a tiny world, with the college even smaller. If she sneezed, within seconds someone would say 'bless you' on the other side of town. 'What made you think Paul Field was in on it?'

'As I was saying. He crashed into my lesson, no invitation, my dear, and started banging on about needing photos from that party. He nearly blew Viv's cover. She's good at her job, that girl, but will never make an artist. Darcy rescued her.'

'Did he?'

Caroline stood to check that Marlene was within calling range and, re-assured, resumed her seat. 'Actually, that jumped up little man wasn't the reason I asked you here, but Darcy.'

'Darcy? Why? What's he done?'

Caroline turned and glared at Steph, 'It's not what he's done. It's you.'

'What are you going on about?'

'You. Using that boy as bait.'

'Sorry?'

'I know what you're up to, and it's disgusting and dangerous. He's struggled to get accepted and now he has a future, you threaten to take it away.'

'What!'

'That boy is talented, and he's bright. He's going to get three As at A level and I'm pushing him to go to Ruskin. He has the brain and the talent to succeed there. That's so rare and you want to jeopardise all that?'

'What are you—'

'If he gets involved in this drugs caper and gets caught, he'll get a criminal record and that will be that, the end of Darcy.

221

You'll ruin his life. And think of Esther. She's already lost one child, her husband's dying and you're dragging her son into criminal gangs.'

How many more times that day was she going to be made to feel like a twelve-year-old getting told off by the teacher? 'But we—'

'But nothing,' Caroline interrupted, 'It's all right for Viv to take risks and become the college dealer – it's her job and she'll leave when you're finished with her. But if Darcy gets that reputation, he'll never recover, and that's how he'll always be known.' Caroline's eyes bored into her. 'At the very least, there'll be gossip and rumour and he could even go to prison.'

At last, Caroline appeared to have finished. Steph sat up straight and looked her in the eye.

'We haven't involved Darcy and we aren't using him or exploiting him. Yes, he wants to be – he volunteered. In fact, begged us to let him help, not once, but several times. He saw what they did to Marianne. They destroyed her life. She was dead from the moment she left Suffolk with Luke. If – and it's a big if – if we ever agree to Darcy helping us, we'll protect him.'

'But these things have a habit of going wrong.'

'How do you know that? Films? TV shows? How many drugs busts have you done? You sit there painting beautiful pictures while Hale lives on the streets in the grime of the gutter, trying to make a difference. I never thought I'd ever hear you say such things. Especially when they're not true.'

Clearly Caroline was amazed by Steph's outburst as she blushed and stood up looking for Marlene once again before sitting down. Steph wondered if she'd said too much. She valued Caroline's friendship and didn't want to risk it over this mess. Caroline, tight-lipped, stared out at the waves now topped by a mass of mercury clouds.

'Look, Caroline, I'm sorry I lost it, but I've seen what they do and how they drag kids into their net and how difficult it is to stop them. I promise, if we ever agree to let Darcy help, he will be safe. He's a good kid and I want to see him do well too.'

There was a long pause while they both became hypnotised by the rising waves, now being pushed up high by the wind. She ought to get Derek out before he got caught by the riptide and sucked out to sea. She rose from her seat to call him, but Caroline touched her arm. 'Sorry if I came on rather strong. Of course, you're right. It needs stopping. When Darcy protected Viv, I assumed he was helping you. You do see that, don't you?'

'Yes. But if he's not involved with us, do you think he's involved with drugs?'

'Darcy? Involved in drugs! No, never. He only wants to help you, and from what I saw today, he's certainly on your team.' Caroline stood and smiled down at Steph. 'Right. I'll keep an eye on him in college and let you know any of the overheards that Viv misses. Now, call Derek back and let's walk to The Sail Loft for a small glass of wine or even two. It's ages since I've been there and Margaret's making supper, so I can truant for once!'

Trying not to let Caroline see her checking the time on her watch, Steph decided it would be better to risk being late than to refuse Caroline's invitation. And she'd better have a word with Darcy if he was going round giving the impression that he was working with the police.

'That would be lovely. Come on, Derek!'

35

WEDNESDAY 18TH OCTOBER: 8.00 PM
STEPH

STEPH KICKED Hale under the table in an attempt to stop his antagonism towards Peter. He ignored it. The team had responded to Hale's urgent request for another meeting. Elizabeth complained that she'd moved an important commitment to attend, and her fixed frown signalled her irritation.

'Let me get this right. Paul Field revealed that the police are watching Fred, whom he accused of being a drugs dealer in front of the entire class, and asked for photos as he was investigating who might have been responsible for David's stabbing?'

'And he revealed to everyone that I have a full book of pencil sketches and implied that I hadn't done them. It was only Darcy's intervention that stopped him blowing my cover completely.' Red faced, Viv got in before Peter replied, and joined the accusing stares aimed at him.

'What a shit show! I knew this wouldn't work.' Elizabeth glowered at Peter, then Hale.

'But that's what Paul Field's like. He always has to be at the centre of things and makes an almighty fuss. But he means well.' Steph nodded at Peter and tried to be as calm as possible to de-fuse the growing tension as he looked more and more uncomfortable. It wasn't Peter's fault, after all. He didn't control every word that came out of Field's mouth, but she knew it was another consequence of not keeping Peter fully involved.

'Thank you, Steph, but I think I can manage to defend my own staff.'

'It's a shame you can't manage them!' Hale had to dig it in, didn't he?

Peter's voice became louder, and he sat up, erect and ready to fight back. 'Look, Hale, Paul Field does his best and it may not be my way, or even the most diplomatic way. But he doesn't want our students to die because of drugs in the college. Maybe I should have taken him into my confidence and I'm sorry if he almost compromised Viv, but his heart's in the right place.'

'A shame his tongue isn't!' Hale slapped a file of surveillance photos on the table to make his point, and several of them fanned out across the tabletop. Steph gathered them into a pile and replaced them in the folder.

Elizabeth was furious. 'I wonder if we should pull you out, Viv.'

Hale nodded. 'I was about to suggest the same. According to our latest intel, Julie's cuckoo has flown, and her house is empty. All that work down the drain. We'll need to start again when they return.'

'Return? You think they'll return?' Panicked, Peter looked across at Hale as if he was the one inviting them back.

'Of course, they'll return. This is fallow ground. Market forces – they want drugs so Luke will provide them or another big shot from London will step in and take over the line and his territory.'

'And did I mention that Darcy told me he was working with the police?' said Viv. 'Perhaps we could—'

'He said what? I don't believe this fuck up.' Elizabeth's voice was getting louder.

Hale blushed under the handler's gaze, and he ran his fingers through his hair, frustrated. He was about to boil over.

Steph tried to calm him down and decided not to mention her conversation with Caroline, who had also formed the same impression. 'He did offer when we drove him back from London, remember? And he's given us all that information from Marianne, so you could say he's helping us.'

Hale didn't look convinced. 'Great! We have a surveillance team to shut down, two dead kids and one body we haven't identified, and we're still no nearer getting anyone for any of it. We'll have to start all over again.'

'Not necessarily,' said Steph. She took a deep breath. It was worth a risk. Elizabeth glared at her. 'Why not take Darcy up on his offer and have him working with Viv? He appears to have a contact with Luke, who owes him for his sister. Maybe he can suggest taking over her line? You'll have two pairs of eyes in college. They can work together, so all won't be wasted.'

The silence was broken by Elizabeth. 'Have you any idea of the level of authority and the paperwork required to achieve this lunatic idea? Of course you don't. I keep forgetting your rank when you retired from the force.' She slammed her pen down on the table. Feeling stupid and humiliated for opening her mouth, Steph was convinced her idea was a good one. She might be ace at the admin and protocols required of a Cover Officer, but Elizabeth would never be mistaken for a people person.

Hale doodled on the side of his notebook, creating a group of boxes, growing them into a small block of flats. Clearly, he was thinking it through. They waited for him to speak. It was his operation after all.

Eventually Elizabeth broke the silence. 'Hale, this isn't the best way forward. He'd have to be properly briefed and protected through a risk assessment and as he's a sixth form student we'd need a shit load of safeguards.'

'He's eighteen, so a young adult who's volunteered to help. And the gang know him, and his sister was running a line for them. It would take much longer for them to accept an outsider like Viv.' Steph felt pleased she'd punctured Elizabeth's argument a little, but she was right – the procedures to involve Darcy were mind blowing.

At last Hale looked up. 'Elizabeth is right that it's complicated to say the least but it's worth considering – we've put so much effort into this. Let's think it through.'

As no one interrupted he continued. 'Right, on the pro side we have Darcy, who is known by Luke and his crew and has a family history of being involved in drugs.' Steph winced at the sudden labelling of the Woodards, once the perfect family, now druggies. 'We have Viv, who, apart from Paul Field's big mouth, has been accepted in college and could give Fred Castle and his chums confidence to continue being involved. Agreed, Viv?'

Viv nodded. 'No one, except Darcy, has said a word. No, I'm fine.'

Elizabeth tutted and shook her head, clearly annoyed that Hale was even considering using Darcy.

Hale ignored her and went on. 'Thanks, Viv. If – and it's a big if – if we can get the authority we need, Darcy could be a participating informant – that's if we can persuade the Authorising Officer to agree.'

Steph knew this would need to go up to the Assistant Chief

Constable and probably agreed by Dorset, Viv's force, as well as Suffolk. Hale would have to put up a convincing case, and if it went wrong...

'If Luke could convince Darcy to take over Marianne's line,' Hale said thoughtfully. 'Viv can help him set up the runners in college and we could tempt Luke back to help set up his empire, then we can get him. Yes, that might work.' Hale shaded in alternate boxes, evidently waiting for Elizabeth to explode. She didn't.

'Do you think Luke would go back to Julie's after David's death? He must know we're on to him?' Clearly, Viv was flattered that Hale was talking to her and was desperate to appear positive and involved. Steph squeezed her lips together, stopping herself from saying something she might regret later.

'No idea. Could do. He's arrogant enough. Probably thinks we're stupid country plods and won't get him. Have to wait and see.' Hale sneaked a look at Elizabeth, her frown deeper than ever, her lips tight.

Peter looked uncomfortable; he hesitated, then spoke directly to Hale. 'Let me get this straight – you're going to retain Viv as one of my students then implicate another as a drugs dealer to tempt more of my students to become users or runners? Suddenly I feel like that goat in *Jurassic Park* – you're using my college as bait and I'm not sure I like it much.'

Elizabeth nodded to Peter before turning to Hale. 'He's right, Hale.'

Hale looked up, making eye contact with Peter. 'Well, Peter, you, or rather we, have a choice, don't we? We set up the trap and try to get the main man behind it, or we walk away and you have a college ripe for picking by any big drugs dealer and we – and that includes you – will have no idea it's happening and no way of stopping it.'

'So, I'm damned if I do and damned if I don't.'

'As I said, it's up to you. Whatever happens, drugs will get into your college, and you may see more deaths. If you want to be with us and fight, that's great. If you want to pretend it isn't happening, well, that's your call. I'm prepared to jump through all the hoops to make it happen, but if you don't agree, that's that.'

All of them appeared to be considering Hale's stark summary and stared at the table. Steph knew that what happened in college was Peter's decision, and if he didn't agree, Hale would be back to square one, having spent a great deal of time and resources for no results. If he did, Hale would have a hell of a job persuading his bosses. The silence stretched.

They waited. Peter sighed and looked across at Hale. 'It's not really a choice at all, is it? You're right, Hale, the best way is to have you involved. If Darcy is prepared to take the risk, I think you should use him, making sure Viv is there to look after him. I'll take Paul Field out for a drink and tell him what we're up to. To keep him on-side, he needs to feel informed and involved. He's a good man underneath, you know.'

'Thanks, Peter. You've made the right decision. Now let's get down to some detailed planning.'

Steph was relieved as peace was declared between her two bosses. But for how long?

36

THURSDAY 19TH OCTOBER: 1.00 PM

DARCY

DARCY WALKED THROUGH OAKWOOD, heading for Julie's house. At last, Hale had seen sense and involved him in getting Luke. Hale had picked him up at eight and he'd spent the morning in a cold flat the far side of Oakwood being briefed and what Hale called 'risk assessed'. Hale had explained that he'd managed to get permission to include him through some complicated process with HQ, which was obviously a big deal. He looked exhausted and Darcy assumed he hadn't slept much.

Without Marianne, his life had been sucked dry and his mother had rejected him altogether. She cooked his meals and asked for his dirty washing, but the daily chat had gone. She showed no interest in him. She lived with Jane Austen.

Whenever he came home – if that's what he could still call it – she was sunk in reading. She'd read those novels so many times she'd probably be able to recite them by heart. Or she was watching a DVD, which showed a perfect landscape, with men and women wasting their time posing in posh clothes, while absent servants worked hard somewhere off stage to make their masters' self-indulgence possible. Several times he'd even tried to talk to her about her Jane Austen life, as he'd come to think of it, but his questions were blocked by her single word answers. He kept out as much as possible.

He parked his car behind the High Street, where Viv should be waiting for him outside the pizza parlour. She'd phoned him to make sure he was happy with it all and they'd decided it would work if they became boy and girl friend and hang around college together. Darcy was pleased that Viv would take Marianne's place; she wasn't as beautiful or intelligent, but she'd be beside him as he walked into the canteen and help him fill the time he no longer spent at home.

She'd been pleased with the video he'd given her of the stabbing; although it was pretty blurred and dark. she thought it might be enhanced to get an image of who'd done it. He told a few of the kids who were at the party that the guy who stabbed David was also involved in Marianne's death, and if they sent him the videos, he would pass them to the police anonymously and they'd be able to catch the killer. He was surprised how easy it was to talk to them when he was asking about something specific, and they didn't appear to think anything of it. Perhaps at last he was being accepted.

'Hey! You almost walked past me!' Viv stepped in front of him, put her arms around his shoulders and kissed him hard on the lips. This part of their act was cool, as she didn't hold back but made most of the moves. Wrapping his arm around her shoulders, they walked in step down the High Street and through the Victorian terraces that led to the sixties streets on the edge of town.

'Your jacket's great.' Darcy flicked one the of pocket flaps on her combat jacket. 'Is it specially for this?'

She smiled up into his face and laughed. 'Don't be silly, it's me.'

'But don't you have to wear proper clothes at other times?'

'Proper clothes? You have an old-fashioned view of what plain clothes means. I always dress like this.'

He glanced at her torn jeans, bright tee shirt and the line of about ten earrings tracing the outside edge of her ears. The diamond stud in the side of her nose glinted in the sunlight and he felt dull beside this streetwise woman who'd belong in any festival or beside any street food stall.

Her voice low, she leaned towards his ear. 'Now remember. No heroics. We're in this for the long haul and to collect enough evidence to get Luke, so we have to take it slow and get his confidence. You introduce me and don't be tempted to suggest you run a line or take any action. That would finish the op – you'd be conspiring as an agent provocateur. They did explain this to you?'

'Yeah, I understand. I listen and wait for Luke to suggest it.'

Viv squeezed his arm and grinned at him. For a moment she looked nervous. Perhaps she wasn't used to working with a partner? He was sure he'd be fine.

They'd reached the dump of Julie's front garden. Since the party, more crap had made its way among the long tufts of grass and nettles, and the supermarket trolley, now upright, was full of cans and bottles and plastic bags of rubbish. The door was ajar, and music was pounding out somewhere in the back of the house, not as loud as it had been at the party, but it still vibrated the windowpanes. An old brown leather sofa and chair had been returned to the party room along with the dark blue carpet, the edges curled up at the chipped skirting boards. Darcy sniffed and took in the stale smell of booze and skunk smoke and couldn't help coughing. Viv, behind him, nudged him on to the kitchen.

Once again Julie was out of it, lolled in a kitchen chair propped up by the wall. Luke was on his phone in the kitchen doorway, staring at the mud patch garden. His voice rose at the end of his call. '—and get that flip-flop crew sorted. I don't want to fucking come back up there and sort your shit, know what I'm saying? You get that dickhead back in line... tell him it's smokin' season and I won't fuck with him, man. I'm not playing games. Sorting your shit out... I don't need the stress, understand? It's your shit. Get respect, understand? Smoke him.'

Aware of Darcy's arrival, Luke finished his call and faced him. He was wearing the same stuff as at the party; black leather jacket, dark hoodie and jeans. Once again, Darcy was hit by his charisma. He ruled wherever he was. Darcy was well over six feet, but Luke stood over him by a head.

'My man, you got over that shit party?' Luke took a step forward and pulled Darcy to him in a man hug. Darcy thought it strange how Luke sometimes became 'one of the crew', his language reflecting urban street talk, not his public-school background. So different to when he'd charmed Marianne and Esther. 'Sharks, that's what I have to work with, know what I mean? Come up country and shit happens. She's clean, is she?' Luke stepped beside Darcy and ran his eyes over Viv, who rebuffed his undressing by staring him out.

'Yeah, my girl, Viv.'

'Nice. You want food or what?'

'Yeah.' How was he to get Luke to suggest that he could run a line? Luke appeared to be waiting for something. What? 'Hey mate, I came on a bit strong at that party the other night. I was grieving. I know you looked out for Marianne. She must've got the bad stuff from the other crew.'

'Pleased you've seen sense. She was mint, your sister. Great line she started up here. Would have been my lieutenant the way she was going.'

'Really?'

'Yeah. That college she went to, you go there too?'

'Yeah, why?'

'She said that college was ripe and she had a crew set up, ready. I was going to send her the gear and we'd be running.'

'Yeah, she said that to me too. Perhaps I—' Darcy felt a sharp poke in his back. Viv had played the obedient girl so far and said nothing, but her prod reminded hm to be careful.

'What?' Luke was all attention.

'Nothing. Marianne just told me, that's all.'

Luke's penetrating gaze forced him to look away. Luke was the boss, and he had no idea what would happen next.

'You think you could take over the line from Marianne?'

Darcy kept his expression neutral, trying not to encourage Luke in any way. He was aware of Viv tensing up behind him. He paused, as if thinking it over while counting to five. It worked.

Luke couldn't resist the sales talk. 'Not for pussies, you know. You'd need to get respect from your crew, build up your contacts.'

Darcy looked at the floor. Counted to four. Raised his head and scrutinised Luke. Luke's eyes narrowed. 'Well? What do you think?'

'Give it a go.' Darcy hoped that this wouldn't sound like he was conspiring on the recording Viv was bound to be making.

'If you are half as good as Marianne, you'll do great, bro. I'll send you the gear and we're running.'

Darcy felt no prod from Viv so assumed he was OK. 'Right.'

'I'll get you burners and everything? Know what I mean?'

'Sure. Whatever.' Darcy hoped he sounded cool, despite his hammering pulse.

Luke was not to be rushed and appeared to be considering his next step. He took out his blade, flicked it open, and started cleaning his fingernails. Subtle or what? Now it appeared it was Luke who was waiting. For what?

'OK? Good to go then or what?' Darcy risked it, trying to show he wasn't intimidated but still allowing Luke to make the running. He spoke in a matter-of-fact tone and shifted back a little, ready to walk out. Movement wouldn't show on a recording.

Luke stared at Viv before turning his gaze on Darcy. With a slick, practised movement, he closed his blade and slid it back into his pocket. 'Who'll vouch for you?'

'Don't need no one. Marianne didn't play games, did she? I'm her brother.'

'Always wondered about that.'

'Adopted.'

Luke frowned, as if this was new information. Darcy was surprised at his reaction. Was he performing for Viv? But then, all Luke ever thought about was Luke. He appeared to make up his mind.

'Right, get this clear. This is my patch, but you get to run it for me, know what I'm saying? If you violate, know what I mean, you're smoked.'

'Yeah, great.'

Julie moaned; her bloodshot eyes scanned the kitchen, but she appeared not to see anything. Her lips moved. She reached out her hand and flicked at something in front of her face, then let it fall onto the table. Flopping forward, she laid her head on her arm, the other dangling by her side. She was well out of it.

For a moment, they stopped talking as they watched her slow-motion movements. Horrified by the change in David's mother from the bright woman he'd often seen at the school gate to this thin skeleton lost in her own nightmare, Darcy struggled to keep a straight face and not let his disgust show. Had Marianne understood what she was doing, destroying people and families like this?

Luke looked bored and irritated by the interruption. 'Back to business. I'll get a car here tomorrow. Station car park, four o'clock. Pick up the gear, let's start at...' As he was speaking, Luke draped his arm around Darcy's shoulder and steered him outside. Clearly, the financial details were not to be shared with Viv.

Darcy was amazed at Luke's slick business brain and the professional operation he described in his City voice. Luke recited the number of wraps of cannabis he would send and the full menu of the drugs he'd supply, offered to increase the amount if Darcy's sales were good, then agreed to discuss moving from brown to white, from cannabis to crack cocaine. He promised Darcy he could earn up to eight thousand pounds a day and when he increased his lines, it could go up as high as one hundred thousand. Once again, Luke threatened that if Darcy betrayed his trust, he would kill him. Business discussion over, they returned to the kitchen to find Viv looking pissed off, sitting on the kitchen chair opposite the unconscious Julie, necking beer from a bottle.

'You going back tomorrow?' said Darcy.

'Not sure. May stick around to see how you get on.'

'Here?'

'Not sure. Need to keep moving. Take this. I'll call to confirm the time.' Luke handed Darcy a burner phone. He nodded. They were finished. Luke held out his fist and Darcy punched it, then turned round, and nudged Viv out of the house.

As they walked down the road, Viv patted his arm. 'Hey, that was great! Even I thought you could be one of them.'

Darcy grinned at her. 'How do you know I'm not?'

37

THURSDAY 19TH OCTOBER: 5.30 PM
STEPH

DEREK TORE the lead out of Steph's hand and galloped towards Hale, who was getting out of his car. The bright day had ripened into a balmy evening with the fluttering copper leaves on the silver birches vivid against a clear blue sky.

Hale, having made a fuss of Derek, leaned across to Steph and pecked her on the cheek. 'How great to be out in the air! Come on, we've got... let's see...' He checked his watch. 'Yes, forty minutes, so we need to leave here in thirty.'

'Forty minutes until what?'

'Until Jim arrives for a chat.'

'At the station?'

'No, your flat.'

Steph stopped, horrified. 'What! I haven't cleared up the breakfast things yet. We should get back there now!'

'No need. Jim won't notice, and anyway, I want some air.'

Derek concluded the debate by chasing a small terrier around the edge of the pond. They ran after him, Hale shouting and Steph apologising to the hysterical owner, who caught her dog, stuffed it under her arms and stormed off towards the car park. With Derek safely under control, they strolled around the edge of the pond, now full with the autumn rains, which drowned the litter chucked in it over the summer.

Hale looked around and made sure there was no one within hearing distance. 'Elizabeth made contact today and told me how impressed Viv was by Darcy setting up the line with Luke – said he behaved like a pro. '

'That's good.'

'Umm... She thought... perhaps just a little too much.'

Steph glanced at Hale's profile. 'What does that mean?'

Hale frowned. 'Well, apparently he made a strange comment as they left and, having watched him this afternoon in college, she thinks he seems to have slipped into his role all too easily and contacted a rather large number of students.'

'Isn't that what we wanted him to do?'

'Yes, but only so we could get evidence against Luke, not so he's tempting more students to start using.'

Steph got out her phone. 'You ought to see this.' She touched the photo app and handed it to Hale. A video appeared that showed a close-up image of Luke chasing David from the back garden of his house.

'That's much sharper than the one Viv gave me.'

'Yes. Darcy got it. He's been asking around for photos or videos and this was the latest sent to him. I'm sure he wants to nail Luke for Marianne's death, not run a county line here. I'll send it to you.'

'Shame it's blurred at the actual point of the stabbing.'

Steph looked at her watch and turned towards the car park. 'Let's get back.'

They loaded Derek in the back of the car and drove towards the flat. Steph had never been house-proud, but in her open-plan flat all domestic life was on show and she needed a few minutes to shove the dishes in the dishwasher. As they drew up outside the flat, they saw Jim had beaten them to it and was standing beside his car, stretching his legs and back.

Hale held out his hand. 'OK, Jim?'

Jim shook it. 'Yeah, fine. Getting a stiff back when I've been in the car a long time – age creeping up, that's all.'

They went in, and after Steph had fed Derek, cleared away the breakfast dishes and made them cups of tea, they sat around the table.

'Well? What have you got for us?' said Hale.

Jim opened the file he'd been carrying and handed round some reports. 'You'll see at last we've discovered the identity of the body we found in the bath. A Jez Stewart, known to the drugs squad as one of Luke's lieutenants who controlled the Battersea patch, including the Latchmere. They were old school friends, apparently. He was killed with the gun we found had been wiped, but they're still examining other evidence for DNA. We have, however, had a result in some of the crack houses Luke runs – or we think he does. He's clever that man and doesn't leave much of a trail.'

'So we've noticed.' Hale topped up Jim's cup and turned to Steph, who shook her head.

Jim turned over a page and pointed to a paragraph halfway down. 'In three of the dens, we found prints and DNA from your boy, Darcy, and in one of them, a large amount of blood. We assume someone was killed there, and the body moved.'

Hale looked up from his reading. 'Another shooting?'

'No, from the blood spatter pattern our chaps think it was a pretty brutal killing with a large knife or machete. Haven't found the body yet.'

Having re-read the paragraph that mentioned Darcy, Steph

interrupted. 'But we already know Darcy had gone to these places to look for Luke, so his DNA would be there.'

Jim pointed to a sentence further down. 'Yes, that's true, but look where they found it. On mugs, plastic bags and wraps, so it suggests he was handling drugs and spent some time in more than one of the dens.'

'Do you think he's involved in Luke's operation?' said Hale.

'That's what we'd like to ask him. Have you got any evidence that he's involved up here?'

Hale glanced across at Steph and sighed. 'We've just involved him.'

'You've what?'

Hale raised his eyebrows. 'Yeah. We've made him a participating informant. He's setting up a line as one of Luke's dealers in Oakwood and we're hoping to catch him handing over the drugs and charge him for murder. My officer said Darcy was convincing; now we know why.'

38

THURSDAY 19TH OCTOBER: 7.30 PM
STEPH

THE FLAT DOOR flew open and bashed a dent in the plaster as Hale rushed in. 'Right, get your coat, we're off. *Now!*'

'Where?'

'Esther's. Stop talking and let's get going – it's urgent.'

He dashed out to the car while Steph locked the flat and jogged after him. What could have happened since he'd left to take Jim down to the police station less than an hour ago?

'Right, all set?' Hale squealed off from the kerb.

'What's happened?'

'It's a total clusterfuck is what's happened.'

Gripping her seat to remain upright as he overtook a delivery lorry heading for the supermarket outside town, she held her breath while she pushed her brake pedal foot hard into the floor.

He must have sensed her panic. 'For goodness' sake, woman! Get a grip!'

They slowed down as they got through the town and approached Southwold.

'What's wrong?'

'Where do you want to start? The incompetence of the lab, the inefficiency of the Crime Scene Manager, the inadequacies of our IT system? I couldn't have organised this fuck up if I'd tried.'

'What?'

'Look, we're here.'

Hale really got up her nose when he was in this mood. One minute she was in the centre of everything, one of the team; the next, information wasn't shared with her and she was on the outside. And her relationship with Peter was now fragile, to say the least. If they ever sorted this out, would she still have a job at the college?

Hale grabbed a file from the back seat and strode to the front door, which opened as soon as he touched it. With the door ajar, he shouted down the hall, 'Esther, it's Steph and Hale! May we come in?'

A weak 'Yes' could be heard from the direction of the sitting room.

As usual, Esther was sitting in her armchair, this time in a long, dark green velvet dress. Steph wondered if she'd had all these dresses made at the same time in a variety of colours, then stopped herself from thinking such flippant thoughts. There were dark bags under Esther's eyes, and this thin woman appeared to get even thinner each time Steph saw her. The usually pristine room was gloomy and smelt musty and it appeared Esther had been sitting in the dark.

'Sorry. I'll switch on some lights.'

They sat on the sofa waiting, while Esther toured the room switching on the table lamps, which helped to make the room feel warmer but highlighted the unfamiliar mess.

'Sorry. Not much good at social stuff at the moment. Tea? Coffee? Something stronger? Sorry.' Her words offered action, but her body showed there was no way she had the energy to go to the kitchen.

'May I get you anything, Esther?' Steph wondered when she had last eaten.

'That's kind, but no thanks.'

Esther fell back into her chair, continuing to stare at the television screen as if they weren't there and where, as usual, a Jane Austen DVD was playing out the lives and loves of her long-frocked heroines.

This time, Steph was surprised to see the cramped and dark interior of a poor kitchen on the screen, instead of the usual grand country house, followed by a sea scene that looked like Lyme Regis. They both waited. Esther made no attempt to turn it off, and the volume was too high for them to talk over. Hale made eye contact with Steph and glanced at the TV.

Steph acknowledged his unspoken message – so she was good for something then! 'Esther, would you mind if we turned this off for a while so we can talk, please?'

'How rude of me! Sorry, not myself.' She fiddled with the TV remote. The screen went black, and she returned to the present. Esther sat up straight and looked across at them, waiting to hear what they wanted. Steph observed Hale, as she too had no idea what they were here to talk about.

'Some additional information about Marianne's death has come into my possession.'

Esther sat forward to listen to Hale, who pulled a few sheets of paper from the file on his lap, got up and handed a copy to Esther. Steph looked over his shoulder as he sat down. It was a post-mortem report. Esther held the paper in her fingers but didn't read it and continued to stare at Hale.

'This is the full post-mortem report following Marianne's death. First of all, I must apologise for the delay. It should have been with us several days ago, but it got stuck in the system. I'm sorry it wasn't here sooner and I'm investigating what happened.' He paused and looked across at Esther, who hadn't moved and looked dazed. 'There are two parts to it, the initial pathologist's report then the results of the follow-up toxicology tests.'

Hale paused again, apparently thinking Esther might comment or want to read it, but she ignored the paper on her lap and fixed him with the same confused expression.

'Right. Let's skip all the scientific jargon and get to the conclusions. You'll see from the initial examination that Marianne's death was caused by an overdose.'

'But we knew that, the same drugs that caused the coma you saw.' Esther nodded at Steph.

Hale ignored her interruption. 'And, as you already know, they also discovered Marianne was in the early stages of pregnancy.'

Apparently uncomfortable, Esther raised herself, brushed her hands behind her long skirt to smooth it and pulled it straight underneath her, before resuming her seat. She sighed and bit the side of her lip, then raised her head and looked across at Steph. 'I suppose now is the time to tell you. I'm sorry Steph, you did a great job but... I already knew. So did Marianne. But she didn't know I did.'

Steph couldn't react. Shocked, she didn't know what to say as she replayed those hours on the beach when she'd struggled so hard to break the news to Esther. Had she really known all the time? Why hadn't she said anything instead of pretending Steph was telling her something she didn't know? What was she playing at?

Hale too, was silent, clearly leaving Esther space to tell them more before he needed to prompt her. At last, she raised her head. 'The morning she left hospital, she discharged herself and they were all in a frightful flurry. She had to go off to the nurses' office to sign some papers and her medical notes were left on the bed. I read them. They'd found she was pregnant when they examined her.'

'Did you ever discuss it with her?' said Hale.

'To find out who the father was, you mean?'

'Not necessarily that but... you know... to discuss if she would change her plans or anything because of the baby...'

'You mean abort it.' The steely tone hit Steph. This was a new Esther.

'Yes.' Hale squared up to her sudden aggression. 'Or other things girls who are pregnant talk to their mothers about.'

Esther said nothing but lowered her head, apparently attempting to hide the blush that flashed across her cheeks.

'Right. Let's move on. The other important finding is in the toxicology report. The pathologist was puzzled by some of the early blood results. They found a large amount of the drug that caused her first coma, but she also had abnormally low blood sugar.'

Hale waited, and Esther started to read the report. The ticking clock measured the uncomfortable silence. She stared at it but didn't appear to be reading it, then she folded the report and placed it on the table beside her.

'Well, that doesn't tell us much, does it? You know the sort of girl Marianne was, always on a diet, never eating enough.' A defensive note had crept into Esther's voice.

'Then do you know where she may have got the insulin from?'

'Sorry?'

'Insulin.' Slow and with an emphasis on each word, Hale recited the findings from the last page of the report. 'High levels of insulin, five times above normal, were found in her vitreous humour.'

It sounded brutal telling a mother they had dissected her daughter's eyes. Even when Marianne was dead, it made Steph shiver to picture her eyes being sliced, but Steph realised Hale's intention was to shock Esther. 'That's the gel behind our eyes, you know. You see insulin is natural and if it's used to kill someone, it disappears from the body quickly, but it remains longer in some places, such as the vitreous humour, and that's where they found it.'

Esther's expression didn't change.

'Then they checked her body again to find evidence of injection sites and discovered that as well as her right arm, she'd been injected between the big and second toe on her left foot. We now know she was murdered and, as far as we can tell, here, in this house.'

The shattering news hit Esther at last, and she half collapsed over the arm of the chair. Hale indicated to Steph, who got up and went to the kitchen for a glass of water. She returned to a sobbing Esther, a serious Hale scrutinising her from the sofa; and once again the ticking clock filled the room. Esther sipped the water, wiped her face with a tissue, and sat up.

'You can't think I murdered my daughter?'

Hale waited and said nothing.

'How could you? I loved Marianne, and I didn't care if she was pregnant by some low life drugs dealer or up to her ears in drugs. She was still my daughter. I loved her and would never have wanted her dead. I was – am – torn apart by her death. How can you possibly think I could have murdered her?'

'I'm sorry, Esther, but you must see that the evidence points that way. She died here in your house and no one from outside your family appears to have been involved. I'm sorry but we need to search your house. I've applied for a warrant, and we'll need to wait here until my colleagues bring it.'

'But they've searched already! When they searched Marianne's room, they found no evidence of anything, apart from a few of those little plastic bags they use for passing drugs.'

'As I said, we'll need to search—'

'You don't need a warrant to search the house. I know exactly where you'll find a large stock of insulin and a whole box of needles. Darcy's been diabetic since he was nine and controls it with insulin. He always has several insulin pens, which get replaced each month on his prescription. Look, I'll show you.'

Esther pulled herself up and led them up the stairs, past Marianne's closed bedroom door, to Darcy's room. They entered a typical teenage boy's room and were hit by the unmistakable smell of unwashed socks. Jeans, hoodies, socks and trainers littered the wood floor, revealing specks of a dark red rug beneath the jumble.

The walls were covered with Darcy's vibrant paintings of leaves, shells and feathers, transformed into bright abstracts, and confirmed Caroline's view that he was a talented artist. Painting equipment on his desk and a small bookcase of art books filled the window wall, and opposite was his unmade double bed.

Following Esther, they picked their way across the room, stepping in the gaps between the scattered clothes to an antique walnut tallboy. She pulled open the top drawer and revealed an insulin pen, a box of small needles and a testing kit in an open case.

Esther tutted and turned the case over. 'He should carry this kit around with him to test his blood levels, but he never does. He feels different enough already without everyone knowing he's diabetic too. You'll find another two packs of insulin in the fridge in the kitchen.' She picked up the pen and held it out to Hale. 'The stuff he uses is a mixture of long and short-term acting insulin. You're welcome to take one to check if it's the same as... what you've found. There are lots of different sorts of insulin, but I expect you know that.'

Esther reached into the drawer, pulled out a box and extracted a few sealed needles that fitted onto the end of the pen. 'Will that be enough for you to find out what you need to know?'

'Thank you, Esther,' said Hale. 'I think we now need to speak to Darcy. He obviously isn't here. Do you know where he is?'

'No idea.'

'But you've got that tracker app on his phone.' Hale was clearly becoming irritated.

'He found it and removed it.' She shook her head and sighed. 'That boy has suddenly gone crazy. I blame him for all this, you know. For not looking after Marianne at Latitude and getting her involved with that Luke. He's always out now. Suddenly, he has lots of friends he needs to see. Before, he was always in his room painting.'

'Please phone us as soon as he returns; we'd like to talk to him.' Hale led the way downstairs. What was he playing at? Steph knew he had Darcy's mobile and could contact him at any time. Maybe he was trying to see which side Esther was on.

Esther sighed and showed them to the front door. As she was turning the knob, she paused and looked up at them, sighing. 'How quickly my life has crumbled. Dickie dying in the hospice, Marianne murdered and as for Darcy – goodness knows what he's up to.'

39

THURSDAY 19TH OCTOBER: 10.30 PM
DARCY

'WHERE HAVE YOU BEEN?'

Darcy hoped to creep in without disturbing his mother, but she appeared as soon as the front door clicked shut.

'I'm sorry to disturb you, Mother, but I had things to sort out.'

She stepped in front of him, blocking his way, and stared long and hard at his eyes. 'Hmm! What things?'

'Sorry I disturbed you. I'm tired and I want to go to bed.'

'I, I, I – that's all you think about, isn't it?' Her screaming accusation made his ears hurt. She shoved him back against the wall and moved in close. 'You selfish pig, you never think about me – what I've been going through, do you?'

As she prodded him further back into the wall, he tasted her whisky breath. 'First you take my Marianne to that festival and let her go to London with that drug dealer—'

'You didn't exactly stop her, did you?'

'How dare you!' She slapped his face, hard. He raised his hand to his left cheek. Shocked, he turned away from her poisonous stare. He pushed past her towards the kitchen.

Looking exhausted, she threw herself on the hall chair, her head bowed. He tried to feel sorry for her, but he'd done nothing wrong – had he? He grabbed a glass from the cupboard, filled it from the tap and gulped. Mother was always angry with him now and had been ever since Marianne's coma.

He felt desperate. Most of the time, they avoided each other. She left a room as soon as he entered it. As far as his mother was concerned, he'd always been the extra, the additional child, not Marianne, the favourite. But it had never been as painful as it was now.

It got worse after Dad went into the hospice. Now her seething rejection had boiled over into major fury as she blamed him for all that happened to Marianne. He'd just tried his best to help her. Couldn't she see that?

Without warning, she rushed at him, swiping the glass out of his hand. It crashed to the floor between them, the splinters of glass cascading around his feet and spreading across the puddle of water.

'I'll get a brush—'

'Leave it! Now look what you've done! Not content with ruining my life, you break up my home! A home I've given you all your life and now you throw it back in my face.'

With her in this hysterical state, it was better not to say anything but get out and go to bed. As he tried to squeeze past her, she hit him hard on his shoulder. Off balance, he slipped on the water and smashed back to the floor, hitting the side of his head on the hard worktop of the island. As he tried to get up, his hands pressed into the sharp glass fragments and he yelled out in pain.

She kicked his arm. It slid away from him and left a smear of blood on the limestone floor. Dizzy from hitting his head, his right hand stinging, he cried out at a sharp pain on his left arm.

She'd sliced across his arm, below his elbow, with a large kitchen knife. Horrified, he couldn't believe what his mother had done. The deep cut filled with blood, overflowed the edges and dripped to form a dark red puddle on the floor. Shocked, he couldn't move.

She too, appeared to be fascinated by the amount of blood oozing from the cut. Surely she would help him now? Be sorry for her temper?

Coming to life, she screamed, an animal scream, and he fell back to the floor, trying to protect himself by lifting his right arm, terrified she'd cut him again.

Holding the knife in front of her, her voice cold, 'The police have been here – that Steph woman from college and her inspector friend.'

Darcy tried to get up, but she bent down, thrusting the knife closer to his chest. He lay back, holding himself up, leaning on his right arm with his eyes fixed on the blade. Poised, ready to attack, she glared down at him for what seemed like minutes. Pins and needles moved up his hand, but he daren't move it. Slowly she stood back, lowering the knife a little. Was she sobering up?

'They brought the post mortem report on my Marianne. Yes, they cut up my Marianne after she died. They cut her up and found out what you'd done to her.'

'Me? I'd done nothing! She died from those drugs.'

'That's what you wanted us to think, wasn't it? That it was suicide or an overdose from that poison Luke gave her.'

Darcy's right arm was stiff with cold. He could no longer feel his hand and wriggled it around to get the blood flowing again. He wished she would let him get up, but every time he made a move, she aimed the knife closer to his neck.

'No, it wasn't suicide. It was an overdose.' The knife came closer.

'Yes—'

'No, not with those drugs but from the ones you gave her.' She jabbed him and the point cut through his tee shirt.

'I didn't give her anything.'

'Yes, you did. It was insulin – your insulin. They've found where you injected it and they've found it in her eyes. Her eyes sliced open – my Marianne. You killed her. You should have loved her, not killed her. You've been jealous all these years, haven't you? Resented her because she belonged to us, not like you, a black cuckoo.'

He fell back. Her words stung, cut him harder than the knife had.

'Mother—'

'Don't call me that. I'm not your mother.'

'I wish I'd never been born.'

'I wish you'd never been born. You were a mistake, right from the start. You've been a mistake all your life.'

Darcy felt desolate, hollowed out as her words sliced into him.

'Now, listen to me.' She took a step back, holding the knife in front of her, ready to strike. 'I want you to leave now and never, ever come back. The police told me to phone them, but I'm giving you some time. Go back to where you belong, with those druggies in London. Do you hear me?' She screamed again. 'Do you hear me? Get out! Get out now! I never want to see you again. Get out!'

She kicked him hard on his thigh. The pain made him cry out. How could his mother be doing this to him? Arm up above his head to stop further blows, he seized the edge of the island, pulled himself up and limped out of the kitchen, along the hall and out of the front door. She tracked him, knife held erect to stop him turning back, until he was in the porch. The slam of the door behind him shook the black trees as he stepped out into the dark. Now where was he to go?

40

FRIDAY 20TH OCTOBER: 6.30 AM

STEPH

STEPH FINISHED TOWELLING herself dry after her shower, wrapped her dressing gown around her, fed Derek and put the coffee on. She jumped as the doorbell invaded the silence of the early morning. Derek dutifully barked before returning to inhale his breakfast.

'Darcy! What are you doing here?'

The elegant Darcy had been replaced by a dishevelled, blood-stained boy who looked as if he'd got the worst of a fight. He must be freezing cold in his thin short-sleeved top, with no coat or jacket.

'Come in. You look as if you've been in the wars. Sit down. I'll get you a coffee.'

She ushered him to the dining table, pulling out a chair, and he slumped down.

Hale appeared from the bedroom, fully dressed and ready for work. 'What's happened to you?'

Steph placed a mug of coffee in front of Darcy, who sipped it.

'Now – something to eat? Some toast?'

'Yes, please.' He sounded defeated, exhausted and lost.

Hale poured himself some coffee and sat at the table opposite, waiting for Darcy to speak. He had a bruise under his left eye, a cut above it and plasters on the inside of his right hand, with four butterfly plasters spanning a deep cut on his left arm. He noticed Hale looking at his wounds and let his left arm drop onto his lap.

'Thanks. That looks great.' He bit into the thick slice of buttered toast and honey, swallowed more coffee and relaxed a little.

'OK, lad, in your own time,' said Hale.

Darcy took another mouthful of coffee, placed his mug on the table and sighed. 'I went home last night and Mother lost her temper with me. She blames me for what happened to Marianne.'

'Surely she didn't do that to you?' Steph gestured to his arm and face.

'I hit my head against a kitchen unit and fell on broken glass on the floor.' He took another gulp of coffee.

'That cut's been made by a knife.' said Hale.

'When I got back last night, Mother was so angry and blamed me for – for it all.'

Steph and Hale stayed silent, waiting for him to continue.

'She threw me out. Said she never wanted to see me again.' He pulled his arm across his eyes, not wanting the tears to spill over his eyelids. 'I went to talk it over with Dad.'

'Last night?'

'Yes, they let me sit with him. I often go in the evenings, especially since Marianne... The nurses patched me up.' He paused, touched the plasters on his left arm and took another gulp of coffee.

'Well, last night when Dad heard what she'd said to me, he told me who I was.'

'Sorry?' said Hale.

Darcy pulled an old tissue from his jeans pocket and blotted his eyes.

'You said 'he told you who you were'. What did he mean?' said Steph.

'I already knew my mother, a Nigerian director in the oil company, died when I was born, but Dad told me last night he's my real father. He and Mother adopted me, but they've never told me I am – was – Marianne's half-brother. No wonder Mother hates me.'

'Why should that make her hate you? She must have known all the time.' Steph pushed another slice of toast onto his plate.

'Thanks.' He took a large bite and chewed it ravenously. 'She thinks I've been jealous of Marianne all these years. I didn't kill her. I wouldn't do anything to harm her. You've got to believe me. I wouldn't. We – I loved her. I'm lost without her.'

His eyes moved from Steph to Hale, unflinching, not blinking, as if he thought by staring them out, he could convince them. He looked desperate and clearly wanted them to believe his story as he sat up straight and continued. 'You were right. Last night Mother attacked me with a knife.' As he spoke, he lifted his left arm on the table, so the extent of the cut was visible.

'She was so angry and drunk. I think she wanted to kill me and she said I should go... go back to London, where I belonged, with the drugs gangs. But I'm not part of them, honest. I'm on your side.' He shifted and pulled something out of his jeans pocket. 'Dad said I had to give you this.' He held out some folded pieces of paper towards Hale.

'What is it? More information you've withheld from us?' Hale's voice was cold.

'This is all of it, honestly.' Clearly Darcy realised how bad this appeared and once again he blushed.

Hale reached across and took the dog-eared paper, flattened the two sheets on the table and ran his hand over them, ironing out the creases, then moved them towards Steph.

'It's an email from Marianne before she died. She told me to give it to the police if anything happened to her. She wanted to make sure Luke was punished.'

Darcy's blush ripened as he must have known this wasn't a great reason for not handing it over much earlier. 'She thought the email and date would prove that she'd written it and it could be used as a sort of statement?' His voice rose at the end, as if pleading with them to agree with him.

'Right. Steph, read it out, will you? The print's too small for both of us to read it.' Hale glared at Darcy but tried to keep his voice as calm as possible. Evidently, this slow reveal was becoming annoying.

Steph picked up the papers and cleared her throat.

If anything happens to me, take this to the police. I'm worried Luke will get out of this mess without taking the blame, as usual. He's so clever, getting others to do his dirty work for him. This is dated and you can forward it to people to show that it wasn't me who shot Jez Stewart, even though Luke set it up to look like it was.

'Hang on. Let's get this straight. This is an email Marianne wrote to you weeks ago?' Hale's slow, deliberate speech was a sure sign he could be about to explode.

'Yeah, that's right. There's the date on the top, see?' Darcy pointed to the top of the page. 'And you can print a copy off my email account to prove it.'

'So, written and sent to you before she was in a coma and before she died then?' Hale glared at Darcy. 'Has it occurred to you that if you'd given it to us and we'd got Luke at that stage, she might still be alive?'

Steph gave his foot a warning nudge under the table. He moved his foot.

Darcy gave Hale a poison glare. 'Don't you think I've gone over and over that since she died? If I'd known what was going to happen, I'd have handed it over, but I couldn't see into the future. I did what she said and kept it, in case something happened.'

'Something happened! Huh! You can say that again!'

They stared each other out. Darcy gave in first. Steph decided to continue, hoping to de-fuse the tension.

We'd been going round his dens to check on everyone, and some kids were scared stiff. Luke noticed it too. When we went to one with a group of really young kids, he took the smallest, grabbed him by the collar and held him up against a wall. The kid looked terrified. He squeaked he hadn't done nothing but then Luke got his blade out and held it up to the kid's throat. He couldn't have been more than seven or eight and I knew Luke would cut the kid without thinking twice.

Hale squirmed in his chair. Steph glanced across at him. It was obvious he shared her horror as they imagined the scene with this kid.

How could I have been conned by him? He used the same voice to threaten that kid he used with me in bed. Low, almost a whisper, a total snake. He told the kid he'd cut him so he couldn't plug anymore and he'd bleed to death and he'd stop anyone helping him. Did he want to die on the floor? Wouldn't it be better to tell him what was going on? The others watched, shocked, silent as he bullied the boy, who wet himself.

'Darcy, this is dreadful! What did that poor girl go through?' Steph couldn't help herself as the story became more horrific by the word. Darcy didn't look up. He pulled the well-used tissue out of his pocket and rubbed his eyes.

The boy found it difficult to speak but begged Luke not to cut him and said he'd tell him everything. Jez had been creaming off the top and getting the kids to deliver to his list, and they'd given him the money. The kid was hysterical and started sobbing. He couldn't go on. So another one, a bit older, stepped beside him and said that Jez had been doing this for a few weeks and had told them Luke had agreed it. Luke moved to the corner of the room where he could see them all and in a really quiet voice said if they did it again, he'd be back and they knew what he'd do to them. They all nodded, terrified. He left, pushing me out of the door before him.

He was furious. I've never seen him so angry. He grabbed me by the arm and dragged me away from the den. The next day, I had dark bruises where his fingers had been on my arm. He said I had to come with him and he was going to sort Jez and he couldn't believe how an old friend, a school friend, could have done this to him. If he'd been doing it that long, he must have stolen thousands. Didn't he reward him enough?

We got to the flat near the Latchmere—

'This was the basement flat where we saw you, right?' Hale raised his left eyebrow to emphasise his question. Darcy nodded. Steph observed the exchange. This was not the time to remind him of his lie.

We got to the flat near the Latchmere. He walked in and started chatting to Jez as if nothing was wrong. It was like normal. They joked and laughed about the kids and shared a few Jack Daniels and Luke said he had some good gear for them later. I thought he wasn't going to do anything and it would be fine.

Without warning, Luke grabbed me, held me in front of him, pulled out a gun from the back of his jeans and held it to the side of my forehead. He gripped me so tight. I was terrified. It was difficult to breathe, and I thought I was going to throw up. What had I done? Had he found the stuff on my computer?

'The files your mother downloaded, and we saw?' Again, Darcy nodded and agreed with Hale.

In that creepy voice, he asked Jez what he should do with me. Should he smoke me or cut me? Jez looked confused and asked what I'd done. Luke said I'd betrayed him and what did he think should happen to someone who'd betrayed him? I was convinced he'd found the recordings, and it was all over. He was going to shoot me.

Before Jez could say anything, Luke threw himself on Jez, who was on a chair. It fell over backwards, and Luke was on top of Jez, holding the gun to his head. Again, in that nightmare voice, he told him it wasn't me who'd betrayed him but Jez, his best friend, who'd been in it with him from the beginning. Jez was the first friend he'd made in his dorm. How could he do this? He was Luke's lieutenant, and he'd trusted him totally.

Jez started crying, snot dripped down his nose and he begged Luke not to shoot, he'd do anything he asked, take a smaller cut, anything. He said he'd already planned to leave the country and pleaded with Luke to let him leave. Luke spent a long time holding that gun over him. He was a total bastard, making Jez suffer like that.

He climbed off Jez and sat beside him on the floor and patted his head like he was a pet dog. Without warning, Luke leaned behind him and pulled the trigger. The top of his head came off and bits flew onto the mattress. I can still see the look of horror in that split second when Jez knew this was it.

'Oh! Why the hell didn't you tell us... Is there more?' Hale shook his head and looked across to Steph, who nodded. Hale pulled his fingers through his hair, the usual sign of his bubbling frustration.

Luke stood up, picked up a rag from the floor, wiped the gun and, holding the barrel, handed it to me, telling me to hang on to it for a few minutes. He bent down, picked up Jez under his arms, told me to put the gun on the floor and grab Jez's legs. We moved him into the bathroom and dumped him in the bath. I daren't say anything or argue. I just did what he said.

As the body fell in the bath, Luke said it was the best place to leave him. There was enough mess for me to clear up. He told me to stay there, clean the flat, and he'd be back the next morning. He said if any runners came to see Jez, I was to say that Jez had left me there to take his messages and check the texts on his phone. He'd see to them later.

He kissed me and left. I sat outside on the bottom step for a while, hoping someone had heard the shot and the police would come and it would all be over, but nothing happened. I went back inside and knew I couldn't stay in there. Having packed my bag, I phoned you and sat out there on the step until you came. Please tell them I didn't shoot Jez, it was Luke.

'Well, your sister could certainly tell a story, lad. That was grim. A real shame you didn't give it to us earlier. You know you could be accused of—'

Steph jumped as her phone rang and the screen showed Esther was calling. She walked out into the garden to take the call.

'Hello... When did he get home? ... Oh, I see. Are you all right? ... Right, we'll come straight over.'

Steph came back inside and stood in front of Darcy.

'That was your mother. She said you stabbed her.'

41

FRIDAY 20TH OCTOBER: 8.30 AM
STEPH

HAVING TAKEN Darcy to the police station, Steph and Hale drove on to Esther's house. They'd informed Darcy that, although he was a suspect, he wouldn't be arrested for Marianne's murder yet. But he must stay in police custody and give a statement under caution about Esther's alleged attack and his whereabouts during the evening of Marianne's death.

Despite protesting his innocence, he acquiesced, and they left him in an interview room waiting for Johnson, a sergeant on Hale's team, to take his statement and to check his alibi for the night Marianne was murdered. Hale planned to discuss any other charges with Jim.

Peter agreed that Steph should spend the day working with Hale, as she convinced him they were getting somewhere at last. She explained what they were doing, with an impatient Hale, desperate to talk to Esther, making 'wind up' gestures while she was on the phone. Ignoring him, she turned her head away to continue her conversation and stared out at Southwold marshland beyond Might's Bridge, convinced that Peter should know what they were up to, if she was to keep her job.

At last, phone call over, they walked up to the house. Esther opened the front door in the same dark green velvet dress she'd worn the day before. Tight bandages bound her left arm from her wrist to her elbow. Her lips made a brave smile, which didn't get as far as her eyes, and this time she didn't attempt the social niceties of offering tea or coffee.

They trooped through to the sitting room and sat in their usual chairs. In the Jane Austen world Esther inhabited, she appeared to be on a visit to Bath, but this time she turned the TV off without prompting. On the way over, Hale had suggested that Steph should lead on the questions and get as much as she could from her.

Esther stared at the black screen, not volunteering anything, but stroking her left arm as if comforting a cat.

Steph leaned towards her from her seat on the sofa, closing the gap between them and creating a more intimate tone. 'Esther, tell me what happened last night after we left.'

With closed eyes, Esther appeared to be picturing the events or putting off having to describe them. Steph wasn't sure which. When she spoke, it was in a wavery whisper they had to strain hard to hear.

'Well, after you left, I sat here, not knowing what else to do. Waiting, just waiting for him. I must have fallen asleep, as I was freezing cold when I was woken up by the front door clicking shut.'

'What time was that?'

'Oh, I'm not sure... but it was late. I went out to the hall and saw Darcy trying to creep in. He was shocked to see me waiting for him.' She paused, eyes closed again. Steph was about to prompt her when she continued in the same low monotone. 'He was out of it on something, something he must have taken. His eyes were huge, and he was tense... twitchy,

265

you know. I could feel the electricity sort of fizzing from him... Or maybe he was drunk?'

Esther paused, closed her eyes, and sighed.

'He talked rubbish and became angry and kept saying I wasn't trying to understand him and wouldn't listen to him. I told him Marianne had been murdered, and you wanted to see him because of the insulin.'

Once again Esther paused, as if it was too painful to continue, but she lifted her head and looked across at them. 'I told him I'd promised to phone you and he should stay here, but he went mad. He pulled out one of those knives, you know, the ones that pop out of their handles...'

'Do you mean a flick knife?' asked Steph.

'Yes, that's it. One of those.' She nodded at Steph. 'He went crazy. I really don't think he meant to hurt me. I know he didn't. He wouldn't. But he screamed at me not to go near the phone and ran into the kitchen to pull the socket out of the wall.'

Esther turned to Hale. 'That's the main one, you know. And he's so big I couldn't get near it. I couldn't phone you. I couldn't.' Hale nodded, clearly wanting her to continue.

She paused, then extracted a tissue from the box beside her and, dabbing at her eyes, took a deep breath.

'In the kitchen, he had a glass of water, which he threw on the floor. He slipped over and cut himself on the glass and hit his head on the edge of the kitchen unit and... and blamed me.' Esther wept and through her tears, she whispered, 'He blamed me!' She looked at them both, appearing to need their support or approval.

'Oh?' said Steph, hoping her neutral tone would encourage Esther further.

Esther, appearing to re-gain her strength, continued. 'I

think his arm may have been cut too.' She blew her nose and glanced at Hale. 'He said he was going back to London, and as I went to hug him... that was all, I wanted to hug him... he fell over again and that's when his knife went into my arm.'

As she lifted the bandaged arm to show them, she winced. They both stared at it but said nothing. Esther lowered her arm to her lap and once again began to stroke it.

'It was an accident. He didn't mean to hurt me. It was an accident. Honestly. He didn't know what he was doing. When he saw what he'd done, he ran. I couldn't stop him.'

The silence stretched. At last Esther spoke.

'And I thought I ought to get it seen to, so I got in the car and drove to the hospital and they sewed it up.' Once again, she searched their faces for a reaction. 'Sorry, I should have phoned you and told you before I went to A&E, but I did as soon as I got back.'

Esther burst into tears and sobbed. Steph darted an enquiring glance at Hale. He shrugged his shoulders. Both stories sounded plausible. At last Esther stopped crying and shuddering. Above the soaked tissue, Esther peered at them. 'And it's all my fault you've not got him.'

Hale got up and stood in front of Esther's chair. 'But we have. Darcy's at the station now giving a statement.' Surprise rippled over Esther's face. Her frown deepened as Hale explained, 'We haven't charged him yet, but we're investigating his role in all this. We'll need a statement from you.'

'Of course. Whatever you need. I'll be here or at the hospice as I must visit Dickie. I don't know how he'll take all this. He mustn't have any stress; it makes his condition worse. Maybe I shouldn't tell him. What would you do?'

'If you want my honest opinion, I wouldn't trouble your husband until we know exactly what's happened. You may upset him unnecessarily. We're very close to reaching a conclusion.'

Steph moved towards Esther. 'If I were you, I'd stay here and rest all day. You've had a shock and you shouldn't underestimate the impact of all you've been through.'

Esther appeared to be re-assured and relieved by their words. She looked up at Hale. 'You're right. I wasn't looking forward to telling Dickie, and when you've solved it, I can tell him once. You're right, I do feel rather fragile. I'll stay here. But you will let me know what happens to Darcy, won't you?'

'Don't worry Esther, we'll be in touch. I'll get someone to phone you about making that statement.' Hale raised his hand to stop her from getting to her feet. 'Don't get up. We'll see ourselves out.'

42

FRIDAY 20TH OCTOBER: 10.30 AM
STEPH

HALE'S PHONE rang as they were on their way to the station. It was Johnson requesting an urgent meeting. Steph held onto the edge of her seat and clamped her mouth shut tight as he pushed his foot to the floor. 'OK?' He challenged her, clearly aware of her tension.

'Fine, thanks,' she lied. They drove in silence the rest of the way.

As they walked into the police station Steph and Hale were greeted by an anxious-looking Johnson. 'Can we go into this interview room? I've something to tell you.'

Hale opened the door nearest to them and they sat around the table in the cold grey room. There were no cameras or tape recordings on this time.

'Sorry, Guv. I thought it was best to come here rather than the incident room – we can't risk leaks.'

Steph was taken aback by this dramatic opening – leaks? Had there been any? Hale hadn't said. She sat beside him opposite Johnson, waiting for the news, which he appeared desperate to share.

'OK – what's happened.' Hale took a small notebook and pen out of his pocket and turned over a page, ready to write.

'Well, Guv, at ten o'clock this morning your mate Jim, from the Met, left a message for you to phone him urgently.' Hale frowned and Johnson quickly added, 'He couldn't get through to you – your phone was off – so I phoned him back' Hale nodded.

'He said the car carrying Luke and the drugs had left the Winstanley and would probably arrive up here about two o'clock, which gives us about three hours to get it sorted. He was convinced Luke was in the car and they're following it. I talked to Darcy who said it was due at four, but they've obviously changed the time.'

'He wouldn't know about it, as you've got his phone. We'd better check it,' said Steph.

'Poor Jim. Must've got home, only to turn round and come back again. Right, let's get the team going.' Hale stood, ready for action.

Johnson moved in front of them. 'And bad news, I'm afraid. That latest video of the stabbing has come back – they can't enhance it so there's no way we can arrest Luke for murder.'

'Oh, I really thought we'd get him on that evidence.' Hale sighed. 'That man seems to evade us whatever we do. At least we can pick him up and do him for possession with intent to supply.'

Steph bent down to pick up her bag, ready to go. 'What a shame. That video Darcy gave us looked possible. Now he'll only be looking at a few years and he'll literally get away with murder. From what we've heard, he'll claim he knew nothing about the drugs and blame the driver, who'll roll over and agree so he'll walk away. Again.'

Johnson fidgeted with his phone, then spoke. 'Guv, instead

of going after the car, if Darcy picks up the drugs as planned and goes to the house with Luke, we'll get them all and he's caught in the act.'

'Think we can trust Darcy? You interviewed him. What do you think?'

'I think he's mint. He's lost, Guv. He's got no family, no future and no idea what will happen to him.'

'Did you believe his story?'

'Yes, I did.'

'Well, we've just come from his mother, who tells an equally plausible but very different version of what happened last night.'

Steph, who'd been listening intently, decided to speak up. 'I believe him, and if he's involved in this op, he'll be under constant observation, and it's not as if he's going anywhere, is it?'

Johnson's phone rang. He looked at Hale, who indicated he should take it out in the corridor.

Hale shut the door, paused, and leaned his back against it. The blood drained from his face as he was evidently weighing up their options and assessing the enormous risk he'd be taking. He took a deep breath then exhaled noisily and looked into Steph's eyes. 'This is a massive risk.'

'And we can't get him for the murder Marianne witnessed in the London basement?'

'His brief would claim it was a fairy story she'd made up – she's not here and there's no one to corroborate her version. The CPS would never let it go to court without more evidence. As I was saying, it's a one hell of a risk.'

'I know it is.' Steph knew exactly what would happen to Hale if it went pear-shaped, but she also felt confident that Darcy could do it. She put her hand on his shoulder. 'You've gone this far, and it's worked. To pull out now would be to waste everything you've done. We're so close to shutting down this line and saving more kids.'

'Come on, Steph, you know another line will replace it in a couple of months at most.'

'That's not a reason for doing nothing, is it? Even a couple of months could make the difference to building up your intel and—'

'Look, you do know what's at stake here! This is really, really going out on a limb. If it went wrong...'

'At least you'll know you didn't walk away and let that bastard get away with it. Stop that car and he'll wriggle out of it somehow. Jim could have stopped him when the car left London, but he knows you can nail him up here. It's the right thing to do, Hale.'

Once again, he paused. He pulled himself upright, put his hands on her shoulders and gently shifted her to the left. Suddenly energised, his voice filled with conviction. 'Right, I'll get urgent authority.' He looked at his watch. 'We've just got time. You go to Darcy and explain what we want him to do. You'll need to give him his phone – hope Luke hasn't already become suspicious. We'll have the car followed, and we'll wait up at the house and go in after the whole crew. Steph, will you arrange with Jake's mum to use her front bedroom for surveillance?'

DARCY

Darcy drew in a deep breath of fresh air as he waited for Viv outside the pizza restaurant. The cell had reeked of disinfectant, which failed to hide the acrid body odour of the previous occupant. After a few hours in the tiny room and the interrogation, he was so scared. Scared he could not prove his innocence. Scared they'd find him guilty of something and lock him away in a filthy cell for most of his life. At least this would be a way of doing something good, of avenging Marianne's death, of getting Luke put away.

Viv had left her car about a mile from the railway station and, as they walked, she was on constant look-out in case they were being followed.

'Now, when we get to Luke's car, it's important you do as we planned, but you must be careful not to instigate anything or you'll be implicated. Just follow Luke's lead. Oh, and don't forget you were expecting him two hours later, so don't be afraid to let him know you're pissed off that he doesn't trust you. Anything else you'd feel?'

'I suppose, er...' he paused to think, 'I'd be surprised to see him and want to know what he wants to do differently, as this might be a change of plan.'

'Good. Think your way into the part and you'll be fine. Don't worry, we're being watched, and if it becomes dodgy, they'll move in.'

She patted his arm, which was meant to re-assure him. On the TV cop shows he'd watched, he'd seen lots of these safe traps go very wrong, and he knew Luke carried a gun and wasn't afraid to use it. He shook the idea out of his head. He mustn't show weakness or fear, or Luke would sense something was wrong. Luke was sharp and had an uncanny ability to know what people were thinking before they spoke. He thought about what he'd say and looked down at Viv as they walked in silence towards the railway station.

Smaller than him, she just about reached up to his chest. She looked the part though – lots of piercings, a tattoo creeping above her collar – and Darcy wondered what other body art she might have lower down. He felt safe, as her gym muscles suggested she could hold her own, but she didn't appear to be armed. Perhaps it was a good thing, as Luke might have spotted it under her tight denim jacket.

He knew he looked a mess. Wearing yesterday's clothes, his face bruised and scabby, his dark top spattered with blobs of blood. Hale had found him a hoodie in lost property, so at least his arms were covered, and he pulled the zip up to cover his top.

'Cold?'

'No, want to hide the blood.'

'That'll help! You certainly look the part of a street fighter.'

He laughed, knowing she was trying to get him to relax, but then he'd be pretty tense in this situation anyway, wouldn't he?

Just before two o'clock, they arrived at the Victorian station. The commuters to Norwich, Ipswich and even London had caught the early trains and their cars filled all the spaces closest to the station entrance. They walked past the brightly lit ticket office and round the side of the brick building to the long, narrow car park alongside the tracks.

Darcy looked along the wire fence, threaded with nettles and brambles, to the end of the potholed cinders, where he saw a gap at the far end for about three cars. Beyond that, in the last space, was the black BMW with tinted windows. He glanced at Viv, who smiled at him, then he strode out purposefully and knocked on the driver's window.

As it rolled down, he recognised the guy from the party who'd given Marianne the drugs. Struggling to keep his face straight and his hands by his sides, he nodded. Beyond him, Luke sat looking smug and, as usual, in control.

'Hey Luke, wasn't expecting you 'til four.'

'A couple of hours won't make much difference. My plans changed.'

'Anything wrong?'

'No. Thought I'd come along for your first trip.'

Darcy frowned and assumed a hurt expression. 'You mean you don't trust me? It's all set up. You didn't need to be here.'

'Don't take it like that. I want it to be good for you. First time. This'll be a good line for both of us.'

'Right.' He lowered his head, as if sulking at Luke's lack of trust. He kicked at the crunchy cinders. A stone flew against the door of the Lexus next in line. He hoped he hadn't dinged its door.

'You didn't answer your phone.'

'Turned off. I was in college.'

Darcy turned his face away from Luke. Mother said she could always tell when he was lying. He hoped Luke couldn't. But, as he turned away to look up the car park to check no one was watching, he revealed Viv.

'Didn't know you were bringing your girlfriend.' Luke sounded annoyed. 'This isn't a party. It's business.'

'She's good. Been working the college, getting her list and contacts. She's well in. My line – I run it my way. You provide the goods, I provide the money. What we arranged. Right?' He'd adopted Luke's staccato style of speech in an attempt to sound tough.

'Get in,' Luke ordered.

It had worked – so far. He glanced at Viv, who dropped her phone, so it was just out of sight behind the car. As they both bent down to pick it up, Viv whispered, 'That guy's Dude, the college dealer.'

'At that party – gave Marianne the drugs.'

They climbed into the back of the car and were smothered

by the sweet, heavy smell of skunk. They'd be wearing it for hours.

Luke swivelled in his seat, scrutinised them, then turned back to Dude and mumbled something Darcy couldn't make out. The driver grunted. With a screech of tyres, the car sped out of the car park in a cloud of black dust. Dude didn't hang around; he put his foot to the metal all right. So far, so good – or was it?

43

FRIDAY 20TH OCTOBER: 2.20 PM
STEPH

STEPH HAD FORGOTTEN the tension surveillance creates. The need to be ready to leap into action after hours of sitting around staring at a door or window, just in case. Jim and his sergeant had arrived. They'd followed the Beamer all the way up the A12 to the railway station entrance but left the local surveillance to Hale and joined them in Jake's house. Luckily, Jake was at college, his sister at school and his mother working at the Bistro, so they had the run of the house with no interruptions or distractions.

Just before two thirty, Hale's radio crackled into life with the news that Luke's car was arriving at Julie's house. The four of them adjusted their stab vests, ready to move. Hale radioed the sergeant in charge of the armed back-up team, waiting in a van parked around the corner, and warned them to be ready to go in.

The earlier lively gossip between Hale and Jim shut down, and they now stared at the space outside Julie's house, alert and adrenaline fuelled. Steph felt slightly sick and her stomach turned as the knot there tightened. Although she was pleased to be included, she'd got out of the habit of living with this stress and concentrated on keeping her breathing steady, as she couldn't afford a panic attack. She mustn't let Hale down, especially not in front of Jim.

The spotless BMW swept into the space outside Julie's house and made a stark contrast with the jungle of rubbish and weeds in her garden. There was a brief pause when no one emerged from the car. Luke must be sussing out if it was safe. After an endless minute, the doors opened and its four occupants climbed out. Luke said something to Darcy, who went to the back of the car, opened the boot and took out two black sports bags. Looking around to check all was quiet, they walked up the path. The door opened as they reached it and they went inside.

DARCY

Darcy carried the bags through to the kitchen, where he was met by an anxious Julie.

'Oh – it's you!' Her words were soaked in disappointment before she noticed Luke loping in behind him. 'My Lucky Luke-y, I've missed you. And where's the little treat for your Jules?'

Julie rushed at Luke, clawing at his jacket, rubbing her face against his chest and smiling up at him while searching his pockets. 'Found it!' He grinned and rolled his eyes at her delight as she scuttled off to the front room to open the little packet and escape from her life. She'd lost more weight and her eyes had sunk deeper into their grey sockets since Darcy had seen her at the party when David was stabbed. Had she noticed he'd died?

The kitchen stank of rotting rubbish. Dried food spattered

the floor, which was growing mould, and the sink and draining board were overflowing with stained crockery and full ashtrays. As he moved towards the filthy table to dump the bags, his feet stuck to the tacky floor tiles. Her daughter must be at school, but imagine coming home to this dump. No wonder she spent a lot of time over at Jake's.

A hand dug him in his back, and he turned to find Luke, their faces almost touching, frowning down at him. He breathed in the weed, and Luke's bleached teeth glinted in the thin sunlight that forced its way through the grimy window.

'Where's your crew, man?'

'Coming after college.' He found himself becoming resentful; must be getting into role. 'You were two hours early. Orders in, cutting at four, deliveries after that.'

'Right.'

'You staying then?'

'That a problem?'

'No. Wannna help?'

'Don't handle this shit anymore. Grunt work. I do the business end.'

No, Darcy couldn't see him getting his hands dirty or doing any of the hard work. Luke was the chief executive of his empire. Darcy started unloading the nearest sports bag and piling the sugar-bag sized packages on the table. When he'd emptied the first holdall, he pulled off the gaffer tape around the black bin bags that protected each two-kilo pack, ready for sorting.

He felt the sweat pulling his top close to his skin and hoped Hale and his men would come in soon. As he'd come straight from the police station, he hadn't got scales nor a pile of small plastic bags for sorting the food. How could he look convincing? Desperate, his eyes darted up to the shelf beside the greasy

279

gas oven where he noticed a roll of tinfoil. That would have to do with a spoon to measure it out. Surely, they wouldn't need to get that far?

Clearly, Viv understood his concern and joined him at the table to unload the second bag. 'OK, boss?'

He ignored her, assuming that's how a drugs boss would behave to his girl. The bag was emptied and stashed on the floor under the table. They unwrapped the second batch of parcels. When they'd finished, Luke stood over them grinning.

'No scales?' Of course, Luke had noticed.

'At home. Didn't have time to pick them up. You were early.'

'Yeah.' Luke didn't look convinced. He took out his knife, flicked it open, and with the tip, started cleaning under his nails. This casual gesture made Darcy feel sick. How much longer were they going to have to continue this charade?

Luke turned to Dude, who was leaning against the sink, and mumbled something. Again, they couldn't hear, but Darcy used the opportunity to pull a face at Viv to show his stress. She touched his hand as she leaned across to rearrange the packs.

Darcy became aware that Luke had finished manicuring his nails and had slipped his knife back in his jacket pocket. It felt as if he was preparing to move or take some sort of action. It would be an hour before the non-existent gang of foot soldiers failed to appear and if the police didn't get in before that, he was dead. He'd seen the bulge beneath Luke's jacket as they climbed out of the car.

Viv nudged him with her foot and moved her eyes across the kitchen to a door standing ajar. Through it, he could see the corner of a loo and a small washbasin. He took the hint.

'Need a slash.' Why had he said that? He didn't normally

announce his intention to pee. No one appeared to notice. Maybe she'd got him out of the way so the police could barge in. He stood with his back against the wall, closed his eyes, took a deep breath and felt his heart rate slow. How had Marianne lived this life even for a few weeks? A day was killing him.

As he flushed the loo, he heard a piercing scream from Viv, followed by furniture being smashed. Throwing the door open, he saw Luke standing Viv up against the wall, his knife pressed into her neck, the table overturned, the drugs scattered across the floor.

44

FRIDAY 20TH OCTOBER: 3.00 PM
DARCY

'Now, let's have a little chat.' Luke gave a quick nod to Dude, who rammed Darcy back against the loo door, slamming it shut, and flicking out his knife, pushed it into Darcy's neck. Darcy yelped at the sting. How deep was it? Already he could feel blood trickling from the wound. Dude moved the blade to the left. Was that his jugular vein?

Luke glanced across and laughed. 'Not so cool now, eh?' His hands swooped down to Viv's blouse, ripping it open. A tiny button bounced along the kitchen floor. Luke grinned and picked it up.

'Now, what's this?'

He waved it around in triumph before shouting into it 'You come in and they get it. Over and out.'

He let it drop to the floor and crunched it under his foot, all the time pinning Viv up against the wall, the knife against her neck.

'Nice try, Darcy. Almost took me in with your little performance. Your sister said you were a pussy. She was right. And as for your pretty little piggy here...' Without warning, he slashed the knife across Viv's neck. Not deep, but enough to free a necklace of blood.

Dude laughed and pushed his blade in deeper. Darcy felt it puncture his skin, but the real pain came from what Luke had said about Marianne. She'd never say that to Luke, would she?

As Luke moved the knife to his left hand so he could reach for the gun with his right, Viv kneed him hard in the groin. In agony, he bent over, wheezed and fell to his knees. 'You bitch!'

She followed up with a vicious kick to his chin. The force of it knocked him to the ground. The knife slid across the floor. Darcy and Dude dived for it. Dude beat him to it and, with his head down, barged Viv, slammed her into the wall and pushed the knife into her stomach. She slipped down the wall to the floor, groaning.

Furious, Darcy seized a kitchen chair and smashed it over Dude's head. Losing his balance, Dude fell to the floor. He stayed there. Was he dead? Darcy grabbed the knife and turned to face Luke, who was struggling to his feet. Viv moaned, a crumpled heap. Her eyes were closed. Had they killed her?

Distracted for a moment, Darcy turned to find himself confronted with Luke, now upright, knife erect, ready to strike. He was grinning.

'Marianne was right – you're a wet pussy. She had real spunk, could do anything. Shame she wanted out – could've been great. Was in the sack.' All the time that clown's grin.

They stood a few feet apart, knives out, braced, ready for a fight. 'It was you, wasn't it, gave her those drugs?'

'You don't understand how it works, do you, pussy boy? You join my crew, that's it. Total loyalty. No way out. She knew that – chose her path.'

He made it sound as if it was her fault. How could Luke

blame Marianne for what he'd done to her? He hadn't finished, 'And you – the useless big brother. I'm going to wet you up, pussy.'

'You used her then... then threw her away.'

'The word is wasted. Yeah, it was a waste. She was a great fuck.'

'You bastard, you killed her—'

'Thought you were the bastard.' Mocking, provoking.

It worked.

As Luke went for his gun, Darcy leaped forward. A powerful rugby tackle took away Luke's breath as he fell back over the legs of the upturned kitchen table. The top two legs broke. He threw himself on Luke and swung at his face. His hand connected with bone. A thrill ran through him. He wanted to hurt this bastard, really hurt him.

Punching Luke's face with the same force as he hit the training bag in the gym, he watched the grin disappear and panic fill Luke's eyes. It felt so good. He pummelled Luke's face with quick, sharp punches. A crack! Luke's nose was broken. Darcy felt ecstatic – it was like scoring a try! At last, he was paying him back for Marianne.

A perfect right hook broke the skin on Luke's cheekbone and blood flowed down his left cheek, merging with the stream pumping out of his nose. Darcy punched harder and kept up the rhythmic pounding until he felt something slam into his left arm. The knife? Luke had cut him!

The knife moved towards his stomach. Acting fast to stop Luke thrusting it in him, Darcy threw himself forward and knelt hard on Luke's right arm. He screamed in agony as Darcy's knee crushed his muscle. The knife clattered to the floor. A flash of light crossed his face. The knife glinting in the sun? No, a shower of glass reflecting the light. Tiny shards of glass covered them as the back door shattered.

He felt himself being pulled off Luke and lifted to his knees.

'On the floor, face down, now!' Two officers were pointing their guns at him. Another two stood over Luke and Dude, guns aimed, ready. Darcy threw himself to the ground and felt his hands being forced into handcuffs.

The two men handcuffed Luke, pulled him up and dragged him out to the garden, his feet making skid marks through the blood and mouldy food on the floor. Another two handcuffed Dude, hauled him upright and marched him outside too. Darcy felt himself yanked to his feet and pushed towards the back door.

'Hang on! We need him in here. He's a witness,' Hale shouted to the two officers. They looked at Hale who indicated they should remove the cuffs, which were agony.

Shaking the glass fragments out of his clothes and hair, Darcy leaped across to Viv, who appeared to have lost consciousness. He fell to the floor beside her. As he lifted her head up to cradle it, the growing pool of blood was revealed beneath her. Hale knelt beside him and having grabbed a towel, pushed it at the hole in her stomach, shouting 'Viv, Viv!'

She opened her eyes a little and, seeing Darcy, mumbled something he couldn't make out. At least she was alive.

'Hold on Viv. Ambulance is on its way.' Darcy held her hand. 'Stay with me, Viv.'

Why do they always say that in films? At once, he knew why. He wanted her to stay, not leave him too. He'd already lost Marianne; he couldn't lose Viv. A drop of blood from the cut on his neck fell on her forehead. He stroked it away and felt her cooling skin. Was she going?

285

45

FRIDAY 20TH OCTOBER: 3.15 PM

DARCY

'You OK? He's stabbed your arm by the look of it.' Steph was standing beside him.

Darcy looked down at the end of his left sleeve to the spatters of blood on the floor. Were they coming from him? Strange, he couldn't feel anything. At once, a burning pain filled his arm and he gasped.

Two paramedics dashed in, threw the broken table out of the door to make space, and dumping their bags on the floor, knelt beside Viv, pushing him out of the way. Steph stood back and helped Darcy to stand. Feeling stubborn, he refused to let his feet be moved but stood at Viv's head, watching the men working on her, stabilising her before they could move her out to the ambulance.

Exposed and cleaned, the wound in her stomach was packed with gauze and sealed with a large square plaster by one of the men. The other gave her an injection, fixed a bag of liquid to her and placed an oxygen mask over her face. They were so quick. Relief ran through him as at last he started to believe she might get through this.

Darcy wiped his face with his sleeve.

Steph put her arm on his shoulder. 'Let's get Viv sorted, then it looks like you need attention.'

At last, Viv was stable and as they carried her out, she opened her eyes, pulled down the oxygen mask and smiled up at Darcy. Her other hand trailed over the edge of the stretcher and, gently lifting it up, he squeezed it lightly, then covered it with the red blanket. A few moments later, the siren cut through the autumn afternoon and faded away as the ambulance screamed off into the distance.

'Will she be all right?' Darcy turned to Hale.

'She'd better be.' He sighed. 'She must.' Was he re-assuring Darcy or himself? His voice changed, stronger, back to business. 'Now, let's have a look at you.'

Steph pulled Darcy towards the window and eased off his hoodie. A sharp pain shot up his arm. He felt faint. Steph ignored his moan and Hale handed her a strip of rag, which she tied above the cut. Darcy didn't know which was worse, the cut or the tight tourniquet. 'Shit! That hurts!'

'Sorry. You bleed a lot, don't you?' She examined the wound, which was above the one from the night before. 'Not as bad as I thought. You've been lucky. More paramedics on their way – they'll see to it.'

Tears were running down his cheeks, and feeling embarrassed, Darcy wiped his face with his sleeve again. Steph rinsed a tea towel under the tap and wrung it out. 'Cleanest one I could find. Use this. All you've done is spread the blood.'

'Thanks.' He wiped the damp cloth over his face and, as he held it there, cut out the chaotic room. Closing his eyes, all he wanted was to get out of this nightmare, to be alone, to think through what had happened, to stop the throbbing pain and to slow his frantic heartbeat. He felt a hand on his shoulder.

'You OK?' Hale's voice penetrated the dark. Darcy lowered the towel and found Hale's eyes searching his face. 'You've missed rather a lot of that mess. Here, give it to me.'

Darcy handed over the wet cloth and Hale gently patted the wide line of blood stretched across his neck. It stung. Darcy drew back, wincing and pulling a face. Feeling like a child again when Dad had 'kissed it better', he was desperate for the reassuring comfort of a hug. What was happening to him? He was supposed to be a grown-up. He took a deep breath, but once again feeling dizzy, he swayed.

Steph pulled a chair out and helped him to sit down. He closed his eyes, not wanting to talk any more. When he opened them, his view was filled by a large bald head. Another paramedic had come from somewhere and his lips were moving. Why couldn't he hear what the man was saying?

'Darcy, is it?' At last, his northern voice penetrated. 'I'm going to clean the cuts on your arm and neck – see if we can fix them here. I think you might get away without stitches. Then there's your hands – a right mess you've made of them.'

He closed his eyes again while the paramedic swabbed and probed and fiddled around with his arm and neck. It felt like it went on forever. He opened his eyes. The man was prodding at the butterfly plasters on his arm. 'Do this a lot, do you?'

The pain in his hands alternated between burning and throbbing. The checks the man made were probably gentle but felt like torture. 'Amazing, but I don't think you've broken any bones. Lucky that. We'll get you patched up, then off to A&E and check.'

Darcy glanced at his deformed hands. They were swollen and his fingers were stiffening up. But the last thing he wanted was to go to the hospital. 'No, I'll be fine. I'm not going to hospital.'

'But that's where you're headed, son. We can't leave you like this. You need to be checked over and those hands x-rayed.'

'I'm not—'

'Look mate, we need him to help us to sort out this mess. We'll look after him and see that he gets to A&E.' Hale rescued him once again.

'Well then, until you do, put a couple of bags of frozen peas on his hands and if the swelling doesn't go down, they go numb or you can't make a fist, you need to get him to A&E immediately.' He bent down so he was in Darcy's face. '*Immediately* – do you hear me?'

'Yes, thank you.'

'And I'm holding *you* responsible for him.' He stabbed his finger at Hale.

'Now, a slight scratch.' Looking down on his right arm, Darcy saw that the bald man was injecting him with something. Too tired to react, he let it happen. Tetanus? Pain killers? He no longer cared. He wanted to get away and pull the duvet over his head.

'Right, Darcy. Almost there. Take two pills now and the rest every four hours. If you start bleeding again or that hand doesn't improve, you,' staring at Hale, 'get him to the hospital. *At once!*' Tetanus, then. The man handed him a little blister pack containing the pills.

He felt a tight plaster collar around his neck and another swath of plaster around his upper arm and both hands, across his knuckles. 'Thank you so much.' He heard a low voice, which seemed to come from his mouth.

'You're welcome. Wouldn't like to upset you, after what you did to that guy in the garden.'

He patted Darcy's back and went through to the sitting room, where he could hear voices getting louder, then a grey-faced Julie, still out of it, was stretchered past him. Once again, a siren dissolved into the distance. Silence. Pools of drying blood, spattered and smudged across the filthy floor were all that remained of the horror he'd lived through. He was desperate for Viv to survive.

He felt dizzy and closed his eyes. A mug of tea was thrust into his hand. 'Drink this, Darcy. You'll feel better and, if it's not too hot, take those pills with it.' Steph held out her hand, pushed the pills through their plastic bubbles and handed them back to him. He swallowed the warm, sweet drink gratefully.

Feeling better, he opened his eyes to find he was surrounded by Hale, Steph and the man he'd met in London – Jim Connolly? He felt hemmed in but didn't have the strength to get up.

Hale spoke first. 'Well, lad, you certainly saw to that Luke. He might just survive the beating you gave him.'

'What!' Darcy was horrified. Jim and Hale laughed.

'I didn't have you down as a bare-knuckle fighter. Don't worry – he'll be fine. May affect his blond good looks for a while, but he got what was coming to him after what he did to Viv.'

A picture of Luke's mangled face forced its way into Darcy's mind, and he felt ashamed of what he'd done. He was as bad as Luke and his crew, wasn't he? But then, did he have a choice? He knew Luke would have killed them both as soon as look. Marianne had told him so, hadn't she?

Darcy took another mouthful of tea. 'What will happen to Luke and Dude now?'

'We'll charge them both with the attempted murder of Viv and GBH of you for today's little episode. We've evidence of Dude dealing at college and suspect he kicked that other dealer to death and left him on the rubbish heap.'

'I saw him at the party chasing that guy and he's been dealing contaminated drugs.'

'Shame you didn't tell us earlier, eh?' Hale's sing-song voice pushed his point home.

Darcy lowered his eyes.

Hale continued. 'There's enough evidence to charge Luke with supplying Class A—'

'And murder? He stabbed David – it was on the video.' Darcy protested.

'Unfortunately, it wasn't clear enough to identify him.'

Jim stepped forward. 'But we do have him for shooting Jez Stewart, that's the body in the basement you identified as Luke.'

'But the gun was wiped,' said Darcy. At last, he felt his brain returning.

Jim interrupted, 'They found Luke's DNA on the bullet casing. Clever stuff, eh?'

Without warning, a laser gaze replaced Hale's fatherly benevolence. 'How d'you know the gun was wiped, lad?' Darcy looked away from Hale's penetrating glare and became aware of Jim standing to his right, alert and paying attention to his answer. He took another gulp of tea, thankful the pain killers were starting to do their job.

'I went there to rescue Marianne. I thought she'd killed him, so I wiped the gun. She saw it all and only told me on the way home. After Luke had done it, he left her in the flat, alone. Alone with the body. She phoned me and I drove down to get her.'

'Why didn't you tell us? Wasted a lot of time and money sorting that mess out,' said Jim.

'Then there's Marianne,' said Hale.

'Sorry?' Darcy was confused. Hale knew all this from the

email Marianne had written. Why did he need him to keep saying it?

'We suspect Luke sent one of his crew up here to give her contaminated drugs, hoping they'd finish her off and get rid of a witness.'

Was that the guy he saw running away from the party, or was it Dude? Darcy realised what a complicated world he'd lived in for the last few weeks.

'We think it may have been the dealer we found beaten to death on the rubbish dump up the road, but we don't have any evidence, apart from a few vague statements from some kids at the party. Maybe we'll find something on Luke's phone.'

Darcy decided to keep his mouth shut, but knew they'd find nothing on Luke's phone. He was too careful to leave a trail. He thought they'd finished and got up, ready to leave.

Hale swivelled round to Darcy. 'So, that just leaves you we have to deal with.'

From the tone of Hale's voice, this would not be a pat on the back. Darcy's stomach lurched. 'But I wasn't one of his crew. I did it to help you get him!'

'Oh, we know that lad, but now we have to clear up how Marianne was murdered with your insulin, don't we?'

46

FRIDAY 20TH OCTOBER: 7.00 PM
STEPH

'What's he doing here?' Esther frowned as she opened the door. 'I thought he was in custody. And where did he get that vile outfit?'

'May we come in? We need to have a chat.' Steph smiled as if this was a social call. Her calm demeanour seemed to reassure Esther and her aggression dissolved a little.

'Of course, please. You know where to go.'

Clearly devastated by the chill in Esther's greeting, Darcy hesitated, and for a moment, Steph thought he wouldn't go in with them. He looked a sight. The cheap grey tracksuit, provided by the police when they'd taken his clothes for examination at the station where he'd given his statement, did him no favours.

Dark blue bruises were developing across his face, his swollen eye would be black in a few hours and a wide collar of plasters hid the cut along his neck. He needed a hug from his mother, not cold rejection. Nudging him through the front door, Steph patted his shoulder, trying to re-assure him.

Esther led the way to the sitting room and lowered herself

into her usual chair, while the others sat side by side on the large sofa, with a dejected Darcy beside Hale on the farthest seat away from Esther.

Esther turned off the inevitable Jane Austen DVD as she sat down.

'There are a few questions we need answers to before we tie this case up.' Steph, the closest to Esther, kept her voice calm hoping she wouldn't feel pushed to be defensive.

The layer of dust on every surface appeared to be getting thicker each time they visited, and the room smelled rank, of stale flower vase water. A plate on the far side of Esther's chair contained half-eaten sandwiches, the edges of the bread curling up to reveal dried out purple slices of something that might have been ham.

Steph wasn't keen on housework and would do anything to avoid it, but she couldn't live in this mess. It hadn't been like this on her first visit. Esther must have given up and spent all her time living in her Jane Austen world. Perhaps it was her way of coping with her grief, of managing her loss.

'We've checked the insulin that killed Marianne and it's the same composition as the one you gave us.' Hale's formal tone made Esther tense up again and she glared across at Darcy. He sank lower in the sofa cushions. Steph kept her face straight but thought it was quick work by the lab; they'd had it less than twenty-four hours. Esther's eyes moved from Darcy to Hale, but she said nothing.

'What Hale means is we're sure the insulin came from one of Darcy's pens or one like it.' Steph's explanation made Hale emit a quiet grunt and she could feel his annoyance. Apparently, he didn't feel that her intervention was necessary. Steph moved her hand behind her and prodded his thigh. He got the message and let her get on with it.

'We knew that. So why is that boy here and not in prison?' Esther darted a poison glare at Darcy, who shrank under her gaze. She was becoming aggressive again.

'Could anyone have got in and taken one of Darcy's pens?' Steph leaned forward, trying to prevent Esther's anger erupting.

Esther shook her head and spoke as if explaining something to a child. 'Of course not. So, it must be Darcy or me who killed Marianne. It wasn't me, so it must be Darcy.'

Steph could hear Darcy's sharp intake of breath at Esther's accusation and the desperation in his voice. 'But I loved Marianne. I'd never kill her. I loved her—'

'Hmm!' Esther grunted and shot another disapproving look at Darcy. 'You certainly did that all right.'

'Then the question is, how did Darcy do it?' Steph interrupted the tense exchange.

'What do you mean, "how"? He waited until she was out of it with the drugs, then injected her with his insulin and left her to die.' Esther was becoming impatient.

'That's not quite how it happened though, is it? That night, you called us and we sat down here together after Marianne died. Darcy wasn't here, was he?' Steph's calm, unemotional tone injected reason once again.

Esther paused as if the thought had struck her for the first time. 'No, he wasn't here when you arrived, was he? He'd left again.'

'No, Esther, the truth is, he wasn't here at all that night. We know he'd gone back to London. We brought him back on the Saturday night but he left again on Sunday evening, as he was determined to find Luke and we'd stopped him. He left before Marianne died and didn't come back until Monday night.' Steph waited for Esther's reaction she knew would come.

'You don't know that! That's just what he's told you. He tells lies.' Steph saw Hale put his hand on Darcy's arm, preventing him from getting up and interrupting her.

Steph continued in her calm, professional voice. 'This afternoon we received time-stamped photographs of him early on Sunday evening at Oakwood station, getting on the train and at Liverpool Street, getting off. Then the same on Monday for his return trip, so it couldn't have been Darcy. He was miles away.' Steph left this to sink in and Esther made no reaction. The silence grew between them.

Steph broke it. 'Were you here all evening?'

Esther rubbed her forehead with her hand as if to soothe a headache. 'I can't remember... Oh! I may have gone to visit Dickie earlier...er... Yes, I think I did. No, I'm sure I visited Dickie.'

'So, while you were visiting your husband, someone broke in, knew where to find Darcy's insulin and killed Marianne? Is that what you're saying?' Hale sounded irritated.

'I don't know what I'm saying! I've lost my daughter, my husband is dying. Why can't you leave me alone?' Esther was becoming hysterical.

'We need to find out how Marianne died. Are you going to tell us?' Hale pushed again, his voice cold.

'I've told you, I don't know.' Esther looked desperate.

Hale nudged Steph. She got the message and remained silent. All three watched Esther as she sat with her head in her hands, her eyes closed. The loud tick of the clock measured the silence and increased the tension in the room. Pattering on the windowpane made them turn towards it. It was raining hard. Thunder rumbled in the distance.

Esther took a deep breath. They waited. Her shoulders drooped as she gave in. Clearly, she'd run out of ideas. She lifted her head, and when she spoke it was a whisper. 'I didn't mean to do anything that night, really I didn't. I loved Marianne, but it all became too much and it was the only way out.' She looked over at Steph, a plea for agreement or support.

'The only way out? What do you mean?' She heard a gasp from Darcy. Once again, Hale held him back.

'You don't know what it was like. My beautiful, clever daughter who was going to Oxford, with a wonderful life before her, suddenly lost it all because of that Luke. All it took was a few weeks in the summer, and she was transformed from my little girl into a crazy drug addict.'

'She seemed fine at college.'

'Oh yes, you saw the perfect public Marianne, not the screaming, vicious creature I had to live with. You saw her that night – she was hysterical. Well, that was what she was like most of the time at home. The girl who was always there for me when Dickie became ill, transformed into a selfish monster. How I missed her! We used to talk about everything... books, the news, her friends – anything. We were so close. Oh, I knew it would all change when she went away to college, but I treasured those times we had together.' She sighed. 'When she came back from London, it had all gone. Disappeared. Just like that. She was a different person.'

'But you knew from the videos on her phone she tried to escape, she wanted to escape. You could have got her help – treatment, counselling.' Steph was finding it difficult to understand Esther's reasoning.

'You're right. And she could have had an abortion too but, no, she wouldn't.' Esther's sudden cold, cutting tone made Steph furious.

'Oh, come on, Esther. Pregnancy isn't a big deal now, is it?

297

She could have had the baby and still gone to university. The world has changed.'

'Is that right? And is the world ready for the deformed monster she was carrying?'

'The drugs wouldn't necessarily have affected her baby. It was so early.'

'No. It wasn't the drugs. The baby she was carrying was her brother's.'

'Sorry?'

'Darcy made her pregnant. They didn't know they were brother and sister at the time – the time when they... did it. They thought they'd simply been brought up together, not that they had the same father. That last night when she came back full of drugs once again, we argued like we'd never argued before.'

Her eyes filled, and she dashed the tears away. 'We argued about the drugs, then I told her I knew she was pregnant from her hospital notes and she became so angry, like she was when you were here. I thought she was going to kill me. I was so scared. She screamed at me and said she wouldn't get rid of it, she loved Darcy.'

She stared past Steph to Darcy. 'I couldn't believe what she was telling me. I thought it was Luke's, but she knew it was yours.' She jabbed her finger at him, accusing him.

Steph braced herself, ready in case Esther attacked him. Darcy looked stunned and was clearly having problems taking in all this information. He didn't need Hale's arm to hold him down. He looked if he couldn't move. Esther leaned forward to glare at him, her voice sharp and vicious. 'You seduced your own sister. How vile is that? All this is your fault! I took you in and cared for you as my own and you took my child from me.'

'But we didn't know. You and Dad didn't tell us. He told me the night you threw me out after stabbing me.'

'What do you think people would think? Marianne, the drugs dealer. Oh yes, she said she wanted to escape. She promised me she did, but she did nothing about it, did she? No, she carried on taking the stuff and, even worse, dealing it. How could I live here and face people with my daughter, a drugs dealer? Selling drugs that made kids addicts, go into comas or worse. And then she'd give birth to her brother's child, a deformed horror. You must see, I had no choice. I freed her from her shame.'

Hale stood in front of Esther. 'Stop there. I'm arresting you on suspicion of murdering Marianne Woodard.' He rattled through the caution, then went towards the hall door to call it in.

A moment of shocked silence froze them.

Darcy was the first to speak. 'Her shame? Or was it your shame?' He stood up, his back to the fireplace, facing his mother. 'You've never lived a real life, have you?'

Steph felt tense but remain seated. Out of the corner of her eye, she glimpsed Hale with his notebook out, pen poised ready to record anything Esther said.

'You brought me over here from Nigeria, never told me I was Dad's real son, and expected me to fit in. Look at me. How could I fit in? I've never belonged anywhere. I fell down the crack in the middle, but Marianne loved me and I loved her. If this mess is anyone's fault, it's yours.'

With a disgusted expression, Esther turned her head away as if she couldn't bear to look at him any longer.

'No, you look at me. If you'd been honest with me, none of this would have happened. You buried yourself in that fantasy of long dresses and stately homes and happy ever afters, instead of living a real life. Marianne knew you were a fraud. She told me.'

Esther's head shot back as if Darcy had struck her.

'Oh yes, when she was younger she was your little angel, but she saw you for what you are – a coward, more concerned with what people think than loving the family who once loved you. Thank you for giving me a life, then ruining it!'

Consumed by anger, the tears dripping down over his bruises, he looked exhausted and worn. He turned his back on Esther, walked over to the bay window, and stared out over the marsh. The rain battered the glass, whipped up by the wind. Esther said nothing, but wept and didn't move.

Hale touched Esther on her shoulder. 'Right, we need to get you to custody now.'

A police car pulled up outside. Esther hauled herself up and walked out beside Hale, her head bowed, not once glancing across at Darcy. The silence in the room magnified the sound of the car engine driving up the lane.

When it had disappeared, Steph stood beside Darcy. A magpie was pecking at something disgusting on the rim of a pothole being filled with the driving rain. The solid metal clouds hung low over the marsh, threatening at least a day's worth.

'I'm so sorry, Darcy. This has been such a mess and you've gone through so much.'

He turned to face her. 'And all because we went to a festival last summer.'

'One of those defining moments, all right.'

'Nothing good came from it, did it?'

'Perhaps not for you. No. But the people you helped won't see it that way.'

'Who?'

'People you've never met who've been freed from working for that bastard Luke or escaped becoming addicts. Luke'll be put away for most of his life, along with the others who worked with him. And the information you've given us has broken many of the lines.'

'But someone else will come along and trap those kids, won't they?'

'Perhaps. But doing nothing isn't an option. We have to keep at it.'

He moved from the window and threw himself in Esther's chair. 'And what will happen to me? I've lost everything.'

She turned to face him. 'I suppose you'll have to keep on going. No choice, really. "Keep moving" is what people said to me.'

She moved towards him and sat on the arm of his chair. 'You've got an exceptional talent. Get your A Levels and go to that college. One day the colour will come back and you'll catch yourself feeling happy again.'

'Really?'

'Really.'

He stared beyond her at the bookcase crammed with Jane Austen novels and DVDs. 'One thing's for sure. I won't spend my days in the past, like she did.'

Steph glanced at Esther's massive collection and thought back to where she'd started getting involved in this family only a few weeks ago.

'Would you like to come back with me for a few days? The sofa's comfortable.'

Darcy laughed. 'I bet Hale would love that! No thanks, Steph. I'll stay here. I have to get used to it. And now there's only me to look after Dad.'

'Perhaps I could drop in for coffee sometimes to see how you are?'

'Please. And I'll visit you in reception for a chat.'

'Promise?'

'Promise.'

He stood. She took the hint and moved to the door.

'See you later, Steph, and thanks for everything.'

She drove out of Southwold in a daze. It felt wrong leaving him alone in that enormous house, but he was a strong boy and he needed space to make sense of all that had happened to him over the last few months. She and Caroline would keep an eye on him at college. She hoped he would soon pick up his life and create a future. A future in which he could belong at last.

ACKNOWLEDGMENTS

Thank you

Rebecca Collins and Adrian Hobart, the talented, tireless power-couple behind Hobeck Books, for their excellent feedback, inspiration and encouragement.

Sue Davison, for a sensitive, outstanding edit and spotting details I missed.

Jayne Mapp, for a creative, evocative and sensational cover design.

Graham Bartlett, for his advice on police procedure and suggesting great solutions to the problems I'd created.

Brian Price for sharing his extensive knowledge of dead bodies.

Kate and Charlie, my children, for their love and always being there.

Jo Barry, for her constant encouragement and for asking the right questions.

Helen Jones, for her support and invaluable comments on the drafts and re-writes.

Jayne Camburn, Debby Hurst, Freda Noble, Bob Noble, Gerry Wakelin – my first readers for their enthusiasm and critical appreciation.

All my friends, for continuing to put up with me banging on about being published!

ABOUT THE AUTHOR

Lin Le Versha has drawn on her experience in London and Surrey schools and colleges as the inspiration for the Steph Grant crime series which now includes two books and a novella.

Lin has written over twenty plays exploring issues faced by secondary school and sixth form students. Commissioned to work with Anne Fine on *The Granny Project*, she created English and drama lesson activities for students aged 11 to 14.

While at a sixth form college, she became the major author for *Teaching at Post 16*, a handbook for trainee and newly qualified teachers. In her role as a Local Authority Consultant, she became a School Improvement Partner, working alongside secondary headteachers, work she continued after moving to the Suffolk coast. She is the Director of the Southwold Arts Festival, comprising over thirty events in an eight-day celebration of the Arts.

Creative writing courses at the Arvon Foundation and *Ways with Words* in Italy, encouraged her to enrol at the UEA MA in Creative Writing and her debut novel was submitted as the final assessment for this excellent course. The first book in this series, *Blood Notes*, was based on her final assessment piece.

Lin is now working on the third title in the series.

HOBECK BOOKS - THE HOME OF GREAT STORIES

We hope you've enjoyed reading the second book in Lin Le Versha's crime series. Lin has written a short story prequel to this novel, *A Defining Moment*.

This story, and many other short stories and novellas, is included in the compilation *Crime Bites*. *Crime Bites* is available for free to subscribers of Hobeck Books.

Crime Bites includes:

- *Echo Rock* by Robert Daws
- *Old Dogs, Old Tricks* by AB Morgan
- *The Silence of the Rabbit* by Wendy Turbin
- *Never Mind the Baubles: An Anthology of Twisted Winter Tales* by the Hobeck Team (including all the current Hobeck authors and Hobeck's two publishers)
- *The Clarice Cliff Vase* by Linda Huber
- *Here She Lies* by Kerena Swan
- *The Macnab Principle* by R.D. Nixon
- *Fatal Beginnings* by Brian Price
- *A Defining Moment* by Lin Le Versha
- *Saviour* by Jennie Ensor

Also please visit the Hobeck Books website for details of our other superb authors and their books, and if you would like to get in touch, we would love to hear from you.

Hobeck Books also presents a weekly podcast, the Hobcast,

where founders Adrian Hobart and Rebecca Collins discuss all things book related, key issues from each week, including the ups and downs of running a creative business. Each episode includes an interview with one of the people who make Hobeck possible: the editors, the authors, the cover designers. These are the people who help Hobeck bring great stories to life. Without them, Hobeck wouldn't exist. The Hobcast can be listened to from all the usual platforms but it can also be found on the Hobeck website: **www.hobeck.net/hobcast**.

BLOOD NOTES: THE FIRST STEPH GRANT MURDER MYSTERY

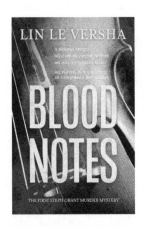

'A wonderful, witty, colourful, debut 'Whodunnit', with a gripping modern twist set in the dark shadows of a Suffolk town.' EMMA FREUD

Edmund Fitzgerald is different.

Sheltered by an over-protective mother, he's a musical prodigy.

Now, against his mother's wishes, he's about to enter formal education for the first time aged sixteen.

Everything is alien to Edmund: teenage style, language and relationships are impossible to understand.

Then there's the searing jealousy his talent inspires, especially when the sixth form college's Head of Music, turns her back on her other students and begins to teach Edmund exclusively.

Observing events is Steph, a former police detective who is rebuilding her life following a bereavement as the college's receptionist. When a student is found dead in the music block, Steph's sleuthing skills help to unravel the dark events engulfing the college community.

PRAISE FOR BLOOD NOTES

'A dark and intriguing thriller.' Jenny McClinton

'I loved this book right from the beginning.' Rachel Revill

'I was completely blown away.' Surjit Parekh

'From the first chapter I was hooked.' Janine Phillips

'Hooked from the first page.' Amazon Customer

'This is a real page turner, from the introduction to the final page. I really enjoyed it.' Amazon Customer

Lightning Source UK Ltd.
Milton Keynes UK
UKHW040709300522
403720UK00004B/405

9 781913 793647